ONLY HER

ONLY HER

A K2 Team Novel

Sandra Owens

Montlake
Romance

Published by Montlake Romance, Seattle

www.apub.com

Amazon, the Amazon logo, and Montlake Romance are trademarks of Amazon.com, Inc., or its affiliates.

ISBN-13: 9781503937550
ISBN-10: 1503937550

Cover design by Eileen Carey

Printed in the United States of America

This is the last book in the K2 Team series, and it seems only right to dedicate it to the men and women of the military, the heroes who keep us safe. Thank you for the sacrifices you make to keep our country free.

CHAPTER ONE

Following his nightly routine, Cody Roberts fed the dogs before pouring a healthy drink, scotch neat. Soon after he'd returned from Afghanistan, the nightmares had started. After a solid month of waking up drenched in sweat, he'd come to the conclusion they weren't going away. After a good degree of experimentation, he'd learned that scotch worked better than vodka, rum, gin, etc. etc. at keeping the dreams away.

Taking into account that it was his first night in his new home in Pensacola, Florida, and in the morning he would report for his first day at K2 Special Services, he cut his normal consumption from six, seven, sometimes eight glasses to no more than two. If nothing else had been left to him, he still had control of his actions—one reason he hadn't stuck the barrel of his gun into his mouth. Plus, his dogs needed him, and that fact alone got him out of bed each morning.

Once Pretty Girl and Sally finished chowing down, he took his drink, picked up his guitar from a chair in the living room, and went out on the front porch, the dogs trotting along behind him. He set the glass on a table and the instrument on the rocking chair. The boxes still to be unpacked could wait. His dogs needed to learn their boundaries.

"Heel." Pretty Girl and Sally took up positions on each side of him and he walked them around the perimeter of the yard, showing them how far they could range. He had them sit at the edge of the sidewalk, told them to stay, then walked into the road, turned to them, and said, "No." Both dogs wanted to come to him, but knew better. Satisfied they understood the street was off-limits, he returned to the porch, followed by his furred friends.

He'd always had a way with dogs, but it had been in Afghanistan that he'd honed his understanding of them. His teammates had called him a dog whisperer. Maybe he was. All he knew was that he preferred their company to most humans since returning home. They never judged him and found him lacking, nor did he have to worry about disappointing them.

From a cloth bag he'd put on the porch earlier, he pulled out two balls and tossed them into the yard. The dogs quivered with excitement—balls being their favorite thing in the whole wide world—but waited for him to give the command.

"Go play." They took off as if shot from a cannon. Cody settled in the rocking chair with his guitar on his lap. Sipping his scotch, he watched them for a few minutes to make sure they were staying on the grass. Normally he would be on his second or third glass by now, but since he'd limited himself to two, he wanted this one to last awhile. It was going to be a long fucking night.

Pretty Girl and Sally tossed the balls up in the air, then caught each other's, a game he had taught them so they weren't dropping the slobbery things at his feet every thirty seconds. He grinned at their antics, one of the few things he smiled about these days. After setting the glass on the table, he began to strum the guitar.

In tribute to Layla—the dog left behind—he always played Eric Clapton's "Layla" first. The e-mail he'd gotten the day before from Wizard, a friend still in Afghanistan, had been discouraging. The possible sighting of Layla hadn't panned out, and as he sat alone in the twilight of a setting sun, he let his despair of ever finding her sink into the music. She had saved his life, had kept him from stepping on an IED, and he owed it to her to find her and bring her home.

To keep from agonizing over Layla's condition and saying to hell with his two-glass limit, he closed his eyes and let the music consume him. The dogs played until they tired themselves out, then brought the balls to him, dropping them at his feet. Both flopped down, panting and tongues hanging out. Not ready to go in, Cody sipped his scotch between playing Eric Clapton songs.

After a while, the scotch was gone. He was contemplating how long to wait for his second and last drink when a car turned into the driveway across the street. "Quiet," he said to the dogs.

The car pulled into the carport, and the engine shut down. Because he sat in the dark, wearing a black T-shirt and jeans, he was confident he wouldn't be seen. A woman got out and headed for the front door.

Her hair was swept up in a ponytail, the tip of which reached halfway down her back. Her height he estimated at a little above average for a female. She was slim and wore a pair of jeans and a blue T-shirt. Something about the slump of her shoulders made him think she was sad.

Not his problem, though. Continuing his impersonation of a statue, he remained still, waiting for her to disappear into her house. She slipped her key into the lock, then turned and stared straight at him.

Cody sucked in his breath. He'd spent countless hours hunkered down in dusty rooms or on rooftops, his sight centered down the barrel of a sniper's rifle, and he knew how to become invisible. He moved not one muscle as she squinted into the dark. There was no way she could see him, but it was as if she sensed him.

Impossible.

He'd served six tours and never once been spotted from whatever hidey-hole he was using. Shaking off the ridiculous notion that she knew he was there, he remained still. The dogs were alert, watching her, and he gave them a hand single to stay quiet. She shook her head, as if she must be imagining things. Cody let out the breath he'd been holding after she entered her house.

Long after she'd disappeared, he remained on the porch, his gaze focused on her windows as she moved around, his yearning for a drink forgotten. Although her blinds were closed, he could track her movements by the lights being turned on or off as she moved from one room to another. He hadn't gotten a clear view of her face, only knew she had long brown hair and that she was sad. The dogs settled down again, and he picked up his guitar, softly strumming "Lonely Stranger."

Was someone watching her? As she slid the key into the lock, Riley Austin glanced over her shoulder. The only unusual thing she noticed was a light on in the kitchen of the house across the street. Ah, so someone had rented the place. That hadn't taken long, but she wasn't surprised. It was a charming bungalow, with its two dormer windows, royal-blue shutters, and—her favorite feature—the wide front porch. Having nothing more than an overhang above her door, she coveted that porch.

The lock clicked open, and blaming her unease on the strange events of the past few days, she hurried inside before the cats reached her. Arthur, as usual, was the first to greet her, soon followed by Merlin and King Pellinore.

The kitten tried to climb her leg, his claws digging through the denim into her skin. "Ouch, Pelli." Her latest acquisition, he'd been left at the no-kill shelter where she spent a few hours each week as a volunteer. Pelli's original owner had shrugged when she'd dropped him off, saying, "I don't want a cross-eyed cat. Creeps me out."

Unable to resist the silly faced, talkative Siamese, Riley had adopted him. Arthur had immediately taken to the kitten, but Merlin, as he did most things new, had turned up his nose, refusing to acknowledge Pelli's existence.

Holding the kitten, she dropped her purse on the foyer table, then shuffled her way to the kitchen, managing not to trip over the two adult cats winding themselves around her legs. At the sound of the can opener, Arthur and Pelli joined in a duet of cat begging. Merlin sat off to the side, his back to the other two as he washed his paws to prepare for dinner.

"I think you're clean enough," she told him, setting down his bowl last.

While the cats ate, she squeezed a slice of lime into a bottle of beer, and then put it in the freezer. In her bedroom, she unhooked her bra and slipped it out from under her T-shirt.

"Ahhh," she moaned, once freed from the evil contraption. Tomorrow was garbage day, so she emptied her bathroom wastebasket and bagged it up with the kitchen trash. The cats were still eating, and she was able to slip out the kitchen door without Pelli trying to follow her. The other two had given up attempting to escape long ago.

After dropping the bag into the can, she paused and inclined her head as the sound of a beautifully played guitar reached her. She recognized the Eric Clapton song, "Bell Bottom Blues." The music seemed to be coming from across the street, and she wondered if it was her new neighbor. The porch was still dark, and she couldn't see anyone. The moment she began to roll the can down her driveway, the music stopped. A dog barked once from the direction of the bungalow, then all went quiet.

It was eerie knowing someone was there, watching her. Had that been what she felt on arriving home? "Hello?" she called. Nothing. So they—a him or a her?—weren't the friendly type. Okay, no problem.

She headed back up the driveway, but paused at the edge of her carport. "You play beautifully. Welcome to the neighborhood." Again nothing.

With a shrug, she went into her house. After retrieving her bottle of beer from the freezer, now slushy and just the way she liked it, she went into her bedroom, flipping the light switch down. The mystery person across the street had caught her interest. Better to wonder about her new neighbor than to dwell on losing another patient.

She pulled over a chair, eased up the window, sat in the dark, and waited. Five minutes passed before he started playing again. When had she begun to think of the person as a he? Maybe it was the way his music spoke to her, as if he were playing just for her. It was as if he stroked her with each pluck of a string. She wouldn't feel that way if it were a woman, would she?

As she sipped her beer, she closed her eyes and tried to imagine his face, but all she saw was the poisoned cat dying on her, and she blinked her eyes open. Her mystery man played into the night so softly that she had to strain to hear him. She wished he would play louder, but then their neighbors likely wouldn't appreciate it as much as she.

When the music stopped, she glanced at the clock, surprised and chagrinned to see it was after midnight. Strangely, she'd forgotten to eat dinner, take a shower, or change into her comfy sweats. Also weird, her cats had curled themselves up under the window and hadn't made a sound.

"You have black magic in those fingertips," she whispered to her mystery man.

The next morning, she sat at her breakfast table, her gaze glued on the house across the street, curious to see him. And he had to be a him, or else she was going to be sorely disappointed in her reasoning.

The top half of a body appeared in the bungalow's kitchen window, and she froze with her coffee cup halfway to her mouth. He was a he!

With a grin, she gave a fist pump. Although she couldn't see his features, the top half of him was built like a freakin' warrior.

"No drooling, Riley," she muttered. With a cup in his hand, he stepped onto his porch, wearing a pair of sweat bottoms and nothing else. She drooled.

Then two dogs followed him out, and she sighed. "My cats are going to hate your dogs, so that means we can't have a hot affair, mystery man."

The dogs, one of them the ugliest thing she'd ever seen, the other a mixed breed that looked to have some German shepherd genes, stayed at either side of him. Because she was a veterinarian and trained to notice animal behavior, she caught the miniscule hand signal he gave them. Ugly dog and mixed-breed dog bounded down the steps and raced around the yard.

Stupid man. Didn't he realize they might run into the road and get hit by a car? She had lost more than her fair share of pets recently and didn't want to see another one die. Damn if she was going to let that happen again.

"Are you crazy?" she yelled at him after going out onto her front lawn. The man gave her body a slow perusal that sent shivers right down to her toes.

"Probably," he said.

What? Was he admitting he was crazy? She backed up a few steps. He took a leisurely sip of what she assumed was coffee, but who knew, maybe he was drinking booze already. She took another few steps back. Why couldn't she learn to mind her own business?

"Excuse my curiosity, but was that just a general observation, or was there a reason for your question?"

The humor—was he laughing at her?—in his voice annoyed her. She marched forward. "Has it not occurred to you that your dogs might run into the road and get hit?"

"Yep," he said.

She waited for more, then continued to wait. Why did the man have to be so freaking hot? Those broad shoulders and his six-pack abs made her want to press her fingers against his chest to see if he was as muscle hard as he looked. Dark brown hair, caramel-colored eyes, a killer body, and a day-old beard made for one potent man. It was the scruff that gave him a bad boy appearance, the kind of bad boy who'd always appealed to her, unfortunately. There wasn't a soft thing about him, not even in his eyes. They were hard and cold.

"Bah," she muttered when he remained silent. Waving a dismissive hand, she turned to go back into her house.

"Call them," he said.

Don't turn around, Riley. She turned. "What?"

"Call them. The ugly one is Pretty Girl and the black and tan one is Sally. Call them by name."

Riley glanced up and down the street to make sure there were no oncoming cars. Okay, she'd show him what an idiot he was by playing his stupid game. "Pretty Girl, Sally, come here." She clapped and crooned to them. They both ran to the edge of the sidewalk, sat their butts on the ground, and swept their tails across the grass. No matter how much she cajoled, they came no farther. Well, that was embarrassing, and the amusement in the man's eyes grated.

"My bad," she said as she slinked back to her house. At hearing his low chuckle, she lifted her hand and gave him her middle finger.

CHAPTER TWO

Cody cracked a rare smile as he watched the woman until she disappeared inside her house. "Did you just give me the finger, darlin'?"

Her hair—hanging straight down her back now—reminded him of a German shepherd's coat with the different shades of dark browns, lighter browns, and the gold streaks. Nice bod, too. Very nice. And he liked the way her eyes had flashed with fire when she'd gotten annoyed with him. He wondered what her name was.

Didn't matter, though. He was better off not knowing. The last thing he needed was the complication of a woman when his life was royally screwed up. He called the dogs in so he could dress for work.

As he headed for his car, his phone buzzed a text message.

```
Have a great first day on your new job,
Sonny Boy. Hope it's what you need to
turn your life around.
```

Cody crammed the cell phone back into his pocket. He got the sub-message. *We hope you're not still drinking.* If he answered his father before he managed to cool off, he'd say something he'd regret. He'd come late to his college professor parents, and they had never quite known what to do with him. Academia was their life, and for that reason, along with not wishing to add to the world's population, they'd elected not to have children. He could just imagine their surprise when at forty-two, his mother had found out she was pregnant.

Someday, he'd tell his father that he hated the nickname Sonny Boy. And someday, he would make them proud of him. That happening had been set back at least ten years when the professors had shown up unannounced a few months before and found him drunk out of his stinking mind. They were one-glass-a-day wine drinkers, anti-war, anti-killing anyone for any reason. That his country considered him a hero for his high kill count embarrassed them.

After witnessing his slurring, they had tried to convince him to return home where they could get him help. The dogs, they'd said, could be taken to a no-kill shelter since his mother couldn't tolerate animal hair. To keep from lashing out at the two people in the world he loved but didn't understand, he'd called on the training and discipline he'd learned as a SEAL sniper and had calmly asked them to leave him alone. What they hadn't understood and still didn't was that the dogs gave him a reason to face another day and another day after that.

A few weeks after his parents had visited, his former commander, Logan Kincaid, had shown up unexpectedly. The next thing Cody knew, he was at a secret location learning all about the *Sealion*, a stealth boat that had only been whispered about among the SEAL teams. Soon after, he'd participated in a K2 mission and hadn't touched a drop of liquor during the operation.

Since then, he'd cut out drinking during the day. Although he'd tried to make it through the nights without the numbing effects of alcohol, the nightmares had driven him back to the scotch bottle. Yet last night, he'd managed a few hours without the dreams. Well, he'd dreamed, but it had been of her, his neighbor with no name. He'd woken up with a massive hard-on, and he'd take that over the nightmares any day.

He pulled into the K2 parking lot at the same time as Ryan O'Connor, the team's medic. The last time he'd seen Doc had been three months before in Helsinki when they'd gotten a defector and his family out of Russia using the *Sealion*.

"Heard you're getting married," he said, bumping Ryan's shoulder hard enough to send the man sideways. "And I thought I was crazy."

His friend came right back at him. "You *are* a crazy son of a bitch."

Fully expecting it, he braced his body against the hard hit. "Oomph."

Ryan laughed. "I heard that. You've gone soft, old man."

It hadn't been that long ago when his body wouldn't have given way, and he sure as hell wouldn't have made a girly sound. Although any civilian looking at him would think him in excellent condition, he'd gotten lax on his training regimen and wasn't in the fighting form that was critical to their job. Time to get back in shape, in more ways than one.

If he didn't get his head screwed on straight, Kincaid wouldn't fire him, but he would ground him and send him to a head doctor. Cody knew this because the boss had been up front with him about his concerns. He appreciated the man's honesty, but Cody would quit before reliving his nightmares with a shrink. That meant he had to get a grip because his sobriety depended on keeping the job and being back with his teammates.

After he spent a half hour with Maria Buchanan, Kincaid's sister and team member Jake Buchanan's wife, getting all his new hire paperwork in order, Maria took him on a tour of the facilities. He was impressed with what his former commander had achieved. K2 Special Services was a state-of-the-art operation, and Cody itched to be included as a valued member of the team. Because Kincaid knew he'd gone a little crazy—more crazy than normal—he'd have to prove he had his act together. He just wished that was actually true.

"Everything's going to work out," Maria said, placing a gentle hand on his arm.

How much had she heard about him? His cheeks heated, and Cody glanced away, pretending to study the open war room where support staff was gathered around Jamie Turner, known as Saint to the team because he didn't drink, cuss, or brag about his conquests. He'd heard Saint had recently gotten married. What was with all the love crap going on with his teammates?

"Unless you're involved in an operation, you'll start each morning here," Maria said, pulling open a door. She led him into the most amazing gym he'd ever seen. Every imaginable exercise machine—treadmill, rowing machine, NordicTrack—you name it, and it was here. Along the back wall were weightlifting benches, and there was even a boxing ring. About a dozen people were inside, working out on the various machines to the sound of high-energy rock music blaring from overhead speakers. Two men Cody pegged as personal trainers were walking around the room, stopping now and then to assist someone.

He spied his other former SEAL teammates, Kincaid, Buchanan, and O'Connor. Kincaid was the first to notice him and gave a slight lift of his chin, indicating Cody should join them.

"Hit the deck," his boss said, when Cody reached them. "Last one to a hundred gets in the ring with me."

Hell. That was going to be him, but he'd be damned if he wouldn't give it all he had. He dropped alongside the others and powered through the first seventy-five push-ups, then with his arm muscles quivering and sweat pouring off him, he got to ninety-two before he collapsed face-down on the floor. What was about to follow was going to hurt.

Kincaid stared down at him, his lips curling in disgust. "Five o'clock, Dog. In the ring."

Cody gave a curt nod, embarrassed about his poor showing. On the plus side, he had until five to recover before he had to step into the ring and get knocked on his ass by the boss.

He spent the rest of the day familiarizing himself with K2 and the current operations going on in various parts of the world. Several times, he caught his thoughts straying to his neighbor, wanting to crack a smile at her giving him the finger. She was a feisty one. If he were in a better place . . . he quickly shut that kind of thinking down. Between being screwed up, starting a new job, and cutting down on the booze, he didn't have any room left for a woman. Even if a certain part of him down below disagreed.

All too soon, the day passed, and he found himself in the ring with Kincaid. Reluctantly in the ring, he amended. The rest of the team, along with other K2 employees, lined the perimeter, and after no one would bet on him, they gave up trying to place wagers. That was a boost to his ego. Not.

The only edge he had was that he was crazy. In their frequent bouts in-country, his team had all been leery of him, including the boss, as they never knew what to expect from "Dog." That would be his only advantage in the fight about to happen. The rules were that there were no rules, and although he'd come out on top more often than not with his teammates, he'd never bested his commander. Even a fool could predict that wasn't going to change today, and he just hoped Kincaid wouldn't hurt him . . . too much. That was his last thought as his vision centered on the fist coming at him.

"What happened?" Cody asked from his position, flat on his back on the mat, as Doc stared down at him. He shook his head in an attempt to clear the cobwebs.

Ryan O'Connor snorted. "First punch, you were out like a baby."

"I'm not a baby."

"You were today. The others left, didn't want to stick around and shame you."

And wasn't that humiliating? Cody pushed up and glanced around. There was no one in sight. "I thought he'd let me play with him for a round or two first, that maybe I'd get a lucky hit in."

"He was teaching you a lesson." Ryan stood. "Since you're not dead, I'm outta here. Got a hot date with my girl."

Alone, Cody tried to stand, only to end up back on his ass. As he sat, waiting for the fuzz in his brain to clear, he bristled at being likened to a baby. Okay, Ryan had intentionally said it to motivate him. Yeah, he got that. Well, he did once the fog lifted. And the boss, same thing. Getting knocked on his ass with the first punch was definitely a motivating message.

He pushed up with one hand while using the other to rub his aching jaw. Getting back in fighting form would be a piece of cake. First thing in the morning, he'd begin a training regimen. Between that and the workouts they all participated in during the workday, in two weeks, three weeks max, he'd be back in shape.

The getting his act together? Whole different story. At least, he could admit his head wasn't where it should be. That was a good thing, right? You couldn't fix a problem if you didn't acknowledge it. The nightmares weren't helping, nor was not sleeping. Damn strange how he had never had a problem with either of those things until he had opted out of the SEALs.

It was like as long as he was doing his job of killing people, he was good with it. He'd followed the ROE to a T, and those Rules of Engagement had been frustrating at best and downright stupid at worst. Too many times, he'd let a man live who he knew down to his toes was a terrorist, because in a military court his only defense for the kill would have been, "I just knew."

Since that would have meant go straight to jail, do not pass go, he'd not pulled the trigger of his sniper rifle without verifiable proof that the terrorist lined up in his sights actually was a terrorist. Maybe what haunted him was the Marine private who had been killed because Cody hadn't acted on his instincts. If there was one he knew of, how many other brothers in arms had died because of a bad guy he'd let live?

Riley glanced in her rearview mirror to see the truck behind her turn into the driveway across the street as she pulled into hers. Her mystery man climbed out of a silver pickup with dark tinted windows. She waved as she walked toward her door, and he responded with a barely discernable nod. Right, got it. Not going to be friendly. Probably for the best, because if sexy mystery man crooked his finger, she'd likely head right for him like the sex-starved woman she was.

All her energy and time the past year had gone into getting her veterinarian clinic up and running so she could pay off her student loans. No time to schedule sex into the appointment book, not even a ten-minute quickie. Before Sexy Mystery Man popped up, she'd not really given sex—or the lack thereof—much thought, being that she was worn out by the time she dragged herself home each night.

But she was thinking of it now—most especially the lack thereof—since her nameless neighbor had stood on his porch that morning, showing off a six-pack that merited serious admiration. Damn him, anyway.

Cats fed, a beer in the freezer, Riley took a quick shower, then slipped on panties and a robe. Although it had grown dark outside, she didn't turn on any lights in her bedroom, but she did open her window. No sound of a guitar, so more disappointed than she'd expected to be, she retrieved her beer-turned-to-slush and spent the next hour trying to catch up on her bookkeeping.

It had only been the month before that she'd finally felt like there was light at the end of the tunnel where her income versus expenses was concerned. *Progress, gotta love it.* Arthur, the most affectionate of her three felines, had curled up on her lap while Merlin perched on the back of a chair watching Pelli bat a ball around on the floor.

Arthur had been the catalyst for giving a lost girl the idea of becoming a veterinarian. Having bounced from foster home to foster home, living with strangers who didn't really want her, she had befriended their pets. Arthur was the only one that had actually belonged to her, a gift

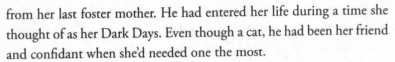
from her last foster mother. He had entered her life during a time she thought of as her Dark Days. Even though a cat, he had been her friend and confidant when she'd needed one the most.

When, as a kitten, he'd refused to eat, she'd checked out books from the library on the care of felines. Those first books had led to more complicated ones, and soon she was devouring any animal books she could get her hands on, including medical textbooks.

"You're my sweet boy, aren't you?" She scratched under his chin, causing him to purr. Yeah, life was pretty good these days, even if lacking in the sex department.

The bills paid, she tossed her empty bottle into the recycling bin. While she'd been busy with the paperwork, she'd managed to put the latest poisoned animal out of her mind, this time a dog. With the first one, she'd assumed it had gotten into someone's garbage or maybe some spilled pool chlorine. The second one had worried her. The third one had alarmed her, but apparently not the police since they hadn't followed up after she'd reported her concerns. Someone in the neighborhood was intentionally killing pets. She'd begun questioning the owners, but so far, she hadn't been able to find a connection. As she'd cried with the distraught owners, she had vowed that she would find the person responsible.

What she needed was to clear her head, and a good, sweaty run would do the trick. She tried to run two or three times a week, usually in the early morning before work, but had let herself get lazy the last few days. Since it was dark out and she wasn't stupid, she would just run up and down the sidewalk in front of her house under the streetlights.

After changing into running clothes, she headed out. She checked her Fitbit, noting the steps she'd taken so far that day. Three thousand more, she decided, clipping the device onto the waist of her shorts.

On the fifth pass by her house, she heard a car coming up the street at the same time she noticed Mystery Man on his lawn, tossing balls to his dogs. She subtly eyed him as she ran past, a thrill coursing through her at seeing him blatantly watching her.

The car's engine revved as it sped up, and Riley considered yelling at the driver to slow down, that there were children and animals living on the block. Better not to, though. Too many crazies behind the wheels of cars these days.

At the very moment she heard the auto's tires bump over the sidewalk, she was tackled from behind by a pair of strong arms, pulled back against a rock-hard body, and rolled across her lawn until finally being pulled behind a magnolia tree.

Acting on instinct, she bit down on the arm holding her. When the man swore and let go, she twisted and brought up her knee, aiming for his junk like she'd been taught in her self-defense class.

"Easy, darlin'," the man said, catching her leg and holding it with a strength she couldn't match. "I'm rather fond of that part."

Heart pounding as if she'd run a marathon, she looked into the caramel-colored eyes of her mystery man. He let her go, and she scooted away. As she became aware of her surroundings, she heard the squeal of tires as the car raced away. The man's dogs were furiously barking, and she glanced across the street to see them running back and forth along the edge of the sidewalk.

"What the hell's wrong with you?" she yelled.

The blasted man rolled onto his back and laughed. "Now there's a question."

"Are you crazy?" Great, her new neighbor was a wacko. He lifted onto an elbow, and she couldn't help but notice how the muscles in his arm flexed. And then he smiled, showing off a dimple on the right side of his cheek, which made her stomach twitchy. Okay, he was a hot wacko.

"You keep asking me that," he said. "Same answer as before. Probably."

Ooh-kay then. The sexy smile faded, and his intense focus on her made her want to squirm. "What? Why are you looking at me like that? Why did you tackle me?"

"Enough," he said, raising his voice.

Just as Riley decided she really was in the company of an unbalanced man and it was time to make her exit, the dogs quieted. "Oh, you were talking to them." There went that dimpled smile again.

"I'd never yell at you, darlin'." He pushed up to a sitting position. "Know who'd like to see you dead?"

Well, hell. Just when she was beginning to think he was sane, he went and ruined her hope. Hope, because her stomach was still doing that fluttery-twitchy thing, and really, she was way overdue for some playtime. She just bet he was a man who could teach her a few new tricks.

She shook her head. "Of course not. Why would you even ask such a question?"

As if used to scoping out his surroundings, he scanned the area around them. "Because whoever was driving that car aimed right at you."

"Huh?"

He reached over and put his fingers under her chin, closing her mouth. "Someone just tried to kill you, darlin'."

"Stop calling me that. My name's Riley. Riley Austin." Although she actually liked how the endearment sounded when he said it, she would never admit it. She had the feeling he was a man who pushed the boundaries of how far he could go. She swallowed a snort. *Admit it, Riley. You'd like him to push your boundaries.*

"Riley," he said, his voice caressing her name. "Nice to meet you. I'm Cody Roberts."

And of course, he would have a sexy cowboy name. "That car, it was just someone not paying attention, probably texting."

"Sorry, darlin' . . . ah, Riley, but no. They were looking right at you and aimed for you. Whoever it was had on a knit hat and dark glasses even though it's night. Couldn't tell if it was a man or woman. I should have gotten the plate number, but I was too busy saving your pretty ass. It was an older model Chrysler, a Sebring maybe, so we know that much."

He thought her ass was pretty? *Pay attention, Riley.* Did someone really try to run her over? She couldn't think of a soul who had it out for her. "No, no one's trying to kill me." On top of her patients dying of poison, that would just be too much. "No," she said with conviction, "you're wrong."

"I don't think—"

Those eyes. She could drown in them. Before she thought better of it, she leaned forward and, oh God, she was kissing him.

CHAPTER THREE

Cody was not a man easily shocked, but Riley Austin managed to do just that when, without warning, her mouth covered his. It had been months—a lot of months—since he'd touched a woman, and her taste was as sweet as a cool drink of spring water to a man lost for years in a godforsaken desert.

Never mind that he was crazy and she shouldn't let him anywhere near her, he needed what she was offering too much to be a gentleman. Hell, he'd never been a gentleman. He cradled the back of her neck with one hand and angled his head, deepening the kiss. Her mouth softened and her eyes slid closed.

Wanting more, he pressed his tongue to the seam of her lips, and her mouth parted. So good, so damn good. It had been too long since he'd had his mouth on a woman's, and he couldn't suppress a moan. At the sound, she pulled away and blinked as if coming out of a trance.

"I'm sorry," she whispered.

"I'm not." It was too dark to see the color of her cheeks, but he'd bet his two drinks for that night that she was blushing. Although he didn't know how to do tender, something inside him felt weirdly soft for this woman, a stranger to him, and it wasn't a feeling he liked.

Riley Austin, kisser of strange men, target of an unknown enemy, stood and brushed the grass from the back of her shorts. He wouldn't at all have minded doing that for her, but doubted she'd appreciate his hands on her ass. And it really was a lovely one. Cody pushed up and waited to see what she would say.

"Well, I guess it's possible you saved me from being hit by a car. That would have just been the last straw on an already crap week. So thank you." She glanced over at his dogs, both on their bellies, their attention glued on him. "I'm a veterinarian and to repay you, I'm offering my services free for a year."

The bad, bad side of his brain almost had his mouth saying that he'd love to have her services for a year. The small part of him that was still civilized managed to stop his mouth from uttering the words.

"Not necessary," he said, "but appreciate the offer. I do need to find a vet for them, and you'll do just fine, but I pay as I go."

"First visit is free then. My clinic is listed. Emerald Coast Animal Care. Night."

And just like that, she was gone. "Good night, darlin'," he softly said as she closed her door behind her. And he would be keeping an eye on her because whether or not she wanted to believe it, there was no doubt in his mind that whoever was driving that car had aimed right for her.

His interest in her had nothing to do with how sweet she'd tasted when he had kissed her. Nope, not a thing. Sally and Pretty Girl, sensing his mood as they so often did, trotted quietly alongside him into his house.

After making the first of his two drinks for the night, he went out to the porch and picked up his guitar. He strummed a few chords, then settled on the Clapton song bouncing around in his head, one he rarely played. As the sound of "Wonderful Tonight" curled around him, he closed his eyes and quietly sang the words while thinking of Riley

Austin and the kiss they'd shared. When the song ended, he sat back and stared at the house across the street. He never should have kissed her.

"Soldier."

The quiet voice stopped Cody. He motioned for his spotter to head on up to the roof of the building they'd scouted out a few days earlier. Cody was familiar with the occupants of the house across the alley. Covered in a burqa, Asra, the teenage girl who lived there with her parents and two brothers, beckoned him before disappearing inside.

He ran low to the other side of the street and ducked into the open door of her home, his Glock palmed in his hand. Taking off on his own was against regulations and foolhardy, but she'd given him good intel on the Taliban twice now. Her only condition had been that no one know about her. He understood. The Taliban would kill her and her family if they ever learned of her treachery.

Adjusting his eyes to the dusty shadows of the house, he zeroed in on Asra, doubled over and holding her stomach. She yanked away the material covering her face. Blood dripped from a cut on her neck. Every hair on his body stood on end. The situation was bad, but he wasn't sure why. Had the Taliban somehow learned that she'd been passing their locations to him? He stepped toward her. It was quiet, too damn quiet.

The air behind him shifted, and he spun . . .

Drenched in sweat, Cody shot up, gasping for air. Nothing about the nightmare made sense. He didn't know anyone named Asra, and was sure he'd never stepped inside her house. Why did he keep having this dream that always ended at the same place?

He'd only been injured once, but had no memory of what had happened. His team had found him unconscious on the street with a large knot on the back of his skull, so they assumed someone had hit him on the back of the head. Cody wasn't so certain, but he had no other explanation. Yet, he couldn't quite accept that anyone could have gotten that close without his sensing danger.

Since he had no desire to go back to sleep and risk the nightmare returning, he untangled his legs from the covers. Gray light poked in around the edges of the window blinds, telling him it was dawn. Plenty of time for a run before he had to leave for work. Pretty Girl and Sally, instantly leaving their beds when seeing him up and slipping on running clothes, pranced around his feet.

"Yeah, we're going running." They raced out of the room, then back in to see if he was coming. "Right behind you." They took off again. At the edge of the yard, he clipped on their leashes, the signal that they could cross the boundary.

The early December morning was chilly, but nothing like Vermont, where he'd grown up and his parents still lived, at this time of year. It was also nothing like the winter nights in Afghanistan. Those were a ballbuster. Sometimes he missed Vermont's winter snow, especially at Christmas, but since his time in the military, he'd become cynical where holidays were concerned.

His parents wanted him to come home for Christmas. He wasn't sure they meant it. For the love of the son they'd never expected to have and didn't understand, they politely sent him invitations to each of their college events, and for the love of them, he politely declined. He knew they'd been relieved he hadn't made an appearance, and he'd been just as relieved to not have been stared at with distaste by his parents' friends and colleagues, the son who'd disappointed the professors by not following them into academia.

If just one person asked how it felt to kill a human being, he feared he'd go ballistic. That question had been pointedly directed at him the last time he'd attended one of his parents' socials. He had walked out the door without answering because his answer would have been, "Would you have rather seen me or one of my teammates killed?"

Don't go there, Dog. Focusing on the sound of his feet slapping on the pavement and that of his dogs' panting breaths, he fell back on his sniper training and let his mind go blank. Nothing else mattered but who was lined up in his sights, or at that moment, putting one foot in front of the other.

Damn, he was fucked up.

Pretty Girl whined, and Cody glanced down at her to see her chocolate-brown eyes were trained on him. Stupid dog was entirely too sensitive to his moods. He looked away from her inquisitive eyes, stumbling at seeing the woman running ahead of him, one whose sexy bottom he recognized. Catch up with her or turn around and pretend he'd not seen her? He slowed, trying to decide what to do. His saner self said to turn around. Kissing her had been too good for his peace of mind. If he got near her, he'd want to do it again.

Pretty Girl took the decision out of his hands by giving a bark of welcome, then Sally echoed her, giving his own deeper bark. Riley turned, jogging backward, and her gaze settled on his dogs as she smiled at them. Damn, he wished she'd smile at him like that. Or, maybe he didn't wish that.

She ran in place, waiting for him to catch up, and when she finally met his eyes, her cheeks flushed and her smile seemed uncertain. Her gaze slid away as she returned her attention to the dogs. Was she embarrassed that she'd kissed him? When she knelt, he let the lines out on the leashes, giving the dogs permission to go to her.

"Hello, sweet things," she said, scratching under their chins, laughing when both tried to lick her face. "You said this one's name is Sally? You do realize he's a boy, right?"

"I noticed. All my dogs are named after Eric Clapton songs. He doesn't sing about men. Doesn't seem to bother Sally, though." He stepped closer, even though he should stay as far away from her as possible. "Behave, you two." The dogs plopped their butts on the ground, peering up at him with their soulful brown eyes, as if he were denying them their fun.

"It's okay. I'm used to being slurped by dogs." She stood, and her eyes focused on the vicinity of his neck. "Listen, about last night, I—"

"Forgotten." An outright lie. It would be a long time, if ever, that he'd forget how soft her lips were, how sweet she tasted. His gaze lowered to her mouth when she chewed on her bottom lip. Damn but he wanted her. But he was not for her. Until he got his head on straight, he wasn't for anyone.

Riley was mortified. He'd already forgotten she had kissed him? Or more like, her kiss had been so out of line that the last thing he wanted to do was remember. His bristled dark cheeks, along with that intense focus he trained on her, made her insides feel like pudding. He probably hated pudding. Gah, just being near him made her silly.

From the haunted look in his eyes, though, he was probably a man she should avoid if she were smart. But there was something about him that tugged at the places inside her too long ignored. What to do about that?

She shook one leg, then the other. "Well, I guess I'll finish my run. Wanna come?" His gaze slid over her, and his eyes darkened. *Smoldering.* There was no other word for the way he looked at her, and when she thought about what she'd said and his reaction, her cheeks felt like they were on fire.

He chuckled as he traced a finger over her bottom lip. "You have no idea how much I *wanna*, darlin', but I'd best be heading home."

"Bye," she whispered to his retreating back. "Nice butt," she added as he and his dogs rounded the corner.

The morning was normal, no emergencies, no poisoned animals. Riley breathed a sigh of relief as she pulled off her lab coat before heading for the small kitchen. Her staff of two, an assistant and an office manager, had gone out to lunch, and she welcomed an hour of quiet. After locking the door behind them, she stuck her head inside the refrigerator, eyeing the contents. Slim pickings. A container of lemon yogurt and a half-full package of cheese sticks were about it. That she'd forgotten to stop at the grocery store to restock on her way to work, she blamed on a man with caramel-colored eyes who had sucked all thoughts but those of him from her mind that morning.

"Damn brain-sucking zombies," she muttered. With her meager lunch in hand, she went to her office. After a few minutes of debate, she picked up the phone and called Maria Buchanan. She had first met Maria when she had brought in her cat, Mouse. After several visits to Riley's clinic with her cat, Maria and Riley had met for lunch one day and hit it off. They had since made lunch a weekly habit. Maybe Maria could talk her out of setting her sights on a man with a sexy cowboy name, a devastating dimple, and smoldering eyes.

A lunch date set up for the next day with her friend, Riley dug into her yogurt and cheese. She'd just finished when there was banging at the door. She glanced at the clock to see there was another thirty minutes until the clinic opened again, but if a pet owner had an emergency, she couldn't ignore whoever wanted in.

Someday, she would be able to afford security cameras, but until then, the only way to see who was on the other side was to open the door, which she did. Janie Forester, with a cat wrapped in a towel, and her young daughter, Kellie, at her side, rushed into the waiting room.

"Please, Max is dying," Kellie said, tears falling down her cheeks.

Riley took the bundle from Janie's arms. The poor cat was seizing and bleeding from the nose, both signs of poisoning. Riley's heart fell at knowing the cat was too far gone to save, but she would try, dammit.

"Stay here," she said, taking Max and running to her exam room. At the moment she set the cat down on the table, he took his last breath. "I'm so sorry, baby." As tears fell down her cheeks, she stroked the still animal's fur. "I swear I'll find out who did this to you. I swear it." She wet a cloth, and after tidying the cat as well as she could, she went to a storage closet and removed one of the small pine boxes. Little caskets.

When she had been fourteen, the foster family where she lived at the time had had a small terrier. The dog had been the only thing in the world she'd been sure actually loved her. When it got sick and had to be euthanized, the veterinarian had handed her the dead animal to take home and bury. Remembering how callously Cricket had been treated, she had bought a supply of the velvet-lined boxes for small animals shortly after opening her practice. She didn't charge anything for them. It was her way of trying to ease the pain of losing a beloved pet. Someday, maybe she could afford some bigger ones for the larger animals.

Or maybe the owners were so grieved that it didn't matter to them. She didn't know, only knew this was the part of her practice that she hated to the depths of her soul. After putting the cat inside, she returned to the waiting room. The little girl was tucked up under her mother's arm, and they both gave Riley hopeful looks when she entered the room.

Riley shook her head, and Kellie burst into tears. "I'm so sorry." Such inadequate words. Taking a seat next to Janie, she said, "I know this is a sad time for you both, but I need to ask you some questions. Would you rather stop back by later?"

"Do you . . . do you know what happened to him?" Kellie asked.

"I think so." Riley took the girl's hand.

Kellie hiccupped. "Can-can I see h-him?"

Brooke and Michelle returned from lunch, and when they saw the obviously upset family, they quietly headed for the back. "Brooke," Riley said to her assistant. "Kellie has the hiccups. Would you take her to the kitchen and get her a glass of water?" She turned to Janie. "Is that all right? I'd like to speak to you privately."

"Of course." After Kellie left, Janie brushed her fingers across her cheeks, wiping away her tears. "You said you knew what killed Max. He was perfectly fine this morning."

Riley went to the counter, leaned over it, and snatched a few tissues, bringing them to Janie. "I think he was poisoned."

"Oh my God! I can't imagine what he could've gotten into."

After a short debate with herself, she decided not to say that she suspected someone was poisoning pets. "That's why I'd like permission to do an autopsy." At Janie's hesitation, Riley added, "At no charge. It's professional curiosity on my part."

"It might upset Kellie."

"She doesn't have to know. In fact, I think it would be better not to tell her what I suspect. Afterward, I'll call you to come get him. I've found that it helps children if they can have some kind of ceremony, and for the first week or two, they like to put flowers on their pet's grave."

"Do you think an autopsy's necessary? I hate to think of any more being done to him. He was such a good cat."

"I really do. Was Max an outside cat?"

Janie shook her head. "No, but he escaped sometimes. Usually when Kellie left for school. He'd go looking for her, which he did early this morning. I left soon after her to run some errands and didn't even notice he had gotten out. I feel so bad. If only I'd searched for him."

"Cats are the best of escape artists. You can't blame yourself. Did you notice anything unusual? Anyone in your neighborhood that you didn't recognize?"

"No, nothing. After Kellie came home from school, she found Max in the bushes. I have no idea where he spent his day."

Although she hadn't expected Janie to be able to point a finger at the bastard killing pets, she'd hoped for a clue of some kind.

"Look, Mama, isn't she cute?" Kellie skipped to her mother, holding the three-month-old black-and-white kitten that had been left in a box at the clinic's door a few days before. "Can I have her? Please? Please? Please?"

"I'm sorry. She heard the kitten meow and wanted to see it," Brooke said, following Kellie back to the waiting room.

After a few minutes of begging by her daughter, Janie gave in. "Has she had her shots?"

Riley assured her that the kitten had all the vaccinations needed at that point.

"I'm going to name her Princess. Can I show her to Max so he'll know I'm not crying too much?" Kellie turned to Riley. "Max hates it when I cry."

"If your mother says it's okay. Just so you know, I need to keep Max with me for a day or two, then your mom's going to come get him so you can—"

"Max has to have a funeral like Grandpa had."

Riley smiled. Kids were so resilient. "I think Max would like that very much."

After Kellie visited with Max, talking to him, telling him about her new kitten, Janie left with her daughter.

"This one makes five," Brooke said, as she and Riley stared at poor Max.

"I know. Somehow I'm going to find out who's doing this. I'm doing an autopsy after we close, see what kind of poison they're using." She'd wanted to perform one on the last animal, the little terrier, but the owner had refused.

"I'll stay and help."

Riley gave her assistant a tired smile. "Thanks. I'd appreciate it."

CHAPTER FOUR

Riley Austin was late coming home. Cody checked his watch for what seemed like the hundredth time. A last-minute operation to track down a runaway teenage couple had popped up that afternoon. Some high government dude's daughter and her boyfriend had taken off when the man had forbidden her to see the boy. Although the boss hadn't said so, Cody would bet that Kincaid had agreed to find her because once they did, the man would owe Kincaid. The boss was very good at collecting favors.

Where was his beautiful neighbor? He and Doc would be leaving the next day, and Cody needed to make arrangements to board his dogs. Some thirty minutes later, she arrived home, and he headed over.

"Stay," he said, when his dogs reached the edge of the sidewalk. "Hey, long day?" he asked when he came up next to Riley on the lighted porch. The first thing he noticed when she glanced at him was that she looked tired. The second thing was the sadness in her eyes.

"Very," she answered as she fumbled with her keys.

He took them from her. "You okay?"

"Sure."

At the tears pooling in her eyes, he tsked. "Little liar. Wanna talk about it?" What was he doing? The last thing he needed or wanted was to take on someone else's problems. He was already keeping an eye out for the car that had tried to run her over. That right there was beyond how involved he wanted to get with her. Now who was the liar? He'd like very much to be involved with her, just in a different way.

"Some . . . someone's kil-killing my patients."

The tears she'd been trying to blink away began to roll down her cheeks. As if his arms had stopped taking instructions from his brain, they slid around her even though he'd ordered them not to. And damn, did she ever feel good there.

"I-I stayed late to au-autopsy a little girl's prec-precious p-pet."

Well, hell. It was her trembling lips as she tried hard not to cry that gut punched him. He got her door open, then scooped her up. As he stepped inside, she pushed the door closed behind them.

"Cats," she mumbled against his neck.

At first he wasn't sure what she meant, but a chorus of meows had him glancing down to see three of the little beasties running toward them. The smallest one, a kitten, ran right up his leg, and Cody felt its claws digging in all the way up.

With Riley in his arms, a baby monster halfway up his body, and one adult cat winding around his legs, he shuffled his way to the sofa. The third feline, a sleek, shorthaired black cat, had jumped onto the back of the couch and was watching him through narrowed eyes. Considering the animal obstacles, he congratulated himself for being able to lower Riley down without falling on top of her. Although said obstacles would have made for the perfect excuse for losing his balance. Finding himself on top of her would work for him.

"You got any wine?" he asked. "I'll pour you a glass." The way she was hurting, it was either find something non-touching to do or pull her back into his arms and kiss her tears away.

"Hate wine. There's beer in the fridge. Put a lime slice in it, then put it in the freezer."

She reached up, pulled the black—still glaring at him—cat down, curling herself around it. The kitten and orange-stripped cat followed him into the kitchen. He found the beer and a baggie of lime slices to the tune of cat-kitten whining. He recognized that sound. It was the same begging his dogs gave him when they were hungry and he was late coming home. After opening a few cabinets he found the cans of cat food. The kitten had made its way to Cody's shoulder and was sucking on his ear lobe.

"Damn cats," he muttered. The benefit of having dogs was they'd still be sitting at his feet, not nibbling on him after leaving a trail of puncture holes on his skin. The tiny thing didn't seem to be offended by his curse on them, just kept suckling. It tickled and a laugh escaped.

"You're an idiot," he said, pulling the little demon away and setting him down. At the sight of the three bowls of food he put on the floor, two of Riley's creatures hurried over and busied themselves eating. The one she cuddled in her arms ignored him and the food.

Cody walked to the sofa and, ignoring the hiss from the sleek animal, carried him to the third bowl, which the wicked little monster had already moved to.

"Eat," he said, setting the black cat down. He scooped up the kitten and took it with him to the living room. "We've come to keep you company." He dropped the kitten into her arms. Riley buried her face in its fur, and hearing her quietly weep, he eyed the door with longing, but his feet refused to move.

Unable to leave her alone while she was hurting, he heaved a sigh. Although he knew half his body would hang over the side, he toed off his shoes, and then scooted up behind her, spooning her. She tensed for a few seconds before relaxing against him, and miracle of miracles, stopped crying.

As he held a woman he barely knew, her body curled against his while she clutched her kitten, he let the peacefulness of the moment take him away. She snuggled into him, and he sighed from the pleasure of having her in his arms.

Cody jerked awake to the feel of soft fingers caressing his cheek. It was so familiar that a fuzzy picture hovered at the edge of his mind, one from his past. As he stared—somewhat disoriented—at Riley's face as she leaned over him, he tried to recapture the memory. It seemed important that he do so, but it slipped away.

"Hi," Riley said, her voice soft as if they were lovers and she'd just awakened him on a normal morning day.

As he grew aware of his surroundings, heard the low hum of a refrigerator that wasn't his, he pushed away and sat up. "What time is it?"

"One in the morning. I'm really sorry. I guess I fell asleep."

He blinked his eyes, trying to clear the dewy haze in them. "Guess I did, too. Sorry. I only came over to ask if you could board my dogs for a few days. Got sidetracked, apparently."

At her smile, his heart skipped a beat. He had to get away from her while he still could. She was damn sexy all mussed up. The long hair that reminded him of a German shepherd's coat with all its colors was a tangled mess, putting him in mind of a woman just made love to. Too bad that wasn't the reason, but better that he'd not gone that far. He would only hurt her in the end.

"Stay," she whispered just before she kissed him.

If he'd been a better man, he would get up and leave. Cody Roberts was a bad man, though, and he cradled the back of her neck with his hand, angled his head, and took control of the kiss. Her mouth was hot and sweet, and when he slipped his tongue inside, and she gave a throaty little moan, he flipped their bodies so that she was under him.

He wanted her like he'd never wanted a woman before. But as they stared at each other, both breathless, he looked into those hazel eyes flecked with gold, and knew he couldn't dump his shit on her. If he thought he could make love to her, then disappear from her life, nothing would stop him from taking her right then. But she lived across the street, so there could be no disappearing, and he had the uneasy feeling that if they did make love, he'd never be able to walk away.

She was a good person, a woman who cried over an animal she couldn't save. To Cody, that made her a true hero, and she deserved a man with a mind that wasn't on the brink of insanity. He had to have one more kiss, though. Had to memorize her taste and the warm softness of her lips touching his.

"Riley," he said, covering her mouth with his. She responded by wrapping her arms around his neck and pushing her pelvis against his raging erection. Christ. Before he lost the will to leave her, he levered up and onto his feet.

"Can I drop my dogs off at your clinic tomorrow?" he said as he backed away. Her eyes filled with hurt. He was a bastard, no doubt about it. With any other woman, he would have walked away right then. With Riley, he just couldn't do it.

He forced himself not to look away from those wounded eyes. "If you're wondering if I want you, you have no idea how much I do. I'm not in a good place right now, and I find myself not wanting to hurt you. That right there is new for me. Normally, I don't much care."

No answer. All three of the cats had snuggled up to her after he had left her side, and she turned her back to him, a clear message that she wanted him gone. Before he walked out, he couldn't resist running his gaze over her one last time. She was beautiful and pure of heart. Maybe he'd taken a step toward forgiveness for his sins when he had refused to contaminate her with his black soul.

"Bring your dogs tomorrow. My receptionist will take care of you."

He hated how broken she sounded, but he couldn't help her. "Thank you," he said to the back of her head. Weary of everything—his life, the nightmares, an uncertain future, disappointing a beautiful woman—he trudged home and went straight to the scotch bottle.

His music had never sounded so depressing before. There had always been sadness in the notes he played, but tonight, he was killing her. As she sat at her bedroom window a few hours after he left, listening to Cody play his guitar, Riley swiped at the tears running down her cheeks. She thought she'd cried herself out, but apparently not. Now with Cody's mournful songs tugging at her heart, the tears were flowing again. He wasn't a happy man, couldn't be to play music that made her heart ache for him.

Maybe she should be embarrassed that she'd fallen apart in front of him, but she didn't have the energy for it. When he had wrapped his big body around her, it had seemed as if he were shielding her from the ugliness going on in her world. The last time she had fallen asleep in a man's arms had been in college, and she had forgotten how good that kind of intimacy felt.

She was, however, embarrassed that she'd practically attacked him, and even worse, had begged him to stay. But he had awakened that part of her that had lain dormant since she had broken up with her college boyfriend, and she was afraid it was going to be impossible to stuff that particular genie back into the bottle. Lifting the blinds, she peeked out. Even though he was sitting on his porch playing his guitar, it was too dark to see him.

It was late, and she moved to her bed, but left the window open so she could fall asleep listening to Cody play. After her earlier nap wrapped in his arms, she missed the cocoon of his body surrounding her. That was strange, since she hardly knew him.

The next morning, she blinked her eyes open and stretched. Arthur and Pelli pounced on her as soon as she moved, while Merlin sat at the end of the bed looking on with disdain, clearly not approving of their meows as they begged for breakfast. More refreshed than she'd been in days, Riley picked up Pelli and held him above her head.

"Morning, rotten." He tried to squirm out of her hands. "Right. We want our breakfast, don't we?" She made a quick detour to the bathroom, all three of her furry friends following her, then headed for the kitchen.

With a peek out the window, she saw Cody standing on his porch, a cup in his hand while he watched his dogs. Like the first time she'd seen him, he wore only a pair of sweat pants. The man must be immune to the early morning chill. If he would appear like that every morning, it would give her a fabulous kick-start to her days.

"You're one magnificent man, Cody Roberts," she said, following it up with a sigh. When he called the dogs and went inside his house, she fed the cats, then showered and dressed for work. His silver truck was gone when she backed out of her driveway, so she probably wouldn't see him again until he came back from wherever he was going. She would tell Michelle, her receptionist, not to come get her when he dropped off his dogs, even if he asked for her.

As she turned onto the street leading to her clinic, she sent up a little prayer that no more poisoned pets would turn up. Also, she needed to contact the police again. Not much they could do without any leads, but they could keep an eye out as they patrolled the neighborhood.

She slowed as she approached her building. At the sight of the man leaning against the bed of the silver truck with darkened windows, Riley cursed her stupid heart for doing a happy dance. His two dogs sat at his feet, their attention on him. Maybe she should hire him to give obedience lessons to some of her more rambunctious patients. Giving him a wave as she drove past, she parked in the back. Neither Brooke's nor Michelle's car was in sight, which meant she would have to deal with Cody, so there went her plan to avoid him.

Perversely irritated, she took her time as she turned on the lights, started the coffee pot, booted up the computers at the front desk and in her office, and made a quick check on the three small dogs, two cats, and one extremely vocal potbellied pig being boarded. When she could think of nothing else to delay her, she unlocked the front door.

Mr. Magnificent leaned against a post under the overhang, arms crossed over his chest, dogs again sitting docilely at his feet. For all appearances, her sexy neighbor appeared to be half asleep. Riley wasn't fooled, though. As much as he might wish otherwise, she was beginning to see past the image he projected. Under that lazy stance and deceptive calm a storm brewed. Not good that storms fascinated her.

"Cody."

"Riley."

She sputtered a laugh, and was rewarded with a crooked smile and a flash of that dimple. Yep. The man intrigued her. So much for keeping him at arm's distance. "Come in. My receptionist isn't here yet, so I'll get these guys checked in." Cody and his dogs followed her, stopping at the counter. She went on around.

"Will you use the food I brought for them?"

"Of course." She resisted sliding her hand over his bad boy scruff, and it was close, but she didn't lick her lips either. Yummy was the word of the day, though. He wore an olive-green T-shirt that stretched across broad shoulders, and tan cargo pants covered his bottom half. Testosterone radiated from his every pore, and she lowered her gaze to the check-in sheet to keep him from seeing the lust that was surely shining in her eyes.

"I'll get their stuff out of my truck in a minute then." He glanced down at the dogs. "They need to stay together, okay?"

"No problem." Certain that she'd gain control of her libido, she lifted her head, her gaze falling on the small logo on his shirt. "What's K2?"

"Where I work. Is there someone around at night when you're not here? You know, should one of them get sick or something."

She'd never had anyone ask her that question before, which just went to show how much he loved his dogs. He'd been keeping their conversation all business, and she followed his lead. "I have a college student who sleeps here at night. He leaves at six, so the boarders are only unattended for an hour, until I or one of my staff arrives." Apparently, he wasn't going to explain what K2 was, which made her all the more curious as to what he did.

"I'm not sure when I'll be back. Hopefully in a few days, but I'll keep in touch." He locked gazes with her. "Can I get your cell number? You know, so I can call and check on them. I might not be able to call here during normal hours."

She broke eye contact before she embarrassed herself just staring at him. It made sense to give him her number, but it seemed like they were moving into alien territory. Did she want him to be able to call her anytime he wished? She glanced up to see he was watching her. "Sure." She rattled off her number, and he put it in his phone. "I'll need yours. In case of an emergency, which I don't expect to happen, but better safe than sorry, right?" She waved the boarding form in front of his face. "I need it for our records. That's all." Now she was babbling.

After giving her his number, he ordered the dogs to stay, then left to get the food he'd brought. She used the form to fan herself. "Jeez, Riley, you're behaving like a high school girl with a crush on a cute boy." One she had kissed and who had held her as she cried, and now they were acting as if none of that had happened.

She leaned over the counter and peered down at Pretty Girl and Sally. "Either of you got any insights on your Mr. Magnificent you'd be willing to share?" She would swear that both dogs looked back at her with amusement. "Right. Mum's the word."

"Why are you talking to yourself, and who's Mr. Magnificent?" Brooke asked, walking up behind her.

The front door opened, and Riley turned to Brooke and lifted a brow.

"Ahhh," her assistant drawled, her gaze raking over Cody as he walked in, a slow smile forming on her pretty face.

Riley wanted to hiss like a territorial cat warning off an invader. This was where she should turn him over to Brooke and go on about her business, but her feet refused to move. Her receptionist followed Brooke in, stepping up to the counter.

"Hello," Michelle said. "Can I help you?"

Both of her employees were single, and both were eyeing Cody as if he were a Popsicle they wanted to lick. Not that she blamed them, but it still irritated her.

"I'm helping him," Riley snapped. Three pairs of eyes settled on her. The two females looked at her as if they'd never seen her before, which this side of her they hadn't. Hell, she hadn't even known she had a *this side*. As for Cody, he was unreadable, but then there went the slightest curve of one side of his mouth. Against her will, she smiled back.

"Ahem . . ."

At the sound of Brooke clearing her throat, Riley realized she and Cody were standing there, staring at each other. Heat rushed into her cheeks, and she grabbed the bag he had set on the counter.

"Any instructions?" she asked, getting her professional mask back into place.

"Just that you keep them together. Can I see where they'll be?"

"Sure. Come with me." With any other boarder, she would have had Michelle or Brooke take the owner on a tour, but she wasn't about to leave either of those she-wolves alone with him.

He came up next to her, close enough that her skin warmed where he almost touched her, and God, he smelled good. The man was entirely too potent and sent all of her senses into a frenzy. She was honest enough with herself to admit that she'd never had it this bad for any man before—not since Reed, anyway—which was tough luck as Cody had made it clear that nothing was going to happen between them. His dogs followed along, their toenails clicking on the tiled floor, and she concentrated on them.

When she had remodeled, she'd included four large kennel spaces along with smaller areas for the cats and little dogs. The dog pens had access to individual outdoor fenced-in yards. As she had no large dogs in residence at the moment, Cody could have his pick.

"You have a preference?" She waved a hand at the pens.

After a quick glance, he took the bag from her hands, went to the pen at the end, and opened the gate. "Come," he said in a voice she was learning to recognize as one he only used with his dogs. It was firm, but there was a gentleness in his tone, and she wished all animal owners were like him.

Pretty Girl and Sally trotted into the cage, then turned and looked up at him as if questioning what their next move should be. He squatted in front of them. "I'll come back for you, I promise," he said, a hand on each of their heads. "You be good for Riley, or I'll take your balls away for a week." At the word "balls" both dogs' ears perked up.

From the bag, Cody removed four balls, two large bone chews, and a tug rope. The dogs eyed the balls with longing. "Not yet," Cody said. "We're not done talking. If for some reason I don't come back, it doesn't mean I don't love you. It just means . . ." He bowed his head.

Most pet owners when boarding their animals just dropped them off. A rare few asked to see where their furry people would be kept, and Riley couldn't think of a time when one had talked to their pets the way Cody was with his dogs. Feeling as if she were intruding on a personal moment between him and the dogs, she quietly left the room and waited for him in the hallway. For some reason, tears stung her eyes. What did he mean by implying there was a chance he might not come back? Although she didn't know him well, she knew without doubt that he wouldn't willingly abandon those two animals.

A few minutes later, he came out and stopped in front of her. "I expect to be back in a few days. I'll keep in touch and let you know when to expect me." His gaze moved to the wall behind her shoulder for a few seconds, and by the haunted look in his eyes, she could swear that he was seeing a ghost from his past. Then his eyes focused back on her. "With what I do, there's always the chance I won't return. You don't owe me anything, and you can say no, but I'm going to ask two things of you."

"If it's in my power." She was afraid she wouldn't be able to refuse him anything. The man was tortured by something, and her soft heart had already decided to hurt for him.

"The first thing, promise you'll find good homes for them."

She nodded. "I can do that. And the other?"

The way he hesitated told her that whatever he was about to say, he'd rather not. "There's a dog, Layla, that got left behind in Afghanistan. If she can be found and I'm not able to, my teammates will get her here. I'd like you to reunite her with Pretty Girl and Sally. So should the unexpected happen, and you do have to find a home for these two, just make sure that whoever it is will take a third dog. Will you do that for me?"

Was it possible to fall for a man because of a few words he'd said? She wondered if he realized how much he had revealed about himself

41

just then. Riley swallowed the lump in her throat, and not trusting her voice, she nodded. The bigger-than-life man standing in front of her with pain shining in those dark eyes had a bigger-than-life heart.

"Thank you." He lifted his hand and trailed a finger down her cheek. "Another time, another place, Riley, you and I . . ." He trailed off, his gaze falling to her mouth.

Yes, kiss me. He didn't, though. As he walked away, she said a prayer that he would stay safe, while wondering what was wrong with this time and this place.

CHAPTER FIVE

He'd come close to kissing her again. Almost wished he had. The vibes for this operation weren't good. It was probably because of his state of mind and had nothing to do with any danger he would face tracking down two kids who thought they were in love. Still, he couldn't shake the feeling that what seemed like a piece of cake was going to turn out to be far from it. He should have kissed her good-bye.

"You'll be flying into Des Moines where I'll have a car waiting for you. It's about an hour and a half drive to Fort Dodge, the last place the couple was spotted," Kincaid said, drawing Cody's attention back to the briefing.

Cody eyed the digital map Kincaid had pulled up on the wall. "Who the hell runs away to Iowa?"

Ryan O'Connor, his teammate on this operation, smirked. "What, you don't like potatoes and corn?"

"Corn and potatoes, I don't have a problem with. It's dumb kids I don't like." Cody sat back in his chair. "What's the background on these two?"

Kincaid slid dossiers across the table, one to him and the other to Ryan. "Small problem. The boy's father is an antique gun collector, and several of his pieces are missing."

The bad vibes that had been doing a slow dance in his head decided it was time to do a jig. What the hell was wrong with him? He'd never had misgivings before about walking into any situation. For a millisecond, he considered telling Kincaid that he wasn't ready to return to action, but then he'd probably be ordered to see a head doc. Besides, the mission was just to retrieve two kids, nothing he couldn't handle.

At the Pensacola airport, a Learjet was waiting to fly them to Des Moines, arranged so that they wouldn't have to go through airport security to board a commercial flight. Considering both he and Doc were carrying, and each had knives secreted on their bodies, they would have set off all kinds of alarms.

"When am I gonna get to meet your woman?" he asked, once the Learjet's wheels lifted.

Ryan laughed. "Don't let Charlie hear you call her my woman. She'll punch you in the nose."

"I'll make a note of that. I'm still trying to wrap my head around all my mates getting hitched. No way I'm drinking the water at K2."

"Your turn will come, and it'll have nothing to do with the water. It just takes the right woman."

His friend sounded happy, not like the man who a year ago had mourned the death of his first wife. Cody had sensed that there was more to the story than a simple robbery gone wrong, but if so, Ryan had never shared the details. All of his teammates were disgustingly in love, their eyes lighting up at the slightest mention of their wives or fiancées. It was one of the things that made Cody uneasy coming to K2, like an outsider peering into the windows of their happy homes.

Although his parents had been baffled by their son's love of all things military since the day he'd found a G.I. Joe in the toy box at day school, he couldn't remember the last time they'd hugged him. They'd made it quite clear they didn't approve of his life choices, and displays of affection weren't in their DNA. All the love business going on around him unwillingly fascinated him, but no way was that a poke of envy he felt.

He had met Kincaid's family, and the man they'd called Iceman during their SEAL days, the man he'd once suspected might live out his days alone, had gone all touchy-feely, unable to keep his hands off his wife and children.

Then there was Jake and Maria. Someday he would get Jake drunk enough to learn how he'd gotten up the nerve to go after the boss's sister, risking life and limb. That had to be love, right? Not long after that, Jamie Turner had fallen into the trap with a woman named Sugar. Cody was pretty sure Jamie could entertain him for hours with that story. And now Ryan was about to marry a stunt plane pilot who would punch Cody in the nose if he said the wrong thing to her. Already he liked the woman.

It boggled the mind how each of his teammates had somehow found a woman who perfectly suited him.

"You'll meet Charlie as soon as we get back. Kincaid's having an engagement party at his beach house." Ryan glanced at him. "You're welcome to bring a date."

Hell. Cody Roberts didn't date. Not anymore. Yet, the way Riley's eyes had darkened with desire when he'd kissed her popped into his mind. Since she was the only woman he knew in Pensacola, maybe he'd ask her. It wouldn't mean anything, wouldn't be a real date, just neighbors going somewhere together.

Liar. Not liking that voice in his head, Cody lowered his seat back and closed his eyes, pretending to go to sleep. Problem— behind his closed eyelids, there was Riley's sweet mouth, parting open when he'd almost kissed her. He willed away the image of her leaning against the wall and how he'd wanted to push his body hard against hers and take her right then and there in the hallway of her animal clinic.

A woman who cried at the loss of someone else's pet deserved better than he could ever give her, though. After he got home and picked up his dogs, maybe he'd look for someplace else to live so he wouldn't see her every day.

"We're on the ground," Ryan said, punching Cody's arm.

Cody blinked open his eyes, surprised he'd fallen asleep. Too afraid the nightmares would come, he never slept on planes or wherever someone might hear him call out. Since his teammate wasn't looking at him as if he'd just stepped off a spaceship from Mars, it seemed he hadn't yelled anything.

He'd nodded off thinking of Riley. Maybe she was the answer to keeping his demons at bay. If he could fill his mind with her before going to sleep, there might not be any room for whatever ghosts were haunting him.

"Let's roll," Ryan said, grabbing his bag from under his seat when the plane came to a stop. "I want to get this kindergarten operation over with so I can get home. Charlie has an air show Sunday I don't wanna miss."

And Cody only had his dogs to go home to. But that was the way he wanted it, right? "Yeah, let's get it done."

The pilot opened the cabin door, and Cody followed Ryan out onto the tarmac, where a man wearing a rental car–logoed shirt handed him the keys to a black Range Rover.

"Gimme." Ryan made a grab for the keys.

Cody fisted them. "Nope." He slid behind the wheel before his teammate took it in his head to wrestle for the keys. "Sweet," he said, checking out the interior.

"I'm driving tomorrow." Ryan tapped his phone to bring up the hotel coordinates for the place that Kincaid had booked for them for the first night. Before leaving the Des Moines area, they got a bag of burgers and two large coffees to go at a fast-food restaurant.

After turning onto the highway in the direction of Fort Dodge, Cody took a sip of his black coffee. One thing he liked about a mission was that he didn't crave a drink. He supposed it was ingrained in his brain that alcohol and missions don't mix, not that the one they were on now was risky. But boots on the ground was a whole different mindset, whether it involved dumb love-struck kids or bullets whizzing past his ears in the middle of some hellhole desert. Or maybe being on an operation meant he wasn't sitting at home in the dark, afraid to go to sleep, needing the scotch to dull his mind.

"What's the latest on Layla?" Ryan asked as he munched on a handful of fries.

At the mention of her, Cody swallowed the lump of hamburger that now felt like a jagged rock scraping its way down his throat. He drank some coffee to help it go down before answering. "The dog Wizard thought might be her wasn't. He's got everyone looking for her."

"Wizard won't quit until he finds her."

"If . . . if she's still alive." He was losing hope, but Ryan was right. Cody had saved Wizard's life, and the man believed he owed Cody, so he wouldn't give up. Problem was, Wizard's time in-country was about up. If Layla wasn't found soon, then she wasn't going to be.

Thinking of the dog he'd left behind always sent him to a dark place, and he didn't need to go there in the middle of an operation. He passed a slow-moving car, a classic Mustang, a couple out for an afternoon ride, it appeared. The woman's hair reminded him of Riley's, and he filled his mind with her. As soon as he did, the churning in his gut eased.

"So there Jake and I were, about to get it on for the first time, and in walks Saint."

"No kidding? What did you do?" Riley needed this lunch with Maria. She'd been laughing from almost the time they sat, and it felt good to get her mind off an animal serial killer for a while.

Maria grinned. "Gave my brother a piece of my mind for interfering my love life. He'd sent Saint to replace Jake as my bodyguard 'cause he knew exactly what Jake and I were up to. Logan finally came around when he realized Jake and I loved each other, so we're all good now."

Riley pushed aside the last few bites of her chicken taco salad, while watching Maria devour a platter of cheese enchiladas. "How is it you don't weigh a thousand pounds?"

"Jake makes sure I get a lot of exercise." Maria winked, giving a lecherous grin.

"Lucky you." She'd met Jake once when he came into the clinic with Maria to drop off their cat for boarding. The man was crazypants hot, but he'd only had eyes for Maria, which Riley thought was really cool. Not that she blamed him. Maria was strikingly beautiful with her olive skin, dark sloe-eyes, and wavy black hair.

"Still no love life for you?"

Her sexy neighbor with the cowboy name popped into her mind. Nah. He was heartache on a stick. Still . . . "There's a guy I'm attracted to, but I think he's got issues."

"Those are the kind you want to avoid." Maria signaled for the check. "Although I'm not one to talk. Jake's middle name was *issues* for a while there."

"You're right, but he's my new neighbor, so he's going to be hard to avoid. Not to mention, his picture is in two places in the dictionary. Once under eye candy and then again under, oh my God, he's got a hot bod."

"Want me to check him out?"

"You mean like look at him?"

Their waitress set the check on the table, and Maria grabbed it before Riley could. "You paid last time. No, I'm talking about running his name, see if he's got a record. At least you'd know if he's trouble as far as the law is concerned." She put a credit card on top of the bill and pushed it to the end of the table.

"Isn't it illegal for you to nose into someone's records?" Even though Riley was tempted, it didn't feel right.

"No, records are public knowledge." She shrugged. "Up to you."

"I don't know. I think Cody's the kind of man who wouldn't appreciate me checking on him like that."

Maria's eyes widened. "Cody? What's his last name?"

"Roberts, but let me think about it before you do anything."

A wide grin lit Maria's face. "I don't have to check into him. He works for us. Oh man, this is going to be fun."

"That's your company, K2? You never said exactly where you worked, come to think of it." Wow, she could get the scoop on Cody, but she still felt uneasy about prying into his life. "Exactly what is K2?"

"K2 Special Services. We do a lot of things, some I can tell you about and some I can't as they're classified."

Secret stuff? That made Riley all the more curious about her neighbor. She glanced at her watch. "I'd love to hear more, but time to get back to the clinic."

After signing the credit card receipt, Maria slid out of the booth. "I'll just say that Cody's one of the good ones." She chewed on her bottom lip, making Riley think she was considering her words. "I'll tell you that he was on the SEAL team with my brother and Jake. He was their sniper. Anything else, you'll have to learn from him."

A SEAL? She didn't know much about the military or their branches, but she'd read a few SEAL romances, and those guys were supposed to be the baddest of the bad. And he'd been their sniper, so was his sole job to kill people? She wasn't sure how she felt about that.

Maria was watching her as if waiting for a reaction. Before Riley could think of a response, her cell played the oldies song "Doctor! Doctor!" It would be Brooke or Michelle on the clinic landline, and they would only interrupt her lunch with an emergency.

"Yeah?" she said, the phone to her ear as she walked out with Maria. She listened to Michelle for a moment. "I'll be right there. Tell Brooke to start flushing out his stomach." Dammit, not another one.

"I've got an emergency." She increased her pace, striding ahead of Maria. About to break into a run, she thought of Maria's adorable cat, Mouse. Maria and Jake lived in her part of town. Turning and walking backward, she said, "Don't let your cat out for any reason."

"What?" Maria walked faster, keeping up with her. "Is something wrong?"

"Someone's poisoning animals. Just keep Mouse inside, okay? Gotta run." With that, she turned and jogged to her car.

"Call me tonight," Maria yelled after her. "I might be able to help."

Riley doubted it, but she didn't have time to ask why Maria thought she could be of help. "Sure, okay. Later." She jumped into her car, and backed out of the parking space. Not caring if she was speeding, she pressed her foot down on the gas pedal. If a cop stopped her, she'd just flash her doctor's credentials and deal with the fallout when she arrived at an animal hospital instead of a human one.

"Call Emerald Coast Animal Clinic," she said to Bluetooth.

"Calling Emerald Coast Animal Clinic," the robotic voice confirmed.

"Update," she said when her receptionist answered.

"Brooke's flushing out his stomach. Hold on a sec while I go to your office."

Riley impatiently tapped her thumb on the steering wheel, waiting for Michelle to come back on the line. Who the hell got off on poisoning helpless animals?

Duncan, the male mixed breed having his stomach pumped, had been her patient since his elderly owners had adopted him from an animal shelter two days before he was due to be euthanatized. Some cold-hearted bastard who'd never been caught had shot Duncan in the left eye when he was a stray. No one had wanted a one-eyed older pet until Mr. and Mrs. Vaughn had chosen him. They loved that dog.

"The Vaughns were standing in front of me when I was talking to you. They're really upset," Michelle said, coming back on the line. "I popped my head into the exam room on the way back here. Brooke thinks he'll be okay."

Thank God. "I'm five minutes away. Tell her . . . Never mind, she knows what to do. Find out from the Vaughns how long he's been sick. Be there in a few."

The Vaughns were such a nice couple, and it would break her heart to have to tell them they'd lost Duncan. Arriving at her clinic, Riley slammed the gearshift into Park, and ran straight to the exam room.

"How's he doing?" She slipped on a lab coat.

Brooke finished washing her hands. "I think he's going to make it."

Michelle poked her head in. "The Vaughns said they took him to the dog park to let him run. They'd been there about ten minutes when they noticed him next to a bush, eating something. Mr. Vaughn brought what Duncan didn't get a chance to finish. Looks like hamburger meat. He said he thought it was suspicious that someone would leave a chunk of raw meat at a dog park, so he used his poop bag to scoop it up. I put the bag into a sealed plastic one and stuck it in the fridge. Is that okay?"

The poisoned meat evidence combined with the number of affected pets gave Riley hope that the police would finally take her seriously.

"You did great, Michelle. Thanks. Tell the Vaughns I'll come talk to them in a few." Riley did an exam, checking Duncan's vitals, relieved that all his signs were close to normal.

"You're going to be okay, sweetie," she said when Duncan licked her arm.

Brooke brought a wet cloth over to clean his face. "I'm so glad we can give the Vaughns good news."

So was Riley. "I'll go talk to them. Bring him out when you've got him all pretty again."

After sending Duncan home with his happy owners, she went to her office and called the police again. The dispatcher told her it would probably be the following day before an officer could come by to take a report. That sucked, but not much she could do about it.

She stopped by the front desk. "Michelle, when you get a chance, call the other clinics in the area. Ask if they've treated any poisoned animals."

Thankfully, the remainder of the afternoon was business as usual. "What'd you find out?" she asked Michelle after the last patient of the day had left.

"No, none have had any that appeared to be poisoned. That's good news, anyway."

And maybe narrowed down the search to someone who lived in the area of the clinic. What kind of sick mind did it take to enjoy seeing an animal suffer? It made her sad and angry, and she decided to spend a few minutes with Cody's dogs. That would cheer her up.

"Hey, Sally. You, too, Pretty Girl." Riley opened the kennel door, stepping inside. Tails excitedly sweeping across the concrete, both sat, as if waiting for permission to greet her.

Never had she seen dogs trained so well. She lowered her butt to the floor. "You two doing okay?" Their tails picked up speed, but they didn't approach. She should have thought to ask for command words.

"Come." That seemed to be the magic word, as both bounded into her arms, Sally giving a joyful bark. She'd played with them for a few minutes, tossing their balls up in the air for them to catch, when her phone buzzed.

The caller ID displayed Cody's name.

CHAPTER SIX

After he and Ryan arrived in Fort Dodge and had checked into their adjoining rooms, Cody decided to use the ten minutes before meeting Ryan to call Riley. He pressed her number, flopping onto the bed as he listened to the ring tones.

"Hi, Cody."

Expecting to leave a message because she would be with a patient, he was surprised when she answered.

"You there?" she said.

"Yeah. Yeah, I'm here." Her voice, even with those few words, soothed him better than the finest scotch. With the phone pressed to his ear, he stuffed the second pillow behind his back.

"Guess what I'm doing right now?"

Things he'd like her to do popped into his head, and he willed them away. If she could read his dirty mind, she'd hang up. "I'm not good at guessing." He rolled his eyes. Somewhere along the way, between graduating from college and now, he'd forgotten how to have a conversation with a woman.

A bark he recognized as Sally's happy one sounded. "You're playing with my dogs." She would never know it, but she'd just stolen a piece of his heart.

"I am. Hold on a sec. Okay, you're on speaker. Say something."

That she would think of doing that made him want to kiss her. Not that he needed a reason. "Pretty Girl. Sally. You guys behaving for Riley?" Two excited barks answered him.

She laughed. "They're going crazy trying to sniff you out of the phone."

It was the first time he'd heard her laugh, and he liked thinking of her as happy. There was a knock on his door. "I have to go. Thanks for spending time with them."

"We're having a ball, so don't worry. Um, I wanted to ask, would you mind if I take them to the dog park?"

Something in her voice set off alarm bells, but he couldn't think of a reason to refuse. "They'd love that. They know all the commands, sit, come, heel."

More laughter poured through the phone. "You should have seen them just now. They sat, then came to the phone, then seemed confused about how they were supposed to heel."

"Down," he said. "Did they lie down?"

"They did."

It was the first time he'd given them commands via a phone, and he chuckled. Ryan knocked again. "I'll try to call you tomorrow."

"Okay. It was nice talking to you."

"Same here."

"Cody?"

"Yeah?"

"Be careful, okay?"

"Always am." Her voice had been so soft when she'd said that, and as he hung up, he rubbed his chest, over his heart. The damn thing had gone all fluttery on him. Other than his teammates, and his parents from afar, when was the last time someone had worried about him?

"Coming," he yelled at another series of knocks. He stuck his room key into his wallet, and went to the door.

"There was a robbery at a convenience store three nights ago in Sac City. The description fits this kid," the Fort Dodge police chief said, handing the couple's photo back to Ryan after making a copy. "Got the APB about it this morning." He flipped through some papers on his desk.

And wasn't that just great? Cody exchanged a glance with Ryan. The game had just changed.

"Was the girl with him?" Ryan asked.

Finding what he was looking for, the chief scanned the sheet. "No, just the kid. He had a gun. Clerk said it looked like an old one." He eyed the copy he'd made of the photo. "I'll be sending this out to the other police departments around here, along with the boy's name."

Ryan stuck the photo back into his file folder. "That's fine. Any description of their car?"

Reading the APB again, the chief shook his head. "Not a good one. Dark. Midsized. That's it."

Cody turned to a map on the wall. "Where's Sac City from here?" He scanned the area around Fort Dodge. Kincaid had arranged this meeting with the chief. Otherwise, the cop wouldn't be so willing to share information with two men who'd walked in off the street.

"On the way out to Storm Lake. Take 20 out of Fort Dodge."

Cody found Sac City, a small dot on the map. More interesting was Storm Lake, which was larger and had a big lake. A tourist destination that would appeal to a couple of kids and one they might think they could get lost in. It probably never occurred to the brainless twits that it was December. Although there was no snow yet, it was damned cold in Iowa. Had they even thought to bring winter clothes on their little adventure?

Ryan got the address of the convenience store the kid had robbed, and they both thanked the cop.

The chief came around the corner and walked them out. "You boys are some kind of elite team from what I was told, but don't be going and testing our tolerance, you hear? This isn't the Wild West."

"We're just here to pick up the girl," Ryan said. "What you do with the boy now that he's gone and gotten into trouble is your business. We'll alert the police in whatever town we find them."

"Fair enough, but I'll call on ahead, make sure they know you're coming."

He and Ryan shook hands with the chief, and then headed for the Range Rover, which Ryan had pulled rank on and was driving today.

"Damn kids," Cody said as they left the police station, heading for Sac City.

"Yeah, now he's screwed up his life, getting an armed robbery on his record. Stupid of her parents to forbid her to see him, too. If they'd left things alone, a month from now, the kids probably would have broken up. That age, they get easily bored."

"True." In high school, he'd had the hots for one girl to the next one. He'd been a jock, and that alone had been a chick magnet. As a kid with hormones raging through him, he'd never been able to settle down with a longtime girlfriend. There were just too many pretty girls throwing their sweet little selves at him, so he didn't get this Romeo and Juliet thing going on with these two.

He wasn't particularly proud of his behavior looking back on it. His parents hadn't appreciated all the phone calls from girls asking to talk to him, but he'd considered the professors old-fashioned. Although he had fond memories of those years, as a man and somewhat wiser, he could see their point. If he had a daughter and found out she was calling some boy, begging him to sneak out and meet her somewhere, he'd definitely have a problem with it. A real big one. And if he ever caught his son sneaking out to meet a girl, he'd ground him for a month.

Not that he would ever have a son or daughter. Out of nowhere, a picture formed of a little girl the spitting image of Riley. *Don't go there, Dog.* But it was there in his mind and refused to go away.

"You and Charlie planning to have kids?" he asked.

"Not right away, but yeah. I can't wait to have a little Charlie running around the house, chasing Mr. Bunny while driving Charlie crazy. It's gonna be fun."

"Mr. Bunny?"

Ryan grinned. "Our rabbit."

"Get out. You have a pet rabbit?" As Ryan told the story of how that came about, Cody's mind drifted back to Riley. Although he hadn't planned to, later tonight, when they decided where to get rooms, he would call her to find out how her trip to the dog park went. Just a friendly phone call, that was all. He snorted.

"Let's see if we can learn something new," Ryan said as he pulled into the convenience store parking lot.

Thirty minutes later, they were back in the car. The only new thing they had learned was that before pulling out an antique gun and demanding all the money, the kid had brought a bottle of water to the counter and had asked how far Storm Lake was.

After leaving the convenience store, they stopped by the police department, and after a phone call between Kincaid and the Sac City police chief, they were allowed to view the videotape confiscated from the store's security camera. Sure enough, it was their boy.

Justin Tramore, age seventeen, had politely asked his question, and after the answer was given, he'd pulled a turn-of-the-century Colt Single Action .38 from behind his back, pointing it at the clerk. "I'm sorry," he'd said on his way out the door, after the clerk had handed over a little under two hundred dollars.

"At least he was polite about robbing the man," Cody said. He shouldn't feel sorry for the boy, but he did.

Ryan turned the car toward Storm Lake. "Tell it to the judge." He glanced at Cody. "What's your take?"

"Last place he used his dad's credit card was when they arrived in Fort Dodge, and that was at a burger joint, of all things. I'm guessing it was about that time it occurred to them the card could be traced. They ran out of money, thus the robbery."

"My thinking, too."

"They're probably feeling a little desperate by now, which makes them unpredictable. Don't like that they have a gun." Cody scratched at the tingling going on at the back of his neck.

"Yeah, me either." Ryan slowed the car as they drove into Storm Lake. The sun was setting, and it looked like the town was closing up for the night. "Let's find a place to get something to eat before they roll up the sidewalk."

"I could go for a steak and baked potato with the works."

Ryan put on his blinker and turned into a parking lot. "Ask and ye shall receive."

Turned out the steak house was open until ten, and the food was good.

After a shower, Cody checked the time. Nine-thirty shouldn't be too late to call Riley. Wearing his favorite sweatpants, he settled on the motel room's bed, stuffing the extra pillows behind his back. Phone in hand, he hesitated. Maybe he shouldn't bother her. Things could get busy tomorrow, though, if they managed to find the kids, and he might not have a chance to check in. He called her.

As he listened to the ring, he realized he wanted to hear her voice. He also admitted to himself that even though he couldn't classify her as a girlfriend, if his head was in a better place, he'd be interested in a relationship with her. Very interested.

He got her voice mail. Disappointed, he hung up without leaving a message.

Riley washed the conditioner from her hair. The trip to the dog park had turned up nothing, which she hadn't expected it to, but it was disappointing nevertheless. She had enjoyed playing with Cody's dogs, while watching them closely to make sure they hadn't eaten anything. She'd also posted several signs, warning owners to keep an eye on their animals and not to let them eat foods left behind by someone. It wasn't her desire to panic anyone, but better a warning over seeing their dog get sick, or worse.

A cup of hot tea in hand, she grabbed her latest book, and headed to her bedroom. The cats joined her in bed. Merlin sat on the pillow next to her, where he could keep an eye on things, Arthur made a few turns on her lap before curling up, and Pelli batted a toy mouse across the comforter.

Riley watched Pelli for a few minutes, smiling at his silliness. Her life was coming together finally. It hadn't been easy. As a child who'd grown up in foster care, bouncing from one family to another, she'd had no one to depend on but herself. Her last family, the one she'd lived with her senior year of high school, had been the best, and she still kept in touch with them. They were the only ones, though, that she had any desire to keep in her life.

Pat and John Haywood had helped her through a rough time, when she'd hated herself and the world. Pat was one of the wisest women Riley had ever known, and had given her Arthur and told her that she could whisper all her secrets to him and he would never tell. There were many secrets she'd shared with him, and once she trusted him, she told him her biggest one. Getting it off her chest had done wonders for beginning the healing process, and her surly attitude began to seem too much trouble to hold on to. Eventually, she'd trusted Pat enough to tell her about Reed.

Seeing that she'd not put her phone in the charger, she picked it up from the night table. When she put the plug into it, it lit up with a missed call, Cody's name coming up. Her heartbeat picking up, she punched Call. Had something happened to him?

"Lo," he said, his voice sleep muffled.

"I woke you. I'm sorry. I just now saw that you'd called earlier."

"Hey, no problem."

He sounded alert now, and she guessed he was trained to go from zero to sixty at a moment's notice. "So you're okay?"

"Yeah, why?"

"When I saw your name on the screen, my first thought was that something had happened. I was worried."

"That's damn sweet, Riley. Thank you."

His voice was sexy, all low and rumbly. She wished she could crawl through the phone and snuggle next to him while he murmured naughty things into her ear. "So, I guess you were calling to check on your dogs?" He chuckled, the sound sending a shiver through her.

"No, darlin', just wanted to talk to you. Is that okay?"

Oh. "Yeah, sure. Where are you?" She heard the rustling of sheets and imagined him sitting up to rest his back against the headboard and wondered what he wore to bed. Her guess was nothing; he seemed like the kind of man who slept in the nude. That she'd like to see.

"Some little tourist town in Iowa. Storm Lake. Ever heard of it?"

"No. Can you tell me why you're there?"

"I will when I get back home. Right now, I'd rather talk about you. Did you go to the dog park?"

"I did, and Pretty Girl and Sally tested my ball throwing stamina. They're great dogs, Cody."

"They are, but they took advantage of you. I'll show you why when I get home. Any more trouble with the poison thing?"

"Yeah, had one today, but his owners got him to us in time. He ate some meat that someone left under a bush at the dog park." As soon as she told him the last part, she wanted to take back the words. He was a smart man, and the comment wasn't going to get past him.

"Riley—"

The soft, sexy voice was gone, replaced by one that was full of command. "I didn't risk your dogs," she said, cutting him off. "I never took my eyes off them, I swear."

"That's not my worry. I know you wouldn't put them in danger. It's you I'm worried about. Has it occurred to you that the person poisoning animals might be the same one who tried to run you over?"

She squeezed her eyes shut. No, that had not occurred to her. What had she ever done to anyone to make them hate her so much that they'd want to kill her?

"Riley?"

"Yeah?"

"I'm not saying it is, but it's entirely possible. Would you promise not to go to the dog park alone? It's a good bet that the person hurting your patients is the same one who put the meat there. If you feel you need to keep an eye on the place, I'll go with you when I get back, hopefully, in a day or two. Either that or at least take someone with you. Okay?"

She'd been on her own as far back as she could remember, and with the exception of the year she'd lived with the Haywoods, she'd made her own decisions. A part of her bristled at having to curtail her investigation, but she couldn't argue with his logic.

"Okay, I'll either wait for you or take someone with me. Do they have a command for attack?"

He let out a long breath. "Thank you. I'll sleep better knowing you're safe. And to answer your question, they do, but they're trained not to attack unless it's me giving the command."

"That's probably wise. Listen, you stay safe, too." Whatever he was doing in Iowa, it had to be dangerous, else he would have told her what he was up to.

"I will. Nite, darlin'."

"Nite."

She plugged the phone into the charger, and no longer interested in her book, she turned out the lamp. What was he doing in Iowa, anyway? To the cats, lights out meant that Arthur got to curl up against her stomach, Merlin buried his nose in her hair, and Pelli dived under the covers, worming his way down to her feet. Sticking to his usual bedtime routine, the kitten sucked on her little toe, which, fortunately, wasn't ticklish. In a few minutes, he would fall asleep, and normally, Riley would, too.

Not tonight, apparently. All the things Cody had said to her ran through her mind like a movie reel. He'd kissed her not long after they met, then at her clinic on the day he'd dropped off his dogs, she was sure he'd wanted to, but he hadn't. Instead, he'd said something about the timing being wrong.

The man confused her, but she couldn't deny that he fascinated her. She'd had two boyfriends in college, the first in a relationship that had lasted less than six months. The second, Brad, in her second year of veterinarian school. His pursuit of her had been relentless, and she'd finally given in and agreed to a date with the cute fellow student. She'd even fantasized about them opening a practice together. That dream had ended when she'd skipped a class to deliver a cake and herself, wearing nothing under her raincoat, to wish him a happy birthday.

Surprise! All three of them—her, Brad, and the girl he was screwing—were stunned stupid by her appearance at the off-campus house he rented with two friends. After him, she'd decided to devote all her time and energy to getting her degree. No more men for her who either died or cheated on her.

Cody was the first man she was interested in since what she thought of as Brad's Big Cheating Reveal. Was she willing to risk getting hurt again? For Cody, maybe.

CHAPTER SEVEN

Cody's night was blessedly nightmare-free. As he dressed and repacked his duffel, he wondered if Riley would mind if he called her every evening. He and Ryan ate a hearty breakfast at a place filled with local cars in the parking lot. The waitress they showed the kids' picture to had never seen them, or so she said. They were two strange men in a town that likely didn't trust outsiders easily.

The first stop after breakfast was to a little place on the main drag that advertised cabin rentals. "Hello. I'm Mrs. Waterman. What can I do for you gentlemen?" a silver-haired woman said, sliding the book she was reading into her desk drawer.

Ryan stepped forward. "I'm Ryan O'Connor, and this is Cody Roberts." He showed her the picture of the couple. "Have you by any chance rented them a cabin or seen them around?"

Her gaze flicked from Ryan to him, and Cody could tell she was wary of them. Going on instinct, he decided honesty might be the best policy. "They're a couple of kids who ran away from home. The girl is Megan Sanders, and she's only sixteen. Her parents asked us to find her."

"Are you the police? I know all the officers around these parts, and I've never seen you two." She smiled and mischief danced in her eyes. "Believe me, I'd remember if I had."

"No, ma'am," Ryan said. "We're not the police, just trying to find the girl. Her parents are really worried about her."

"People say I'm a good judge of character, and I don't sense any threat coming from either of you, even though you're about the biggest, strongest men I've ever seen. Swear on something you hold dear that you're being honest with me."

Ryan stuck his hand in a back pocket and pulled out his wallet, opening it to a photo. Cody craned his neck to see it. It was one of Ryan, a pretty woman, and a rabbit.

"You take pictures with your rabbit?" Cody snorted. He'd save that one for a day he needed to razz his friend.

"Totally Charlie's idea." He showed it to Mrs. Waterman. "I swear we're being honest with you. This is my fiancée, who I'd willingly die for."

Mrs. Waterman turned her attention to Cody, her brow raised. Phone in hand, he clicked on a picture of Sally, Pretty Girl, and Layla taken in Afghanistan. In it, his dogs sat at his feet, peering up at him. He remembered that day. Dressed in full battle gear, about to go out on patrol, he was telling them to stay. Anyone could tell by looking at those three that they wanted to go with him.

He didn't look at the picture often because it killed him to see Layla, the prettiest of the three with her wolfhound features, as she stared at him, her eyes begging him to take her so she could protect him from all the evil things. That was his Layla, always worried about him.

"Cody, show her the picture."

His friend knew what it had cost Cody to return home without knowing Layla was safe, and the sympathy in Ryan's eyes about undid him. He shook off the headfirst dive his thoughts had taken. "Right."

He held up his phone. "I swear on these dogs, one of which saved my life, that we're being honest with you."

She stared at it a moment, covering her heart with her hand. "My grandson lost a leg over there. Yes, I've seen your couple. They rented a cabin for two weeks. I felt bad about taking all their money, but the cabin's not mine, so I had no choice."

Cody met Ryan's eyes. As it didn't seem Mrs. Waterman had heard of the convenience store holdup, he didn't mention it. Nor did Ryan.

"Get those kids back to their parents where they belong. They'll never survive up here through the winter."

"Yes, ma'am," Cody said, giving her a warm smile.

"Oh, I almost forgot to warn you boys. It's deer season, so watch out for hunters back in those woods."

Ryan tipped an imaginary hat. "Thanks. We'll keep an eye out."

They left with the address and directions to the cabin. "I can't believe how easy that was," Ryan said.

"Easy makes me nervous." Cody would've knocked on wood, but there was none in sight in the Range Rover. He still couldn't shake the bad vibes. Scanning the directions, he said, "Go halfway around the lake, then we need to watch for a row of mailboxes. A mile past those, there's a dirt road to the right."

"How far down the road to the cabin?"

"About two miles. There're four cabins, and the kids have the one on the far right." Mrs. Waterman had told them that they were one-room cabins, with a small bathroom in the left corner, which was good since there wouldn't be many places to hide.

"We'll park out of sight and go in on foot," Ryan said.

Fortunately, the area was wooded, giving them cover. About a half mile from the cabin, they found a place where they could park the Range Rover. Using the woods as cover, they made their way to the last cabin on the right. Two rocking chairs sat on the front porch, and in one was Megan Sanders. She appeared to be crying.

"Wonder where the boy is," Ryan said.

"The car's here, so he's either inside or out in the woods. Looks like it's not all rainbows and unicorns."

Ryan sighed. "I never know what to do with a crying woman. She's yours. I'll deal with the boy."

Like he knew what to do with one. "Remind me to forget to buy you a Christmas present."

"Fair trade." Ryan took his earpiece from a cargo pocket and put it on. "I'll ease around and come up on the side of the cabin."

Cody put his earpiece in, zipped his coat up to his neck, and kept his eyes trained on the girl as Ryan slipped away. He kept his ears tuned to the back of him. As he settled into his surroundings, he began to feel as one to all that was going on around him—the same as in his sniper days—aware of every little sound, every movement, any alert of danger.

At the back corner of the cabin, Ryan eased his way down the side of the building. He was almost to the front when the girl stood, wiped her nose on the sleeve of her jacket, and then went inside.

Damn. "Target went inside the cabin."

Ryan halted at the front corner. "Roger." He backed up, stopping next to a window. After a minute, he returned to the front. "They're yelling at each other. The curtains are closed, so come to the front door."

"Roger." Cody met Ryan at the steps leading to the porch. They both removed their earbuds. Obviously, all was not well in paradise. Although he could hear the couple arguing, he couldn't make out their words.

"Let's try the door first. Maybe she didn't lock it when she went in, and we can take them by surprise."

Cody nodded. "Sounds like a plan."

The door was unlocked, and Cody followed Ryan in, both coming to a stop just inside. Justin Tramore had his back to them, and appeared to be chopping something, while Megan beat on his back.

"I want to go home!" The boy kept chopping. "Are you even listening to me, Justin? I'm cold, hungry, and bored." She pounded on his back again.

"We can't go home, dammit. You forget I'm wanted for robbery?"

"Well, I'm not going to jail. I told you not to do it." She let out a sob. "I thought running away with you would be fun, but it's not. I'm going home. You can stay here and hide for the rest of your life for all I care."

Cody glanced at Ryan and rolled his eyes. Stupid kids.

"You said you loved me." Justin turned, and his eyes widened. "Who the hell are you?"

Megan glanced over her shoulder, and at seeing them, she screamed. Justin pulled her against him.

"Easy." Cody held up his hand. "I'm Cody Roberts and this is Ryan O'Connor. Megan, your parents sent us to bring you home."

"We're not going." Justin brought the knife up to Megan's neck. "If you don't leave now, I'll do it. I swear I will. Then I'll slit my own throat."

Megan whimpered.

A buzzing sounded in Cody's ears, increasing in volume until it seemed as if a million bees had made a home in his head. His vision blurred, and he cursed the dusty room for making his eyes water. He wouldn't let them kill her, not this time. Asra snared his gaze, fear and pleading in her eyes. The insurgent holding her sliced a thin line across her throat, and her small, trembling hands rose to her neck. Tears streaked down her cheeks, leaving clear lines through the dirt on her face. Dark red blood oozed between her fingers.

Distant rifle fire broke the silence. "It's a trap," he heard someone yell, and he thought it might have been him.

"Roberts!"

Didn't his teammate get it? "It's a trap, Doc," he said, trying to make him understand. "I have to save her."

"Jesus," Doc said. "Stand down, Dog! That's an order. Wait for me outside."

Cody was forcibly pushed out the door. He stumbled across the floor of a porch—where the hell had a porch come from?—and down the steps. Cold hit his face, and he sucked in the frigid air. Why was it cold? The temperature had been over a hundred that day. He clearly remembered sweat dripping down his spine and into his eyes. Everything was fucked up.

He sank to his knees, drawing the biting air into his lungs. Where the hell was he? He blinked his eyes in an attempt to see past the haze. When his vision cleared, he scanned the area around him and saw a forest instead of the desolation of Afghanistan. He covered his face with his hands.

Christ, what have I done?

Riley took Cody's dogs to the park on her lunch break, bringing Brooke with her. The first thing she saw was that all her warning signs had been taken down. Had the person trying to kill people's pets done it or the city? She kept Pretty Girl and Sally on their leashes until she'd checked under the three bushes and around the four trees. Not finding anything suspicious, she unclipped them. Both sat at her feet as if awaiting her command.

"Go play." She took out the two balls she'd put in her purse and threw them. Expecting them to chase the balls and return them to her to throw again, she instead watched in amazement as they tossed them up in the air, catching each other's.

"Wow," Brooke said. "I've never seen dogs entertain themselves like that. You sure I can't have Hot Guy? I like him and his dogs."

So did Riley. "He'd eat you alive."

Brooke collected her long, blonde hair and pulled it so it fell over one shoulder. "And I would have a problem with that because?"

Riley laughed. "Because you're too innocent for him."

"And you're not?"

She hadn't been innocent since the day she'd entered foster care. "I don't think it matters. He's not looking for a relationship."

Brooke's blue eyes narrowed as she tilted her head to stare at Riley. "You know this how?"

"It's just a feeling, okay?" She'd not told Brooke or Michelle that Cody was her neighbor. She hadn't mentioned how he sat in the dark and played his sad songs on his guitar. She'd certainly not told them that he'd spooned his big body around hers to comfort her. And that he'd kissed her? That one was her special memory, not to be shared.

"Pretty Girl. Sally. Come." They each mouthed a ball and raced to her. "Is that trick what your daddy said he'd show me?" she said when they dropped their treasure at her feet. With her thumb and a finger, she picked up the balls, one in each hand. The two dogs danced in anticipation. She threw the balls, but this time they ran back to her and dropped their toys for her to toss again. Had their first game been a fluke? When they came back with their saliva-slimed balls, she repeated what she'd said the first time.

"Go play." Off they went, and this time, they did their tossing-the-balls-to-each-other game. "I'll be damned." Pleased that she had stumbled on the trick Cody had alluded to, she leaned back against the bench and watched them.

"I've never seen dogs so well behaved," Brooke said. "Is he a dog trainer?"

"I have no idea." If he wasn't, he should be. She'd never doubted Cody loved those dogs. Okay, maybe she'd wondered if he did when she'd embarrassed herself that first time she'd taken him to task for letting them play near the street.

She thought back to that first morning when he'd walked out onto his porch wearing nothing but his sweatpants, showing off a male body the likes of which she'd only seen in magazines. What she wouldn't give to slide her fingers over his sculpted chest and muscled arms.

His declaration that it wasn't the right time or place for them had her wondering at his reason for saying such a thing. Maria had said he'd been the SEAL team's sniper, and Riley had the feeling that whatever Cody's issues were, they had something to do with that time in his life. She hadn't planned to watch *American Sniper*, but maybe she should. It might help her understand him better.

Her phone buzzed with a text.

`Police are here to take your report.`

Riley texted Michelle that she'd be there in a few minutes.

"Time to go back. Thanks for coming with me."

"It was fun," Brooke said, sliding the strap of her purse over her shoulder.

Riley called to the dogs and they came running to her, standing still as she clipped their leashes to their collars. As she walked toward her car with Brooke alongside her, she noticed a woman standing outside the fence, watching her. She wore a bulky coat, a ball cap with the brim pulled down, and large sunglasses, hiding her face. The dogs playing with their balls had probably caught her attention. Riley waved, and the woman stared at her for a few more seconds before walking away.

"Weird," Brooke said. "Guess she didn't like you waving to her."

Actually, it had creeped Riley out. She loaded the dogs into her car. On the way back, she glanced into the rearview mirror. "You guys have fun?" Both dogs barked, assuring her that they had.

"Would've been more fun if their daddy had come with us," Brooke grumbled.

What Riley didn't say was that if Cody had been with her, Brooke wouldn't have been invited.

At the clinic, she got Sally and Pretty Girl back into their kennel before going to the waiting room. A uniformed officer awaited her, which was disappointing. She'd hoped for a detective.

"Hi. I'm Dr. Austin." She held out her hand.

"Officer Kilpatrick."

After shaking hands, she led him back to her office. "Would you like something to drink? I've got water and sodas."

"No thank you, ma'am. I understand you think someone's poisoning pets?"

"I don't think, I know. Have a seat." He was maybe a few years older than she, and with his short blond hair worn in what she thought of as a typical cop cut, and cornflower-blue eyes, he was definitely good-looking. Although he wasn't as muscled as Cody, he was close. And why was she comparing him to her neighbor? The two men were as opposite in appearance as could be.

"How about you call me Riley? Ma'am sounds so old."

"Trust me, Riley, you're far from old. I'm Mike."

Well then. That grin he gave her should have melted her bones, and a week ago, it might have. Instead, she had to be hung up on a moody bad boy who couldn't tell her exactly what he did and never seemed to sleep.

"Glad to meet you," she said. "Here's a statement of the timeline and the pets involved, along with all the information I have." She handed him the report she'd created. "Thought it would save time to have it ready."

Mike took the pages. "This is great. Do you mind if I take a few minutes to read it? See if I have any other questions."

"Sure. My first patient is waiting, so why don't I take care of that while you're reading? I won't be long. Just routine vaccinations."

"No problem. If you don't mind, though, I'll take that water you offered."

She took a bottle from the mini fridge and handed it to him. His fingers brushed over hers, intentionally, she was sure. Yep, he was interested. "I'll be back in a few."

"Man, I'm digging all the hot guys coming in here lately," Brooke said after they finished with their first patient of the afternoon. "The cop is like a beautiful angel and the other one is all dark, dangerous, and sexy."

Her assistant had nailed them perfectly, but she wasn't going to admit to noticing. Otherwise, there'd be no end to Brooke's teasing. "They're just men."

"Pfft. Keep telling yourself that. Which one you keeping? I'll take the other one."

Riley winked. "Why can't I keep both?" She walked out before Brooke could respond, returning to her office and the waiting angel.

Mike stood when she walked in. "Good timing. I just finished going through your statement and made a list of questions."

His eyes tracked her as she moved around her desk, and she wished she'd taken a few minutes to run a brush through her ponytail and put on lipstick. Other than the brief kisses with Cody, her dry spell had gone on way too long.

"You'll let me know when you get the results on the meat?" Mike said after she'd answered his questions.

"I will." They'd decided that she would get faster results from the lab she used than if he sent the poisoned meat to the police lab.

He handed her a card. "Until we get a lead on who's doing this, not much we can do other than beef up patrol in this area. I'll make sure everyone keeps an eye out, though. I wrote my cell number on the back. If anything more happens, call me direct instead of going through dispatch."

"Thanks." She walked him out. At the front door, he paused.

"Are you married, Riley?"

"No. Are you?"

"Came close once, but no dice." And there was that killer smile again. "Now that we've established neither of us is married, would you like to go out tomorrow night? Dinner and dancing, maybe? Or a movie . . . or just drinks if that makes you more comfortable."

She pushed away the image of brooding caramel-colored eyes. Cody had made it clear that he wasn't interested, and the truth was, she was ready for a life outside of work. "I'd be good with dinner and a movie. I'll text you my address, and you can let me know what time."

"So I get the dangerous one?" Brooke asked when Riley turned back to the counter.

In your dreams. "Don't you two have something to do?" Her employees were too nosy by far, and the thought of either one of them going after Cody made her want to say something snide.

As she headed for the exam room where her next patient waited, it occurred to her that it was Cody she wished she had a date with, not Mike. Go figure. She was smart, though, so she would put Cody out of her mind. Mike was the perfect choice to begin her foray back into the dating game, and if things went well, who knew? To be on the safe side, she'd stop at the mall on the way home and do some sexy underwear shopping.

CHAPTER EIGHT

———— ✦ ————

Ashamed, Cody kept his gaze on the trees when Ryan sat on the steps next to him. What if the situation had gone south in a really bad way? He couldn't be trusted, and that was the cruel truth. Hell, he wouldn't want himself on an operation, so he couldn't expect his teammates to think any differently.

If Ryan was sitting here, though, that meant he'd talked some sense into the two inside. Cody exhaled a relieved breath. At least he wouldn't have the guilt of his teammate or one of the kids being hurt on his conscience. He should say something, but he had no words to explain what had just gone down.

"Have you had flashbacks before?" Ryan finally asked.

"I don't know what happened in there." His greatest wish was to be able to dig a hole and disappear from sight.

"I think you do."

The words were said so softly that Cody wasn't sure he could bear it. A team that ate, slept, and fought side by side bonded together tighter than glue on glue, and although they never said the words, they loved each other. They were often closer than blood brothers, and he owed Ryan an explanation. As much as Cody wanted to get up and walk away, it was time to own his problem, whatever that might be. He still wasn't sure.

"That was the first flashback . . . if that's what it was, but I've been having nightmares about a girl back in Afghanistan. I don't recognize her. Don't have a clue who she is. She just keeps showing up in my dreams." Elbows on his knees, he stared down at his hands where they dangled between his legs. "Pretty fucked up, right?"

Ryan reached down and retied the laces on one of his boots. "Is it the same dream all the time?"

The door to the cabin opened, and Justin poked his head out. "Hey, man, we leaving or what?"

"Yeah, we're leaving," Ryan said, standing. "Give us a minute." When the kid closed the door, Ryan squatted and put his hand on Cody's knee. "We need to talk, but let's get these two taken care of. Justin's agreed to let us drive him to the police station where he'll turn himself in. Megan used my phone to call her parents, and they're coming to get her. We're to meet them at the Des Moines airport in a few hours."

Cody stared at the hand on his knee, willing away the tears stinging his eyes. He hadn't cried since the day Evan Prescott, one of their SEAL team members, had been killed on an operation, and he'd be damned if he'd cry now. But, fuck, with his touch, Ryan was telling him that he had Cody's six, whether he deserved it or not.

"Let's get this over with." He pushed himself up. "You need help with the kids?"

"Nah. Truth is, they're scared of you. Why don't you go on to the car and we'll be right behind you." Ryan tossed him the keys.

That hurt, but he had it coming. Not that he wanted to stick around and have the couple stare at him like he was the big bad bogeyman, so he gladly headed to the Range Rover. When he reached the vehicle, he slid into the driver's seat, started the ignition, and turned on the heater to warm up the interior. He figured it was better if he drove. That way, he could ignore everyone and they could ignore him.

He scrubbed at his face. What the hell was wrong with him? The dream had haunted him for months now, but he had no memory of meeting a young woman named Asra. Inside that cabin, though, when Justin put the knife to Megan's throat, Cody had been transported back to a dusty room in Afghanistan and had seen Asra's face clear as day.

There was no way he could hide this from Kincaid. If he didn't tell the boss, Ryan would, and rightly so. He didn't want to believe it had been a flashback, but what else could it have been? And why couldn't he remember?

The front passenger door opened and Justin slid in, giving him a wary glance before putting on his seatbelt. Ryan got in the back with the girl so that the couple wasn't sitting behind him and Ryan where they could get up to no good.

"Glad that's over," Ryan said as they watched Megan hugging her parents.

"Yeah, me, too." Justin's parents were on their way to bail him out of jail. The charges against him were going to be tough for the kid to beat, but Cody hoped he'd been scared straight. As they walked out of the Des Moines airport, he tried to get a handle on the bugs crawling under his skin. Ryan had decided they'd spend the night here, have dinner and a long talk. It was the last thing Cody wanted to do.

"Anything particular you want to eat?"

"No." He wasn't even sure he could eat. His head felt like spiders had woven thick webs around his brain, keeping him from being able to think straight. His legs and feet were a hundred pounds heavier, making it hard to put one step in front of the other. His heart had shriveled to the size of a prune. And he was tired, so damn tired.

It was getting harder to deny that something had occurred on his last deployment that he couldn't remember. Ryan probably expected him to try to explain away what had happened in that cabin today, but he wasn't going to do that. It was time to man up and admit something was wrong, letting the chips fall where they may.

They ended up at a diner near the hotel where they'd made a brief stop to book rooms. There hadn't been many cars in the parking lot, and Cody guessed that was why his teammate had chosen it. Easier to talk with no one around. Another reason might be that there was no alcohol available, which Cody would almost kill for.

They took a booth in the far corner, and without looking at the menu Cody ordered scrambled eggs, toast, and a glass of milk. His stomach wasn't feeling so well, and he hoped he could keep the bland meal down.

"You call Kincaid?" he asked after the waitress left.

Ryan leaned back against the booth with one arm stretched across the top. "No. Texted him. Told him we'd be back in the morning."

That surprised Cody. His friend should have called the boss, giving him an update on the operation and Cody's screwup. The waitress returned with Cody's milk and a cup of coffee for Ryan.

"I never told you what went down with my wife."

"You mean besides the robbery?" Ryan's wife had been killed when a druggie had shot her after burglarizing her jewelry shop. Where he was going with this, Cody hadn't a clue.

"Yeah, besides the robbery." He put his elbows on the table and clasped his hands, reminding Cody of someone praying. "She was two months pregnant when she was killed. Do the math."

Cody blinked. They'd been deployed for six or seven months when Ryan had been notified that she was dead. "Fuck, man. You're kidding, right?"

"I wish. The thing is, every one of us on the team has been screwed up in one way or the other. From what I understand, Kincaid couldn't get past the guilt of losing Evan on his watch. Jake lost a man on a K2 operation and went off the deep end for a time. Jamie blamed himself for his parents' deaths, which messed with his mind for years."

"How do you know all this?"

"I just pick up on things here and there mostly. As for me, I spent a year trying to deal with the fact that my wife cheated on me. My point is, you're not the only one on the team who's walked ass deep through shit. We've all been there. You need to trust that not only do we understand better than most, but we'll always have your six. You'll always be our brother. Now tell me about these nightmares you're having."

The reassurance that his team would have his back was fractionally calming, but his craving for a bottle of scotch and a dark room hadn't abated. Problem was, if he started down that road, he might never come back.

Their meal arrived, and Cody tried not to gag at the greasy smell coming from Ryan's burger. Man, his stomach was messed up. He forced a bite of eggs down his throat, following it up with a long drink of milk.

He ate one slice of toast before setting down his fork. No way he could eat and talk about his nightmare at the same time. "So, that dream I keep having. It's always the same. I think what happened in the cabin was triggered by hearing the guns going off at the same time the kid put the knife to Megan's throat. It was like I was back there again."

"I'm guessing those were the deer hunters we were warned about. Go on."

"I'm . . . I'm about to go up on a roof with my spotter when this young girl calls to me. I know her because she's given me intel previously. I tell my spotter to go on up to the rooftop, and then cross the alley and follow her into the house, thinking she's got some new info. It's not until then that I see she's hurt. Then I sense someone behind me. That's it. That's where I wake up drenched in sweat every fucking time."

Ryan pushed his empty plate to the end of the table. "And the flashback was the same as that?"

Cody slid his half-empty plate aside. "Yeah, I saw her clear as day. It wasn't Megan in that room, it was Asra. I swear I don't know anyone named Asra."

"You know this happened for real, right?"

"If so, you'd think I'd remember."

Ryan nodded when the waitress appeared to fill his coffee cup. Alone again, he said, "You were with a new team, but I heard they found you facedown on the street, out cold. A concussion can cause memory loss, especially if you saw something you don't want to remember." He poured a dab of cream into his refreshed coffee. "You have to tell the boss all this." His gaze lifted to Cody's, sympathy in his eyes. "If you don't, I'll have to."

"I'll tell him." And he would, but if he didn't get out of the diner right now, he was going to lose it. How long could he go on denying to himself that Asra was real? He didn't want her to be, because if so, that meant she'd been killed because of him. He slid out of the booth and walked out, sucking in the ice-cold air like a drowning man.

Riley missed her guitar guy. Tomorrow night she had a date with Mike, and she regretted agreeing to go out with him. Well, the side of her that got all hot and bothered by her bad boy neighbor did. The other side, the one lecturing her on finding a nice guy, hadn't shut up about doing the smart thing and swearing off a man who was in the wrong place at the wrong time. Or so he claimed.

On the way home, she'd gone shopping for sexy bras and panties. After she'd had dinner and the cats had been fed, she'd streamed *American Sniper*. As she watched the ending of the movie, she reached for another tissue to wipe away the tears flowing down her cheeks.

God, Cody, was it like that for you? It was a useless question as he wasn't here to answer. Arthur jumped onto her lap, nuzzling his face against hers. "I know, sweetie." He hated when she cried, had from the beginning when she'd been a wounded young girl telling him her deepest, darkest secrets. "It's just that I think he's hurting really bad, and I want to help him."

She thought he needed a friend but didn't know how to ask for one, much less how to let her or anyone else in. It was late, but she was restless after watching the movie. Cody hadn't called, which surprised her as he'd been keeping in touch since he left. Before she could talk herself out of it, she texted him.

Are you awake?

When several minutes passed with no answer, she turned out the light and tried to go to sleep. Scenes from the movie kept running through her head with Cody's face instead of Bradley Cooper's. If Cody was in a bad place like she thought, she could relate to that better than he would ever know.

She didn't often allow herself to think of that time in her life. When she did, it was like her heart was ripped open all over again. *Don't go there, Riley.* She wrapped her pillow around her head and squeezed her eyes shut, but that was a mistake. Reed Decker hovered there in the dark, his hand reaching for her as if begging for help.

Suddenly, she couldn't get air into her lungs, and she shot up, toppling Arthur off her stomach. Lights. She needed the lights on. As she reached for the lamp, her phone buzzed. Grabbing her cell as if she'd been thrown a lifeline, she read the text.

Yes.

She stared at the message, trying to decipher that one word. Did he want to talk? Not talk? She waited a few minutes to see if he'd say more, but nothing came through. Kind of weird. Curiosity won out, and she pushed Call. Besides, she needed to hear his voice so she could replace it with the one in her head belonging to Reed. The phone rang so many times that she was about to hang up when he finally answered.

"Hey," she said. "I didn't wake you, did I?"

"No."

"Good. I guess I got used to you checking in and was worried when I didn't hear from you."

"I'm fine."

Funny, he didn't come across as fine. His tone was clipped, and he sounded nothing like the man who'd called her darlin' during their last phone conversation. "Okay. Good." When he didn't respond, she took a deep breath, wishing she hadn't called him.

"The dogs behaving?"

She nodded before realizing he couldn't see her. "You know they are. You've trained them well." Again, nothing back from him. "Well, I'll let you go. You know when you'll be home?"

"Tomorrow."

"That's good. They'll be happy to see you. Nite." As much as she wanted to ask him what was wrong—because she was certain something was—she didn't. Maybe he was just tired. Who knew? He sure wasn't giving her any hints.

"Riley?"

Her heart stuttered. She knew what pain sounded like, and she heard it in the way he said her name. "Yeah?"

"Thanks for calling."

"Sure. See you tomorrow." He hung up without answering, and she stared at the phone's screen. Maybe she should have said more, but not having any idea what the deal was with him, she hadn't a clue how to offer comfort . . . or whatever he needed.

Didn't mean she wouldn't worry about him.

Riley was going over the instructions for care after spaying with a cat's owner when Michelle opened the door and crooked her finger. Her receptionist wouldn't interrupt if it weren't an emergency.

"That's it," Riley said, handing the woman a sheet that detailed everything she'd just explained. "Call me if you see any of the symptoms on this list."

Michelle rushed into the exam room as soon as Riley was alone. "We have another poisoned pet. Mr. Hatchel's dog. Brooke's in two with him. Doesn't look good."

"Dammit." Riley went to the sink, and as she washed her hands, she scanned the day's appointments pinned to the corkboard. "Tell Lisa that we might be running late. She can either wait or bring Barney back at five, unless she wants to reschedule him for another day." The cockatiel just needed his wings clipped, so it wasn't critical that she see him right away.

"Okay."

Riley followed Michelle out, turning right to go to room two. "How is he?" She could hear the medium-sized mixed-breed dog's labored breathing as soon as she entered. She pressed her stethoscope to his chest, alarmed at the rapid beat of his heart.

"I've got everything ready to flush him," Brooke said.

"It's okay, Sam," Riley said when he convulsed. She kept talking to him, hoping to calm him as they rid the poison from his stomach. Anger that anyone would intentionally harm an animal simmered, but she would get mad later. Right now she had a dog to save.

When his stomach was empty, she washed her hands. "All we can do is wait. Stay with him, and I'll go talk to Mr. Hatchel." Before she went to the waiting room, she made a stop in her office and called Mike.

"Kilpatrick."

"Hi, Mike. This is Riley. You have a minute?"

"For you? Always."

Laying it on a bit too heavy, Mike. "Yeah, okay. Ah . . . listen, I have another poisoned animal. A dog this time. I'm about to go talk to the owner, see what he knows."

"I'm finishing up a late lunch. I'll swing by in a bit."

"Thanks. See you soon."

"Hey, Riley?"

"Yeah?"

"Looking forward to it."

She disconnected, uncomfortable with how personal he'd made the call. Nor did her stomach flutter the same way it did when Cody said her name. Her focus was on finding the person responsible for harming the animals, and maybe she didn't need the complication of a man in her life right now.

"Mr. Hatchel," she said, walking up to the man.

He stood. "How's Sam?"

"He's not out of the woods, but we're doing everything we can." She hated this part of her job. He was a widower, a retired department store buyer, and a nice man. His dog was all he had.

"Please, Dr. Austin—"

"I know." She placed her hand on his arm. "We're doing everything we can for him. I want Sam to stay with us overnight so we can keep an eye on him."

"Whatever you think necessary. What's wrong with him? He's only three years old, so he shouldn't be getting sick, should he?"

"Does he spend time outside?"

"Yes. My back yard is fenced in, and I let him out back there."

She asked a few more questions, learning that he lived on a corner lot, and that he'd not noticed anyone in the neighborhood he didn't recognize. "I think Sam was poisoned," she said. "If you don't mind, I'd like to have an officer stop by and take a look around your yard."

"Poisoned?"

"I think so."

"Who would do such a thing?"

"I wish I knew. Give us a call in the morning, and we'll let you know if you can come pick him up."

He removed his glasses, pulled a handkerchief from his pocket, and cleaned them. "Will you call me if he . . . if he—"

"I promise I'll call if there's any change." Tears pooled in his eyes, and Riley impulsively gave him a hug. He walked out, his shoulders slumped, and she blinked away her own tears. Mike hadn't arrived yet, and she was running behind, so she gave Michelle instructions on what to tell him when he stopped by.

"Give him Mr. Hatchel's address and ask him to take a look around the yard." Seeing that Lisa had chosen to wait with Barney, she took them to an exam room. Mike might be disappointed that she wasn't available, but she wasn't in the mood to be flirted with.

The rest of the afternoon, she played catch up, going from one exam room to the next without a break. Sam seemed to be doing better, and she went to his kennel to check on him one last time. She told Denny, the college student who spent his nights at her clinic, to call her if the dog's condition worsened. Denny was a good kid, reliable and trustworthy. Often when they had a sick animal, he would make a bed near the kennel so he could keep an eye on it.

Before she left, she walked to the big cages, but there were no dogs wagging their tails at the sight of her. "Where're Pretty Girl and Sally?"

Denny shrugged. "They were gone when I got here. Figured the owner picked them up."

Why hadn't Michelle let her know Cody had stopped by? She went to the front. "Cody pick up Pretty Girl and Sally?"

Michelle turned off her computer. "Yeah, about two hours ago. Told him I'd let you know he was here, but he said not to bother you." She slipped her purse strap over her shoulder. "He wanted his dogs, and he got his dogs."

"That's fine." Something was going on with him, but she couldn't imagine what.

When she arrived home, Cody's truck was parked in his driveway, but all his blinds were closed. Once she got the cats fed, she went to her bedroom window and opened it. He never did come out on his porch to play his guitar.

CHAPTER NINE

Friday morning, Cody sat in Kincaid's office, determined not to squirm under the boss's stare. The man was always intense and focused, and Cody hated that kind of attention on him. There was no one he respected more than his former SEAL commander, and there was no one he regretted disappointing more.

"If you mean to fire me, I understand," he said when he finished explaining what had gone down in Iowa.

"I have no intention of firing you if you agree to one condition."

Cody raised a brow, but he knew what was coming. Get help.

"It's obvious that something happened in-country that you don't remember. Probably the concussion played a part in forgetting, but I think whatever it was, subconsciously, you don't want to remember. Which tells me that whatever you witnessed was some bad shit. These dreams you've been having aren't good, Dog. You have to know that. Until you remember and deal with it, I can't risk including you on any operations."

"I understand." And he did. Didn't mean he was any less ashamed and embarrassed. "I guess you want me to take a leave of absence?"

Kincaid stood and went to a mini fridge. "Want a soda or water?"

No, he wanted a full bottle of scotch. "A water, please." He'd been tempted to get so wasted that he couldn't remember his name when he'd arrived home last night, but knowing he had this meeting first thing this morning, he'd resisted. Last thing he needed was to have shown up with red eyes and a hangover. Kincaid handed him the bottle, and Cody twisted the cap, downing half the contents.

Kincaid returned to his chair, setting a bottle of soda on his desk. "To answer your question, there's plenty around here you can do until you're ready to go back on a team. I have a good friend, Tom Bledsoe, who works with vets dealing with PTSD. I'll call him and set up an appointment for next week. He's a vet himself who lost a leg in Iraq, so he can relate."

Swallowing the baseball-sized lump in his throat, Cody let out a breath. Good news: he wasn't fired. Bad news: he had to see a shrink. The last thing he wanted to do was explore his inner psyche. Something told him there was some bad shit in there. He briefly considered quitting, but that would only be the beginning of a downward spiral from which there would be no return.

"Do you agree?" Kincaid asked.

"Not like I have a choice."

Kincaid's eyes narrowed. "You have all kinds of choices, so don't give me that shit. I don't turn my back on my men, but I expect them to do what it takes to be a fully functional member of the team, so lose the attitude. If you don't accept that you have a problem and aren't willing to take the help you're being offered, then we'll part ways right now."

Chastised, and rightfully so, Cody stood and held out his hand. "You're right, but then you always are. I have a problem and I need help." That had been the hardest thing he'd ever admitted to, but in saying it, a seed of hope sprouted in his heart.

Kincaid clasped his hand with Cody's. "Good. For a minute there, I thought I was going to have to beat some sense into you. Go catch up with what operations we have going on and make yourself useful. I'll let you know when your appointment is after I talk to Tom."

"Thank you. Although it might not have sounded like it, I do appreciate—"

"Nothing I wouldn't do for any of you."

And Cody believed him.

"One other thing."

Cody wasn't sure he could take one more thing. "What's that?"

"I'm having a dinner at my house a week from tomorrow to celebrate Ryan and Charlie's upcoming wedding. Bring a date."

"Is that an order, sir?"

Kincaid studied him for a moment. "Yeah, it is. You need to get to know some women now that you live here. I'll have Dani invite someone for you if you want."

He didn't want Kincaid's wife setting him up with a stranger. "I have someone in mind."

"Good. Now get to work."

For the rest of the day, Cody buried himself in catching up with what missions K2 had going on, managing not to think about nightmares, shrinks, and his sexy neighbor.

When he arrived home a little after six, Riley's car was in her carport. He decided to take a shower before walking over and asking if she'd go with him to Kincaid's dinner. Instead of putting on his usual sweatpants once he was cleaned up, he chose a pair of jeans and a blue-and-white striped button-down shirt. After a moment's consideration, he tucked it in and added a belt.

"You're just walking across the street, dude," he said, eyeing himself in the mirror. Yet, he wanted to look halfway presentable. It had been ages since he'd asked a woman out—not that he was asking Riley out exactly—and he was damn nervous. He slapped a little cologne on his face while wondering if he should have shaved.

"Enough." He was making too big a deal over inviting a friend to a celebration dinner. Done with dithering, he walked out onto the porch. Just as he started down the steps, a yellow late-model Mustang turned into Riley's driveway. A man got out and walked up to her door. Cody retreated into his house. He went into the kitchen and watched as Riley came out and got into the car with the dude. Her boyfriend?

Once the car disappeared down the road, he changed into sweats and a long-sleeve T-shirt. In the kitchen, he poured a tumbler half-full of scotch, eyed it, then decided to allow himself this one night of wallowing in his misery. He filled the glass to the top.

Guitar and drink in hand, he went out on the porch with his dogs. "Go play." They both tilted their heads and stared up at him, as if they found him confusing. Sally barked once. "Right, the balls." Cody set the guitar and scotch on the table, reached under it, and pulled out the bag with the balls. He tossed two into the yard and the dogs took off.

For a few minutes, he watched them, but their silliness—which usually cheered him—made him think of Layla. She should be out there with them, fat and happy, but was instead lost somewhere in Afghanistan and likely half-starved, if she was even still alive. He downed a good bit of his drink, and then picked up his guitar. All afternoon, he'd worked to put out of his mind all the shit crashing down on him. Alone on his porch as the sun set, he thought his brain might implode from everything he was trying not to think about.

Where was Layla? Who was Asra? What had he seen in Afghanistan that he couldn't remember? Was he going to have to lie on a couch and share all his inner thoughts with someone he'd never met? Who the hell was the man with Riley?

As he played his sad songs and drank to numb his mind, the night grew dark. At one point, instead of refilling his glass, he brought the bottle out onto the porch. The dogs had long since fallen asleep at his feet. He drank some more, but sober or drunk, his fingers knew the chords, so he played on. Even though he tried not to watch the dark house across the street, his eyes kept straying in that direction. What if she didn't come home all night?

The thought of another man holding her, touching her, made him want to go hunt them down and snatch her away. If she had a boyfriend, then he'd been wrong about thinking she was interested. No surprise there. He was wrong about a lot of things these days.

His pity party continued, the alcohol doing a damn good job of pickling his brain. He wasn't a mean drunk, nor was he a happy one. He got quiet, or even quieter, he should say. Never a talkative man, he had a tendency when drunk to zone out and not think about anything at all, which was why drinking worked for him. He liked that state, probably too much.

A car turned the corner, and Cody watched the Mustang pull into Riley's driveway. It occurred to him that he should go inside so he wouldn't see her bring the dude into her house with her, but he didn't move. The man headed around the front of the car, but Riley didn't wait for him to help her out. The couple walked to her front door, and if Cody wasn't mistaken, she glanced toward his house. Was that a good sign, or was she just worried that he was watching her? He gave his dogs a signal to keep quiet.

Riley took out her keys, and the man said something to which she shook her head. When the dude put his hand on her cheek and leaned in to kiss her, Cody's hand took off on its own and strummed a harsh chord. He made a fist with his wayward hand to keep it from making more mischief.

Riley and her date peered his way. She said something, drawing the man's attention back to her. Pretty Girl and Sally swept their tails over the wood floor of the porch, their necks straining toward the house across the street. Although tempted to let them go to her, Cody managed to refrain. It was up to Riley what happened next. If she

disappeared inside her house with her date, then he'd move tomorrow so he'd never have to watch her with another man again.

If...

The guy spoke again before turning and walking to his car. Riley glanced toward his porch once more, and then disappeared inside her house.

Alone.

Riley greeted her cats as she walked toward her bedroom, Pelli clawing his way up her slacks, Arthur circling her feet, and Merlin racing ahead to greet her from his place on the pillow. They weren't used to her being gone at night and didn't seem to know what to make of this new development.

"It was just a date, guys. Nothing earth-shattering." They didn't seem to agree as they made their displeasure at her absence known, all three begging for her attention in their own way.

Going out with Mike hadn't been awful. He was a nice guy, and she'd enjoyed having dinner and seeing a movie with him, but he didn't make her stomach twitchy. Not like the man who sat on his dark porch and let her know with one sharp note on his guitar that he didn't want another man to kiss her. She'd briefly debated letting Mike kiss her goodnight anyway, but couldn't bring herself to do it knowing Cody was watching. She told Mike that it was late and she had to be at the clinic early when he'd suggested a nightcap.

"Some other time then?" he'd said.

She'd stolen another glance at the dark porch where she knew Cody sat with his dogs. "I think I might be involved with someone, so maybe not."

Mike raised a brow in the way men were born knowing how to do. "You think?"

She nodded. "Yeah, pretty sure." Okay, a small lie. She wasn't sure at all, but the moody man watching them was on her mind twenty-four seven, and she didn't see that changing anytime soon. It wouldn't be fair to Mike to pretend she was interested in him even though she would be if she were smart.

After sending Mike on his way, she changed into a pair of jeans and sweatshirt. Although she should just go to bed and put Cody out of her mind—like forever—she was drawn to him, alone there on his porch. Why she knew that he needed her was anyone's guess, but she thought he did. His heartbreakingly sad music floated over, as if he played just for her. She had to go to him, whether it was a wise thing to do or not.

As soon as she started down her driveway, he stopped playing. If his silence was intended to keep her away, she had news for him. "Ready or not, here I come," she murmured. At the steps to his porch, she paused. The moon was only a sliver in the midnight sky, and all she could see of Cody was the outline of his body. She waited for him to greet her, but he said not a word. At least the dogs seemed happy to see her, both bounding over to her.

"Hey," she said. "Don't stop playing on my account."

Nothing.

Because of the dark, she couldn't see his eyes, couldn't read him. If she asked him to turn on a light, she thought he would refuse. "I forgot my beer. Be right back." She paused. "Don't go anywhere, okay?"

Nothing.

Fine, don't talk, but you have no idea how stubborn I can be. She ran back to her house, grabbed a beer from the fridge and added a lime, then went into her bedroom to get a candle and lighter. Although she'd feared Cody would be locked inside his house when she got back, he was right where she'd left him.

"So, where were we?" She took the seat on the other side of the table from him, set down her beer, and lit the candle. "There, that's better. Not too much light, not too little." He eyed the candle, then glanced up at her, and the word that skittered through her mind was haunted. She was a doctor, and although she worked to heal pets, she wanted to heal him. If he'd lost his way, she wanted to help him find it again, and if she thought he'd let her crawl onto his lap and hold him, she would.

"I'm sorry I missed seeing you yesterday when you came for your dogs." When she picked up her beer, she noticed the almost-empty scotch bottle. Had he been drinking from it all night?

"Didn't want to bother you."

Ooh-kay. At least he was talking, but she heard the slight slur in his words. "I was hoping you would bother me."

No response to that. She tried a different tack. "Would you play for me? I love listening to you."

"How was your date?"

Not expecting that question, she glanced at him. "It was all right. Had dinner and went to the movies."

"Boyfriend?"

"Um, no. First date." He grunted, but she wasn't sure whether it was one of approval or what.

Without another word, he began to play. She could listen to him all night. As his music flowed through her, she leaned her head back and closed her eyes. What was his deal? She had a hundred questions she wanted to ask, but sensed she'd lose him if she asked even one of them. Instead, she settled for being allowed to share this time with him.

Sally and Pretty Girl slept with their chins on his feet, and she'd noticed that for the hour or so that he'd played, he hadn't moved his legs. She smiled, thinking how she would do the same with her cats, no matter how uncomfortable she was.

"Why are you smiling?"

Because you're sweet and you don't even know it. "I guess because I'm enjoying myself."

He seemed to mull that over as he strummed a few chords. "Why?"

There were several answers she could give him. She could tell him that she liked being with him even though he wasn't the happiest person she'd ever met. Far from it, in fact. Or she could tell him that he intrigued her. He was mysterious, which made her curious. The man was downright sexy with that bad boy thing he had going, so that of course appealed to her. Any of those reasons might have him running from her, however, so she thought it best to go with a reason that didn't relate personally to him.

"It's peaceful. Your music, the night, the sleeping dogs. I think I could sit here forever if someone would just deliver us food." His attention was focused on her as she answered, as if whatever she said mattered to him. She could get lost in those sad eyes.

"You're a beautiful woman, Riley. You make me want things I have no business wanting." His eyelids hooded, and he stared down at his fingers as they plucked at the strings of the guitar. "I want you, but I'd hurt you, and that would kill me."

"I think you might be worth the hurt, Cody." Call her crazy, but damn, she wanted him, even though she believed that he probably would hurt her. Okay, no probably about it. But every bone in her body said he was worth the risk, and there was the slightest, tiniest, itty-bittiest chance that each of them could come out on the other end unscathed. They might even fall in love. At least one of them might, namely her.

She didn't care. She wanted him.

"I watched *American Sniper* last night," she said, the thought coming out of nowhere, then wanted to bite off her tongue when his fingers missed whatever chord they had intended and hit a jarring note.

He picked up the bottle that still held at least two glasses of scotch and poured the contents down his throat. Riley thought that if he knew how much he'd just revealed to her that he would never speak to her again. She couldn't stand it any longer. She let her desire to be near him, to touch him, to comfort him fuel her decision to park herself onto his lap. He dropped the empty bottle to the floor with one hand and gently set his guitar down with the other.

The bottle made a clanking sound as it bounced and rolled on the porch's wood floor. Sally and Pretty Girl jerked their heads up in unison, both scrambling to their feet, their noses reaching for the new toy.

"They believe you've invented a new game," Riley said, swallowing her smile at the way Cody's eyes widened at finding her on his lap. "Don't think." He was already worried about hurting her, and the last thing she wanted him doing was thinking of all the reasons she shouldn't be straddling him.

"No thinking," he muttered as he wrapped his fingers around her neck and pulled her head down, his mouth seeking hers. Each time they'd kissed . . . what, three times now? Not that she was counting, but their kisses just got better and better. Her mouth already knew the feel of his tongue seeking entrance, and she welcomed him in. The man didn't know gentle. He demanded—he took—and that she let him was a marvel. Because of her background, she normally needed to be in control.

Wanting him closer, she threaded her fingers through the short spikes of his hair, and pressed her chest against his. Their noses bumped, and he angled his head for better access. A rumbling growl sounded from him when she fought his tongue with hers for supremacy, somehow knowing that he'd like that.

She thought maybe ten minutes of sucking each other's tongues, nibbling on each other's lips, and exploring each other with their hands passed before he pulled away. His head fell back against his chair, and he sucked air into his lungs like a man deprived of oxygen. Her breathing wasn't much better.

"This isn't a good idea, darlin'."

"Tell me why." She didn't doubt that he had a list of reasons, each of which she would debunk. She wanted him, and she would have him. From the hard ridge of his erection pressing against her bottom, she didn't doubt he wanted her. His problem wasn't with down there. It was in his head. He thought he should be honorable, or some such nonsense.

"You watched that movie?"

She nodded.

"I met him once, Chris Kyle." Cody turned his head to the side, watching his dogs paw at the scotch bottle. "On my first deployment. He was already on his way to becoming a legend by then, especially to the other snipers. I got it in my head that I'd beat his numbers."

"Wasn't that a good goal?" she asked when he paused. From what she'd learned watching the movie, the snipers had saved the lives of countless American soldiers.

Cody put his hands around her waist and picked her up as if she weighed no more than a ten-pound sack of potatoes. He deposited her back onto her chair, and then walked to the porch railing, keeping his back to her.

"It would have been a good goal if I hadn't let my ego get ahead of me." He put his hands on the rail, curling his fingers around the wood. "I'm not quite sure what happened, but . . ." He turned and his glare was fierce as he fisted his hand and pounded on his chest. "But I fucked up. I don't know how exactly, that part's buried in my mind. It's trying to come out, though, and I'm not sure I'm going to be able to deal with it when it does. I think you should go home."

Ignoring what was probably sound advice she went to him. She snaked her arms around his waist and pressed her cheek against his chest, right over his heart. He sighed, although she wasn't sure if it was one of relief that she was still there, or if it was one of exasperation at her stubbornness.

"Not going home," she murmured with her lips pressed into his shirt.

"Don't say I didn't warn you, darlin'." He picked her up, carrying her across his porch. They were at the door to his house when he whipped his head around.

"What?" she said when he dropped her feet to the ground and took off. *What the hell?*

CHAPTER TEN

Cody chased the car down the block, the same one that had tried to run over Riley. "Dammit," he swore when the car sped around the corner. He stared at the empty road, willing it to come back so he could catch the bastard trying to hurt her.

It had only been because the car had slowed as it drove by that he'd taken notice. He turned back toward his house, coming to a stop at the edge of the yard where his dogs pranced in agitation. "You ever see that car again, you let me know."

Sensing his tension, they growled at the empty street, wanting to protect him from the unseen evil. Along with Layla, it had been their self-appointed job in Afghanistan, and they didn't like being left out. He knelt and assured them he was fine, receiving licks in the face.

"Was that the same car as before?"

Cody glanced up at Riley. "Yeah. Unfortunately, I only got the first two letters of the license plate, but it's a start." He stood. "Have there been any more sick pets?" The interruption had been timely; otherwise, he'd have her under him by now. He wanted that more than anything, but he couldn't bear the thought of hurting her.

"Can we please talk about this tomorrow? I think you were about to have your way with me, and I'd very much like for that to happen."

She edged closer, her citrusy scent making him want to bury his face in her hair and breathe her in. With her, he could forget all his problems for a few hours, but then what? She lived across the street, so no way he could avoid her. Nor was she sure that after one taste of her he could let her go if kissing her was any indication. Everything about her was a siren call that he'd never experienced with another woman—the way she fit into him, the way her warmth seeped into his skin, the surge that felt like some kind of electricity powering through him when they touched.

"So would I." Unable to resist touching her, he trailed his knuckles down her cheek. "But—"

"I knew there was going to be a but."

"Yeah, darlin', there is. But you deserve better." She clamped her teeth down over her bottom lip, and he grew hard thinking of her biting him, begging him to make her come.

"Don't you think it should be up to me to decide what I deserve?"

"Not tonight." He snapped his fingers, and the dogs followed him as he forced his feet to walk away.

"When?"

His mouth curved into a grin, but he kept his back to her. She was a feisty one, and he liked that. A lot. The woman would be demanding in bed, and on that thought, he almost scooped her up so he could find out which of them would come out on top. Because that was how it would be with her, both of them fighting for dominance. From kissing her, he'd already learned that she liked to be in control.

When he was sure he'd lost his grin, he faced her. "Come over in the morning, and I'll cook you breakfast. We need to talk about who might be driving that damn car. While we're at it, we'll talk about sex. If we can establish some ground rules we both can agree on, then we'll discuss when."

Instead of answering, she marched toward him like a woman on a mission, put her hands on his cheeks and tugged his face down. Her mouth met his in a crash of lips, and she pushed her tongue inside. Hell. How was he supposed to resist her? About the time he decided to throw her over his shoulder and carry her to his bed, she pulled away.

"I have to be at the clinic by eight, so I'll see you at six thirty. I drink my coffee with cream and sugar."

"Damn, woman," he muttered, watching her walk away, his gaze drawn to the long ponytail bouncing against her back. It was like an arrow directing his eyes down to her sweet ass, which he admired until it disappeared from view. After a slight adjustment to his jeans, he headed inside to take an inventory of his refrigerator.

When he reached the porch, he spied the scotch bottle. He'd fully intended to tie one on big time, but then Riley had appeared. Although he'd had a good buzz on, he hadn't yet reached fall-on-his-face-drunk, and for that he was thankful. If she'd seen him in that condition, he never would have been able to face her again.

Now, he had a mission. Figure out what he was going to make her for breakfast while keeping an eye on her. There was no doubt in his mind that someone meant her harm, and he'd be damned if he would let that happen. As for discussing when they'd have sex, his mouth had gotten ahead of his good sense on that one. For her sake, he'd fully intended to leave her alone.

She was a determined little thing, though, and that appealed to him. Maybe she was strong enough not to fall in love or something stupid like that, only taking what she wanted and not expecting more than what they mutually agreed on. If they could come to an agreement, that was. He sure as hell hoped so because he'd never wanted a woman like he wanted Dr. Riley Austin.

What if you're the one who goes and falls in love? He crushed that irritating voice in his head. "So not gonna happen."

He picked up the bottle and his guitar, and ushered his dogs inside. After surveying his food supplies and doing a quick search on the Internet for a recipe that seemed to be easy, he turned out the lights and headed to the bathroom to take a cold shower. Hopefully, that would work in cooling the heat Riley had stirred in his blood.

An hour later, he stared at the ceiling fan, its spinning blades visible in the moonlight shining through the window. There were so many things crowding his mind that he thought there was a good chance he'd levitate right off the bed. In an effort to organize his brain into some semblance of order, he decided to deal with one thing at a time.

First, there was his job and what he was going to have to do to keep it. Staying with K2 was high on his priority list, so no matter how distasteful, he had no choice but to let the head doc in. Since he was damned tired of the nightmares, hopefully they would go away once he remembered whatever it was his mind wanted to forget. Seeing someone who could help him might not be such a bad thing.

He was using the drinking as a crutch to forget what he couldn't remember, and although that shouldn't make sense, it did. He didn't think he had a drinking problem per se, as he didn't crave the scotch. Actually, he could take it or leave it. It was the numbing of his brain cells that he sought. That had to stop. Tonight was his last binge, end of story. With that decision, he felt a little lighter. Not much but some, and that right there was something.

Layla. She was next on his list of things weighing him down. At some point, he was going to have to accept that she was lost to him. Since he wasn't there yet, he needed to make a plan to expand his search for her. Not wanting to bother anyone else about a stray dog among many in that hellhole, he'd only asked Wizard to keep an eye out for her. It was time to make a last ditch effort and contact everyone he knew still in-country to ask for help in the search. Another decision that seemed to lighten the load he'd been carrying.

Last but certainly not least, there was Riley. He honestly didn't know what to do about her. That there was enough chemistry between them to light his bed on fire was a given. He wanted her. She wanted him. Shouldn't be a problem. But there was that miniscule part of him that demanded he leave her alone because he was fucked up, and he'd only contaminate her with his poison.

Cody let out a long sigh as he kicked off the covers. Just thinking about her got him hot and bothered. He wasn't going to leave her alone. The only way that was going to happen was if he was tossed in a cell and the key was thrown away. Even then, he'd find a way out if she were the prize for doing so.

If that was the way it was going to be, then they had to set ground rules, ones that would protect her from getting hurt. He mentally made a list of what those should be. After covering every possibility, including that there would be no falling in love, he turned his mind to finding whoever was trying to hurt her.

Although she didn't know it, she was now under his protection. She didn't seem to want to believe that she was the target of some nutcase. The question was why had she been targeted? It seemed likely that it was the same person poisoning pets. For one, both things had started at the same time, and Cody didn't believe in coincidences.

He had the make and model of the car, along with the first two letters of the plate, which was a start. He'd give them to Maria, see if she could narrow the search. He'd heard that she was downright scary on a computer, able to find things no one else could. That might mean a few questions from his friends at K2 on just what Riley Austin was to him, and he didn't know the answer.

He jerked awake the moment the nightmare started. It was the first time he'd been able to do that. When had he fallen asleep? Glancing at the clock and seeing that it was five, he got up. The last thing he wanted was to nod off again and have the dream take up where it had left off. He dressed, ran eight miles with the dogs, came home, showered, used the trimmer on his shaver to neaten his stubble, and then got out his recipe for the breakfast he planned to make for Riley.

Riley groaned when the alarm clock buzzed, and she slammed her hand down on snooze. When it went off the second time, she blinked her eyes open. Pelli stared back at her from his perch on her chest.

"Hey, you." He let out a plaintive I'm-so-hungry meow. "Poor starving baby."

On Saturdays, she opened her clinic from eight to three for those who worked during the week. Picking up Pelli, she slung her feet over the edge of the bed. Arthur rubbed his body along her legs, and Merlin sat in the doorway with his back to them all. Riley glanced at the clock again, furrowing her brows. Why had it gone off an hour earlier than normal?

Then it hit her. She was having breakfast with Cody, and she jumped up, causing Pelli to dig his claws into her T-shirt to keep from falling to the floor.

"Ouch, Pelli, that hurts." She dislodged him from her shirt and set him down. With a speed she wasn't normally capable of in the mornings, she fed them, and then jumped in the shower. After drying off, she debated what to do with her hair. For work, she always wore it up in a ponytail, but she decided to leave it down for her breakfast with Cody.

Next problem, what to wear to a breakfast date where a discussion of when she and her freaking hot neighbor would have sex was on the menu? That he'd offered to make her breakfast had pretty much blown her mind since he didn't seem like a man who would be comfortable in the kitchen. If he put a bowl of cereal in front of her, though, she planned to praise it like Chef Bobby Flay—her secret crush—had served it to her.

"Concentrate, Riley. Clothes." Normally, she wore an old pair of jeans and a T-shirt to work in, with a lab coat over them. This morning, she wanted something special. She decided on black skinny jeans, black knee-length boots, and a red V-neck sweater. Underneath, she wore her new matching black bra and panties. Not that sex was also on the menu for this date, or whatever the hell it was, but she wanted to feel sexy. The lace trim around their edges felt foreign on her skin, yet stimulating. It was about time she was stimulated by something, and that something was a quick walk across the street.

At six thirty-one, she pushed Cody's doorbell, her heart beating like she was racing in a marathon. Never had she been this excited and this nervous about being with a man. Her date with Mike—had it only been last night?—had been nice, and that had been the problem. She didn't want nice. That was Cody's fault. Before him, she was sure she would have enjoyed Mike's company. Now, there was only one man she wanted.

The door opened, and Pretty Girl and Sally came tumbling out. They took a few moments to greet her before tearing off into the yard. Lifting her gaze to Cody, she sucked in a breath at the way he stared at her, as if he could gobble her up. The stubble on his face gave him the dangerous appearance that she loved on him. He wore a pair of jeans that looked old and soft, a dark blue short-sleeve knit shirt, and a pair of leather flip-flops.

"Hey," she said, pleased that her voice didn't come out sounding all breathy.

"I like your hair down."

"Ah, thanks."

"I like it in a ponytail, too." He stepped back, waving her in.

"And your hair's wet." Gah, was that the best she could come up with?

"Just got out of the shower."

As she walked past him, she could smell the fresh scent of soap. An image of him in the shower, all soaped up with droplets of water glistening their way down his naked body, flashed into her mind. She stumbled.

"Whoa." He caught her arm. "I've got you."

And so he did. She'd been brave last night—forward, more like—kissing him even when he had tried to push her away. Not so much in the light of day, or she'd be kissing him this very minute. Her gaze was drawn to his bare forearms, where the muscles flexed from holding her. She'd always had a weakness for men's arms, and his were downright perfect.

"Riley?"

And by God, his rumbly voice could melt butter in the middle of a blizzard. "Mmm?" She peered up at him only to see amusement dancing in his eyes. Her cheeks heated at getting caught practically drooling because of a pair of arms, and knowing she was blushing only made it worse. There was no doubt in her mind that the color of her face matched the bright red of her sweater.

"Just this." He brushed his lips over hers in the lightest of touches. "Good morning, darlin'." He fingered the hem of her sweater. "This red top you have on . . . it's damn hot."

She was about to melt into a puddle right at his feet. "Good morning, Cody." Well, the control over her voice hadn't lasted long. She sounded like she'd lost all the air in her lungs.

"Come on. Let's go feed you."

"Right. Breakfast. That's what I'm here for."

He chuckled as he started to close the door. "No, you're not, but we'll talk all about that."

"Wait." She glanced over her shoulder. "I don't think you should leave your dogs out if we're not there to keep an eye on them."

"They're trained not to approach strangers without my okay, nor will they eat anything without my permission, but yeah, better safe than sorry." He whistled, and they immediately came bounding up the porch and inside. "Come with me, darlin'."

Yes, she'd go with him wherever he wanted to take her. She'd never been in his house before, and curious, she glanced around. The living room was small, the only furniture a sofa, two comfortable looking theater chairs with a table between them, and a large screen TV mounted on the opposite wall. Underneath the TV was a small stack of boxes.

"Still moving in?"

He eyed the four boxes. "I guess I should get around to doing something with those."

In the kitchen, a pub table was in front of the bay windows. He'd already set it for their meal. "Is that champagne?"

"Yeah. I thought you could handle one glass before work, but if not, no problem."

There were strawberries in the bottom of the flutes, and the champagne was golden and bubbly. "Yum!" She headed straight for the table. From the corner of her eye, she saw the hint of a smile on his face. "I'm impressed that a man would have champagne and strawberries. I mean, you didn't invite me here until late last night, so you had to already have this, right?" She took a sip and moaned from the crisp, cold taste.

"Sorry to disappoint, but I found an all-night store. Sit and enjoy. I'm making you French toast and bacon." He tilted his head as he looked at her. "Is that okay?"

She heard the uncertainty in his voice, which sent a little thrill through her because she interpreted it to mean that serving a woman breakfast wasn't a usual thing for him. His nervousness was endearing. It would have been a definite turnoff if he'd been confident of making a conquest of her.

"It's so okay that I think you deserve a kiss." Without waiting for a sign that a kiss would be welcomed, she walked straight into his arms, and covered his cheeks with her palms. The man's lips were soft and seeking. She'd initiated the kiss, but when he took over, she let him.

She had bounced around from foster home to foster home in her youth, and as a result gave up control to no one. Ever. And although there was something different with Cody, where she was able to let him set the pace, she couldn't resist testing him.

He made a slow slide with his hands down her back, his fingers coming to rest on her hips. His tongue tangled with hers, demanding dominance. She gave him that for a few moments. When she felt like she was drowning, she clamped her teeth down on the tongue exploring all the corners of her mouth.

She peered up at him, needing to see his reaction. Searing heat shimmered in his eyes. The man could take whatever she threw his way. With a last tightening of her teeth, she let go and leaned back, waiting to see what he would do or say.

"Christ, darlin'." He sucked in a breath as he took her hand and pressed it against the bulge in his jeans. "I think he's permanently stuck on hard." Letting go of her hand, he narrowed his eyes. "You bit me. I liked it."

"I liked biting you. I have some other places in mind to bite you." She went to the table and took a seat, hiding her smile.

"I'm screwed."

He said it so low that she didn't think he meant for her to hear, but it was the best compliment she'd ever been paid. "I'm ready for my French toast and bacon."

The man actually saluted her. "Yes ma'am. I'm on it." He made a show of adjusting his jeans. "Just gotta figure out how to walk normally again first."

Riley laughed when he funny walked to the refrigerator. "I could grow to like you, Cody Roberts."

Her sexy-as-all-get-out neighbor turned, and the expression on his face was nothing but serious. "As God is my witness, that's my wildest hope, but you might change your mind once you get to know me. I want you like the very devil, Riley, but I have some conditions before we fall all over each other in bed."

Conditions?

CHAPTER ELEVEN

Riley's face blanked, all the mischief and fun that had been there gone in a flash. Cody mentally regrouped. He should have waited until after they ate to bring up his conditions, but she'd rocked his world with that kiss she'd initiated, and he'd totally lost his bearings. And the thing was, he'd learned something new about himself, something he never would have guessed.

He liked her being the aggressor. Who knew? Although he'd been celibate for—he did a quick calculation in his head—close to six months, he'd been with his fair share of women. Every single one of them had been like putty in his hands, looking to him for direction on what he wanted from them. That hadn't seemed boring before, but now it did.

"What conditions?"

"Nothing big, just some things we need to agree on." He walked to her chair and put his hands on the back, leaning toward her until their faces were only inches apart. Damn, she smelled good. "Let me feed you first, then we'll talk."

She shrugged. "It's your party."

Regretting that he'd spoiled the mood, he rose and went to the fridge, taking out milk, butter, and the eggs he'd already whipped. He tried to think of something amusing to say, but he wasn't an amusing man. As he worked, he listened to her talk to his dogs. She was good with them, but being that she was a veterinarian, it was a given that she loved animals.

"Your feast, darlin'." He slid a plate in front of her, grabbed the second one from the counter, and took a seat across from her. Trained not to beg for food, Sally and Pretty Girl lay on their bellies at his feet.

After pouring a generous amount of syrup over her French toast, she took a bite. "Oh, yum. This is delicious."

At least he'd done something right. "Where are you from originally?" he asked.

"Everywhere and nowhere."

At the flash of sadness in her eyes, he wished he hadn't asked, but her answer intrigued him. He waited to see if she would explain.

She sighed. "It's not my favorite subject, but I don't make it a secret. I grew up in foster care, bouncing from one home to another. I was considered a difficult child."

"I'm sorry." Although as a kid, he'd sometimes wondered if his parents were aliens from another planet, he'd still known that in their own way they loved him, and he'd had a stable home. He couldn't imagine what it must have been like for her.

"Yeah, well, it was what it was. Where are you from?"

"Vermont. My parents are professors at a liberal arts college. I was as foreign to them as they were to me."

"But they loved you?"

Her question sounded like a plea, as if she couldn't bear the thought of another child not loved. "Yeah, they did." The conversation had taken a turn he hadn't expected. He never talked about his personal life to anyone, yet he was telling her.

With a groan, she pushed her plate aside. "I usually only have coffee and yogurt for breakfast." She grinned. "Now I just want to crawl back into bed and go back to sleep with my full tummy."

"I'm glad you liked it." He hadn't been sure if she would, but French toast had seemed safe enough.

She glanced at her watch. "I have about thirty minutes to spare you. Tell me about these conditions of yours."

"More champagne?" he asked, suddenly reluctant to speak about the list he'd made in his head last night.

"Tempting, but no. I have a surgery at ten."

"Okay, here's the thing." He slipped off a flip-flop and stroked the fur on Sally's neck with his foot. He'd always found touching his dogs calming, and at the moment, he was damn nervous. What if she didn't agree to what he needed? Was he willing to let her walk out if she didn't? All he knew was that he wanted her like he'd never wanted anyone before. That both excited him and scared him.

Just spit it out. "Okay . . . I've already told you that I'm messed up. I'm not a man you want to fall in love with, so rule number one, don't fall for me."

She burst out laughing.

Well, that wasn't the reaction he'd expected. "I'm serious."

"I'm sure . . ." More laughter. "I'm sure you are. Go on, what's the rest?"

A bit offended that she hadn't protested rule number one, he said, "Why is that funny?"

She gave a shake of her head, as if indicating he was an idiot. "Like anyone can control their heart. I don't plan to fall in love with you, but if it happens, it happens. Deal with it."

Damn, he liked this woman. "For your own sake, I hope you don't. Next, if we sleep together—"

"When. When we sleep together. It's going to happen, Cody, so you might as well get used to the idea."

Oh yeah, he definitely liked her. "Okay, *when* we do, whether it's here or at your house, no spending the night together."

"That's a bummer. I like waking up with a man in my bed." She tilted her head and studied him. "So, why not?"

Although he didn't want to tell her, it was only fair she understood. "Because I have nightmares, and sometimes I wake up not knowing where I am. I'm afraid I might hurt you."

"That's a good reason. Next?"

It was that easy with her? No delving into his psyche, wanting him to spill his guts? "This is the last one. There will be no others for either of us for as long as it lasts between us. I don't share. When either one of us has had enough it will end. No fights. No tears."

Her lips thinned. "Had enough?"

Christ, he was a moron. That last sounded good in his mind when he'd thought of it last night, not so much when he said the words aloud.

She stood, put her hands flat on the table, and leaned her face toward his. "I should warn you that when someone puts conditions on me, I have a tendency to do the exact opposite. That goes back to the foster homes where there were always conditions on my behavior if I wanted to stay. Most times I didn't, but I won't bore you with my poor, sad childhood. I'll do my best to abide by your rules, but I have one of my own."

He managed not to squirm with those hazel eyes focused on him, while at the same time he was aroused by how the gold flecks in them seemed to flare like a lit match. She was pissed, and being a typical man, all he could think about was burying himself to the hilt in all that fiery heat radiating from her. *Her, I want her!* his dick screamed, snapping to attention.

"And that would be?" Surprised his voice hadn't come out sounding like a croaking bullfrog, he gave in and squirmed. He should've put on sweatpants, not jeans.

"That the time we spend together isn't only in bed. We go out on dates like a real couple."

"I don't date."

"You do now, so ask me out."

He opened his mouth to argue, then remembered the party Kincaid was giving Ryan and his fiancée. "There's a dinner party next Saturday at my boss's house for one of my teammates who's getting married." Not liking being stared down at, he stood. Much better. "Would you please be my date?" Her smile was like the cat who ate the canary, and who could blame her? She thought she'd gotten one over on him, and he let her have the win. She didn't need to know that he'd planned to ask her.

"So we don't see each other until then?"

That was unacceptable. He slipped around behind her, curled a strand of her long hair around his hand the way he'd been fantasizing doing, and tugged her head back. With his mouth brushing her ear, he said, "No, darlin'. That's the beginning of our going-out-together agreement. At the start of our conversation, you wanted to know when we were going to have sex. The answer to that is tonight."

"Oh," she said.

How could one short word sound so breathy? He pressed his erection against her sweet ass. "Yeah, oh. I'll even feed you dinner first. Seven on my porch sound good?"

She tilted her head back, resting it on his chest, and peered up at him. "Sounds really good."

"Then I'll see you tonight." He wanted to kiss her, but if he did, he knew he wouldn't stop, and she needed to go to work. He settled for nipping her earlobe, swallowing a smile when she closed her eyes on a sigh. When she tried to turn in his arms, he stepped back. "Go to work, Riley."

She shook a finger at him. "You're a cruel man, Cody Roberts, sending me off without even a kiss."

"You want a kiss?" He grinned at how vigorously she nodded her head. "Then be here at seven." She needed to go while she still could. It was only by one tenuous thread of control that he didn't go caveman on her, throw her over his shoulder, and carry her to his bed. If he even got that far.

"Maybe I will, and maybe I won't." She tossed her head, let out a huff of aggravated air, and then walked away.

Cody trailed behind her, giving up on keeping his gaze off her ass. Tonight he would see her bare naked, and that particular part of her anatomy was high on his list to touch. At his door, he expected her to turn, to say something, maybe try one last time for a kiss. She didn't. Just kept right on going. The woman was still pissed. He chuckled, and apparently she heard him because she lifted her middle finger without looking back.

That made him laugh. He'd been fascinated by her from the first time she'd done that, and red flags waved a warning as he stepped onto the porch to survey the street. No car turned the corner, aiming to run over her. That she was under his protection as any neighbor who was in danger would be wasn't the reason for the flags demanding his attention. That he'd never met anyone like her, never wanted a woman as much as he wanted Riley, had agreed to date her when his head wasn't even sure it wanted to face another day . . . All of that was almost too much to take in.

"I am so screwed," he said to Sally and Pretty Girl, both of them sitting at his feet, watching their new friend walk away. At hearing him, they lifted brown doggy eyes, looking up at him as if they totally agreed with his assessment.

He eyed the dogs. "You two could argue the point." After Riley drove away, he went back inside to make a list. Wash the sheets, buy beer and limes. Figure out what to feed his . . . what exactly was she to him?

Riley pretended not to notice Cody watching her as she left. He made her feel safe. She would have welcomed a man like him when she was in foster care, fighting off advances from those whose supposed job it was to protect her. With Cody guarding her, she dared whoever was trying to hurt her and the animals under her care to bring it on.

She'd almost walked out when he'd given her his conditions. Like she'd told him, she didn't do well with rules. There had been too many times when the "house rules" laid down by her foster parents had no other purpose than to put her at their mercy. If it wasn't the mother seeing Riley as no more than a slave—someone to clean the house, wash the clothes, do the dishes—it was the father or an older son eyeing her in a way that creeped her out, even when her young self hadn't quite understood why.

It wasn't until living with Pat and John Haywood that she'd felt safe and wanted. If only she'd found them before she'd had to watch Reed die in her arms. He had been her first love, and she'd failed him.

Going there only led to depression and guilt, so she pulled her mind from that dark part of her past, and thought about Cody. It was clear that he was haunted by something, but she'd managed to get past his first wall of defense. How many walls he'd erected that she'd have to blast her way past, she didn't know, but in her heart, she believed he was worth the trouble. And the man was trouble. There was no doubt about that.

She turned into the parking lot of her clinic, and when she saw Jeff and Marla pacing at her front door with their cat, Rascal—with only his head showing from the top of a towel they had wrapped around him—she wanted to scream. Not again.

It was going to be a bitch of a day.

"Stud Two's here," Brooke said from the doorway. "If you're going to keep Stud One, can I have Stud Two?"

Riley rolled her eyes. "You really need to stop calling them that."

"Well, it's true. Anyway, can I?"

"I think that's between you and Mike. Have him wait in my office. I'll be there in a sec."

She washed her hands, slipped off her lab coat, and headed down the hall. At the doorway, she stopped. Brooke stood close to Mike, both of them laughing. They made a cute couple, and Riley checked her jealously meter, happy to see that it registered zero. It would be a complication if she were attracted to both Mike and Cody.

"Hi, Mike. Thanks for stopping by," she said, entering her office. He and Brooke jumped apart, and then Brooke mumbled a good-bye as she left.

He turned from watching her pretty assistant leave. "Brooke said you had another animal come in sick today."

"Poisoned." She walked around her desk and picked up the lab report she'd gotten back that morning. "This is on Max, a cat I couldn't save. He belonged to a little girl who cherished him. Who would do something like that?"

Mike took the paper she held out. "I don't know, Riley. I see some crap in my job that makes me question humanity, but then I meet someone like you who cares. That tells me the world isn't such a bad place after all."

"You care, too," she said, softly. As she had before, she wondered why she wasn't attracted to him instead of Cody, who by his own admission was a hot mess.

He studied her for a moment. "I'm feeling kind of weird about this, but if I ask Brooke out, is that a problem? I mean since we're just going to be friends. That is all we're going to be, right?"

What she wanted to do was talk about the lab report and how the police planned to catch the bastard hurting animals. But this was a conversation they needed to have. "Yes." She gave him a sad smile. "I'm sorry."

"Me, too. Is it because of the guy across the street from you?"

"How do you—"

"Because when I picked you up for our date, you kept looking over there, and when I brought you home, same thing. Like you were afraid he was watching, and you didn't want him to get the wrong idea. I saw him standing on his porch when I came down your street to get you."

"Wow, you're good."

He laughed. "I'm trained to observe. So no reason we can't be friends?"

She really did like him. "No reason at all, and I think you and Brooke are perfect for each other."

The grin spreading across his face was cute. "Thanks. Now, what does this say?"

She stayed silent as he read the report.

"Strychnine," he muttered, looking up at her.

"Found in gopher bait. Mix it into raw meat, leave it where you know an animal will get to it, and walk away."

"That's going to be almost impossible to trace."

She scrubbed her hands over her face. This whole business infuriated her. "I know. I did an Internet search. It's as easy to buy as candy."

"All we can do at this point is what we're already doing. We've put the department on notice to keep an eye out, and we've beefed up patrols in this area. I wish there was more we could do."

"Yeah, me, too." They'd saved Rascal this morning, but would the next dog or cat be brought in fast enough to save? "Thanks for stopping by. I appreciate it." She glanced at her watch. "It's time to close. Go ask Brooke out before she leaves."

Mike shot her a grin. "Yes, ma'am. I'm on it."

After he left, she completed the notes on her last patient. Brooke came bouncing in, followed by Michelle.

"Oh my God. Stud Two asked me out." Brooke grabbed Michelle's hands, dancing them in a circle. "He's so freaking hot. We're going to dinner tonight. Tell Michelle she has to come home with me and help me decide what to wear."

Riley watched them, smiling at Brooke's excitement. "Michelle, go home with Brooke and help her."

Brooke came to a sudden halt and turned to Riley. "Is that okay? I mean, he wouldn't have asked me out if he was going out with you, too, would he?"

"No, Mike wouldn't do that. Michelle, get her out of here before she explodes all over my desk from giddiness."

Brooke grinned. "Thank you."

"You bet. Enjoy your date."

"Oh, I'm gonna. See you Monday."

Riley spent a few more minutes organizing her office, then made the rounds before leaving. Denny wouldn't come until later that night, so she made sure the one cat and three dogs being boarded had water. If Rascal hadn't recovered enough to be sent home, she would have waited for Denny to arrive. But because she was seeing Cody, she was glad she could leave. She had just enough time to go home, take a shower, shave her legs, and dress.

With her purse over her shoulder and her phone in hand, she headed for her car. Her long sex drought was going to end tonight. The hottest bad boy on the planet was going to see to it. Her toes tingled just thinking about it.

She clicked her remote a few feet from her car, and at the sound of footsteps behind her, she started to turn, her heart sinking at the thought of someone rushing their sick pet to her. Before she could see who it was, pain exploded in the back of her skull, and her world faded to black.

CHAPTER TWELVE

The plate of assorted cheeses, paper-thin shaved ham, grapes, strawberries, and blackberries looked good if Cody did say so himself. He visualized feeding those berries to Riley with his fingers. Because he'd noticed that she liked her beer slushy, he had a bottle in the freezer. For dessert, he had the makings for ice cream sundaes. A fun meal, and one he wouldn't have to spend time in the kitchen making.

His plan was for them to eat their dinner on the porch, then watch the sunset while he played for her. She seemed to like that, and other than for his teammates when they had been on deployment, he only played his guitar for his dogs. Until Riley.

Although it seemed like it should be just the opposite, being around her calmed him. She wasn't quiet or meek, so he didn't understand why that was. Where was she? He'd been keeping an eye out the window, thinking she should've been home by now. Hopefully, she hadn't had a last-minute emergency, especially another poisoned pet.

Whether or not Maria could narrow down his search of the suspect's car to a reasonable number with only the first two letters of the license plate remained to be seen. He'd given her the info on the model he thought the car was, and with that and the letters, he hoped she could give him a list to start working on.

He was feeling pretty good about the decisions he'd made. Letting Riley into his life for however long she could put up with him, agreeing to see the head doc, and this morning, e-mailing everyone he knew even vaguely who was still in Afghanistan—sending them a picture of Layla—were all positive steps in getting his head screwed back on right. Seeing the doctor meant he'd have to face whatever had happened that was giving him nightmares, but he was finally ready to deal with it. Yep, he was feeling good that he was finally taking control.

At another glance out the window, he saw that the sun was starting to set, and if she didn't get here soon, they were going to miss watching it together. Where the hell was she? He took the bottle of beer out of the freezer before it exploded and put it in the fridge.

There was nothing left to do until Riley arrived, and he realized that even more than the sex they had put on the agenda for tonight, he just wanted her with him. Not that he wasn't looking forward to the sex. He wasn't going to kid himself about that, but it was more than that with her. Too restless to stay inside, he decided to wait for her on the porch.

"Wanna go out?" Both dogs jumped up and ran to the door. Before he could reach them, his phone buzzed, Riley's name popping up on the screen.

"Hey, darlin'. You get delayed?" At the sound of heavy breathing, he frowned. "Riley?"

"Hel-help."

"Riley! Where are you?" No response. Phone in hand, he grabbed his keys. "Stay," he said when the dogs tried to follow him. Not bothering to lock the door behind him, he slammed it shut on his confused dogs and ran to his truck. The only thing he knew to do was to drive from his house to her clinic, watching for her car.

He was two blocks from his destination when a siren sounded behind him. With a glance in the rearview mirror, he saw a cop car, lights flashing, on his tail. Eyeing his speedometer, he saw that he was traveling far faster than the residential speed limit. Too bad. The cop could just follow him.

His tires squealed when he took the turn into her parking lot, the persistent police car still on his bumper. The front lot was empty, and he sped to the back where she parked her car. If she wasn't there, he didn't know what he'd do.

As soon as he came around the corner and saw Riley facedown on the pavement, his heart fell so hard that he thought he was having some kind of attack. He screeched to a halt, shoved the gear lever into Park, and almost fell out of his door trying to get to her.

"Riley!" he yelled, running to her. When he reached her, he dropped to his knees and put his fingers on her throat, looking for a pulse. "I'm here, darlin'," he said, willing her to respond. She didn't, but he let out a relieved breath when he felt the blood flowing through her neck vein.

"Don't move her."

Cody looked up at the cop standing over them, recognizing him as the man who'd taken her out. "Call for a fucking ambulance."

The officer was already speaking into his radio, giving an address for the rescue squad. Cody petted her shoulder, not knowing where else he could safely touch her. He wished Doc were here. His friend would know what to do.

He leaned close to her ear. "Wake up, darlin'. We were supposed to watch the sunset together, but that's all right. We can do that some other time. You just need to wake up."

She moaned.

Let her be okay, he prayed, something he hadn't done since they'd lost Evan Prescott on an operation in Afghanistan. His prayer hadn't work then, but he refused to go there. Sirens sounded in the distance. The cop knelt on the other side of her, and Cody glared at him for getting close to her.

The cop glared right back. "Hey, man, I know she prefers you, but she's still my friend. Don't be an ass."

Cody gave a terse nod as he took Riley's hand in his. Her skin felt so damn cold and clammy. "Why haven't you caught who's doing this?" he demanded. If the cops had done their job, Riley would be sitting on his porch, drinking her slushy beer while he fed her grapes.

"Why hasn't K2?" the man retorted.

The hell? Cody jerked his gaze up. "What do you know about K2?" And if the dude didn't wipe that smirk off his face, Cody was going to do it for him.

"Not as much as I'd like. When she told me it was her neighbor she was interested in, meaning not me, I ran a check on you. Whoever you people are, you're downright spooky. I'm a cop. I should be able to find out anything I need to know about you, but I was blocked at every turn. That tells me you're a black ops operation."

When the cop paused, no doubt waiting for Cody to confirm his guess, Cody stayed quiet.

"Yeah, I didn't expect an answer. I'm Mike Kilpatrick. Not yet ready to say nice to meet you, Cody Roberts. Depends on how you treat the lady."

If the man didn't shut up, Cody was going to put him flat on his ass. That he'd treat Riley bad in any way was an insult. *So you didn't mean it when you said for however long it lasted? You didn't think that would hurt her?* Okay, so short term he had no intention of hurting her, but long term? He probably would. After he knocked the cop into tomorrow, he'd do the same to himself.

A rescue squad truck sped up, closely followed by an ambulance. The EMTs pushed him aside, checked her vitals, put a neck brace on her, and then loaded her on a stretcher. Cody watched as they closed the back doors of the ambulance behind them, whisking Riley away. He felt like his damn heart had been torn out of his chest.

"Where you going?"

Cody picked up Riley's phone and purse. "To the hospital. Why don't you do your damn job and find out who did this to her."

"I plan to," the man said, not seeming to take offense.

So did Cody, and when he found the person responsible, they were going to have the worst day of their life.

At the emergency room, no one would tell him anything because he wasn't a relation. To keep from going on a rampage and tearing the place apart to get to her, he went to a chair that had a view of anyone coming or going. From there, he could see if they moved her.

He shoved his hands into the pockets of his jeans, his fingers touching her phone. Curious how she'd been coherent enough to dial his number as hurt as she was, he nosed around in her contact list. When he found that her clinic was number one on autodial, that didn't surprise him. What did was that he was number two. All she'd had to do was push one number to call him, which answered one question, anyway. But he had a whole slew of others. He hoped to God that she'd gotten a good look at the bastard's face.

Riley smelled antiseptic, but that was a common odor in her practice. Was she in her clinic? If she'd fallen asleep at her desk and missed her date with Cody, she was going to be royally mad at herself. Although her eyes felt like they'd been glued together, she managed to crack one open, then the other.

The first thing she saw was Cody's face looming over her, and the second thing was Mike's on the opposite side of her bed. Why were they in her bedroom? She tried to frown at them, but gave up when a searing pain in the back of her head made her want to throw up. To hell with them, she thought, and promptly fell back to sleep.

"Go do your job and find who hurt her."

Cody?

"We don't have anything to go on. I need to talk to her when she wakes up, see what she remembers. Why don't you go home? I'll make sure someone calls you when she comes to."

That sounded like Mike.

"I'm not leaving this room, *officer*."

Definitely Cody. Someone took her hand, and she knew it was Cody because she immediately felt safe. "Head hurts."

"Christ, darlin', you scared the life out of me."

She tried to smile but the effort hurt too much, so she settled for forcing her eyes open. "Why?"

"We'll talk about that later. Right now you need to rest."

"Why?" Nothing made sense.

"Riley, can you tell me what happened? Who hurt you?"

Someone hurt her?

"Leave her be, Kilpatrick. Better yet, come back tomorrow. She should be able to answer your questions by then."

She still didn't understand why both Mike and Cody were in her bedroom, but she was too tired to care. With Cody's hand still protectively covering hers, she drifted off.

Riley opened her eyes and surveyed the room. This wasn't her bedroom and she didn't think it was Cody's. Not that she'd ever seen his, so maybe he went for sterile white. She turned her head to the left, wincing when a bolt of pain shot from the back of her skull down her neck.

Dark brown hair was the first thing she saw. She squinted, recognizing that military haircut. Why was Cody sitting in a chair with his face pressed to the bed? As she listened, she recognized the steady breathing of a man asleep. Next to his face, he held her hand in his. Her gaze searched the room. Why was she in a hospital bed?

The door opened, and a nurse padded in on rubber-soled, silent shoes. "Ah, good, you're awake."

Cody's head shot up, and he scrubbed at his face. He yawned, and then turned an intense stare at her. "How do you feel?"

Stubble covered his cheeks and chin, and she reached up and trailed her palm over the bristly hairs. He leaned into her hand the way Arthur did when he needed a pet.

"How about you wait outside for a few minutes, Mr. Roberts, while I check on Miss Austin."

"Dr. Austin," Cody said.

"Actually, Riley works for me." She waved her hand. "Go on."

"I'll be right outside." He leaned down and gave her a quick kiss before leaving.

"Good-looking man," the nurse said.

"He sure is. Why am I in the hospital?"

"You don't know?"

"If I did I wouldn't be asking, would I?" Riley sighed. "I'm sorry. My head's killing me. It feels like someone took a baseball bat to it. What happened to me?" Was it an aneurysm, or dear God, a brain tumor?

"The doctor's on his way and he'll talk to you about your head. After that, there's a police officer waiting to ask you some questions."

"Why?" Had she done something wrong? She tried to remember when the headache had started, but her last memory was of locking her clinic doors, wanting to hurry home so she could get ready to see Cody.

"Mr. Roberts said you're a doctor, but I've never seen you around," the nurse said, not answering Riley's question.

"I'm a veterinarian. I want someone to tell me what happened."

"You have a nasty bump on your head," a man wearing crisp, blue scrubs said, walking up to the bed. "Dr. Austin, I'm Dr. Garrett. Let's take a look. Turn your head to the side, please."

Riley did as requested. Although she was an animal doctor, she was still a doctor, and that was no mere bump on her head. At least it wasn't a brain tumor. "It hurts."

"I'm sure it does. You have a concussion and five stitches. We had to cut your hair around the wound, but you can easily hide the bald spot until it grows back out. We're going to keep you under observation at least one more night. Depending on how you are tomorrow, we'll talk about whether you can go home or not."

"One more night? How long have I been here?" As for her missing hair, she'd deal with that when her head didn't feel like it was going to explode.

"You came in yesterday evening."

She'd lost a whole night? One she was supposed to have spent with Cody? That sucked. "Will someone please tell me what happened?" She was irritated that no one would explain anything to her.

"Officer Kilpatrick is here with a detective. They'll explain everything. I'll be back in the morning, and we'll see how you're doing."

The doctor was all business, no real bedside manner, but all she cared about was seeing Cody and finding out why her head was split open. As soon as he left, Mike and a man she didn't know came in, closely followed by Cody.

"You need to wait outside, Mr. Roberts," the unknown man said.

Cody headed straight for her. "Not happening."

"I want him here." She needed him even though she was only now getting to know him, and why that was she'd think about later. After her head stopped hurting. He took her hand in his large one, and she gave him a squeeze in thanks.

"I'm Detective Margolis. I understand you already know Officer Kilpatrick?"

Riley nodded, immediately regretting it. "Hi, Mike."

He glanced at her hand entwined in Cody's. "Hey. How's the head?"

"Feels like it's twice the size it should be and hurts like crazy."

"You scared us, Riley. What do you remember?"

"Not a thing. I still don't know what happened."

The detective put his little notepad back into his pocket. "We know very little. We found a rock not far from you that had blood on it. We've sent it to the lab to see if it's yours, and fully expect that to be the case. It appears someone came up behind you and hit you on the head with it."

"Why?"

"I understand someone's poisoning pets under your care? We think it's related to that. Who would want to harm you, Dr. Austin?"

She couldn't think of a soul. "I don't know."

"Mr. Roberts mentioned while we were waiting to talk to you that there was an earlier incident. He believes someone tried to run you over." The detective raised a brow as if asking why she hadn't volunteered that information.

"That could have been a driver not paying attention to the road." God, she wanted to believe that. All three men exchanged glances, which irritated the hell out of her. "Stop looking at each other like that. In fact, go away. All of you."

"Not going anywhere, darlin'," Cody said, and although she wouldn't admit it, she was relieved that he wasn't an easy man to run off.

With instructions to try and come up with names, the detective left. Mike leaned down and gave her a kiss on her forehead. "Take care, Riley. I'll check in with you tomorrow."

"Thanks." After he walked away, she glanced at Cody, who was glaring at Mike's back. "He's just a friend."

"One who feels free to kiss you?"

She laughed. "God, my head hurts. Don't make me laugh. Friends do give innocent kisses, you know."

"I don't want to talk about him." Still holding her hand, he toed the chair up to the bed and sat. "Christ, Riley, when I saw you facedown on the pavement, my heart stopped."

"I'm sorry, but mostly I'm sorry for missing last night. I was looking forward to it, you know."

"Hush, darlin'. Concentrate on getting better so you can get out of here. There'll be plenty of nights for us."

"Okay. I'm tired."

He brushed his fingers softly down her eyelids, closing them. "Sleep. I'll watch over you."

"Kay." It was nice knowing he'd be there when she woke up. "Cats?" she said, suddenly thinking of them.

"Taken care of."

"Thank you." She didn't have the energy to ask how as she drifted off, knowing Cody was there, keeping her safe.

CHAPTER THIRTEEN

Riley wasn't happy. That was apparent by the glare she was sending him and Brooke. "You're not returning to work until you get checked out on Wednesday, and that's final," he said. "Doctor's orders."

Brooke gave a vigorous nod. "I rescheduled all your appointments and called Dr. Andrews. If there's an emergency, he'll cover for you."

"Why don't the two of you go away?" Riley made a shooing motion with her hand. "I don't like either of you right now."

Cody grinned. "Funny woman." That got him another glare.

It was Monday afternoon, and the doctor had only agreed to allow her to come home if she promised to rest and had someone with her round the clock. Cody didn't plan to leave her alone, and she was going to rest if he had to sit on her to keep her from going to work like she wanted to do. She was prone on her sofa with a pillow under her head, and her protests that she should be at work were halfhearted. Riley's three cats held positions on her body, sitting like sentinels bent on guarding her. The little one finally grew bored with that task and began to play with the fringe on the afghan covering her.

"Can you stay for a few more minutes?" Cody asked Brooke. "I need to let my dogs out and then feed them."

She nodded, her pretty blonde hair bouncing around her neck. Riley had told him Brooke and the cop were dating, and that news had pleased him because it meant Kilpatrick was no longer going after Riley. Although she was probably better off with the man. Mike, at least, seemed to have his head on straight. Cody didn't care. Riley was his for as long as it lasted, and in his mind, he'd already stretched that time from a few weeks or a month to open-ended. Until she wised up and realized she could do better.

As he made his way across the street, his phone buzzed, and Kincaid's name came up on the screen. "Boss."

"How is she?"

"Grouchy. Doesn't like ordered bed rest." He'd called Kincaid that morning, asking for a few days off so he could stay with Riley, and after he'd explained why, his request had been granted.

"Maria said she'll shoot you over an e-mail list of cars with those first two letters as soon as she has it. She's also going to come stay with Riley tomorrow afternoon so you can keep your appointment."

No way was he leaving Riley. "I appreciate it, but—"

"You will show up at Tom's office promptly on time. Maria and Riley are already friends, so Riley won't have a problem with that."

Cody opened his door and let the dogs out. They raced to the yard to do their business. He'd left them alone too long. "I didn't know that. I guess if it's okay with Riley, that's fine."

"Good. Stop by here after you finish with Tom."

Cody recognized that as an order. "See you tomorrow."

Kincaid hung up without responding. Cody chuckled as he shoved his phone back into his pocket. His former SEAL commander still knew how to get his men to ask how high when he said jump. The thing was, Cody would jump to the moon if the boss gave the order. There was no other man he knew who would take on a screwed-up, PTSD-suffering warrior, while also turning over all his resources to keep a woman who Cody cared for safe.

After the dogs were fed, he told them to stay as he made to head back to Riley's. They both looked so pathetic as they watched him walk to the door that he paused. "If I take you with me, will you promise to behave?" He went back to them and knelt. His team claimed he was a dog whisperer, but that was about to be put to the test. "There're cats where I'm taking you, and they outnumber you by one. If you go after them, you're going to end up with bleeding noses. You can go with me if you promise to ignore them."

Sally and Pretty Girl heard the word "go" and, unable to sit still, their butts bounced on the floor. "That's not the same meaning you're thinking it is." He stood. "I'm telling you right now, the minute you ignore my orders, you're going to prance yourselves right back home. You understand?"

Both barked their understanding, but he didn't quite trust them. He'd never trained them to be around cats because it had never occurred to him that he'd fall for a woman with the creatures. *Fall?* No, he hadn't fallen for her. He just really liked her and wanted to have sex with her. Nothing more to it than that.

"Heel," he said as the dogs followed him down the porch steps. At the end of the yard, they stopped and planted their butts on the ground. He clipped on their leashes. "Come."

Riley was probably going to freak when he walked into her house with his dogs, but if he was going to spend time with her, that was going to include his dogs getting to know her cats. It was going to be an interesting evening.

At Riley's front door, he said, "Sit. Stay." Both obeyed, looking up at him expectantly, as if asking what next? He opened the door and stepped in. Riley was asleep, and he crooked a finger at Brooke. She rose from the chair where she sat and came next to him.

"She conked out about five minutes ago," Brooke whispered. "After telling me what she thought of us both."

Cody chuckled. If nothing else, Riley never hesitated to speak her mind. "Thanks for staying. If there are any further poisonings, call me. Give me your phone." She handed it to him and he put his number in.

"Cool. Now I have Stud One's and Stud Two's phone numbers." She tossed him a wave as she skipped out.

What did that mean? No doubt he was better off not knowing. The three cats were curled up asleep on various parts of Riley's body. He knelt in front of his dogs. "Here's the deal. I don't know if you've ever seen a cat in your life, but I do know that your first instinct's going to be to chase them. You will not do that, or you will be banned from here forever. Got it?"

He was clueless why he wanted Sally and Pretty Girl to make friends with Riley's cats. It was in his head that he might—hopefully might—be spending some time at her house, and he didn't like the thought of his dogs being left alone when he was only across the street.

Although they didn't understand his words, both tilted their heads as if trying hard to get his drift. "Just do what I tell you and we'll be good." He stepped back into her living room. "Come." Apparently, they sensed his concern, because they crept up next to him. He put his hands on both their heads. "Stay with me."

He moved to a chair near Riley, his dogs slinking along with him. They sat at his feet. "Have either of you seen a cat before?" he whispered to keep from waking Riley. He didn't know their backgrounds, but considering their country of birth, it probably wasn't a good one. If they'd never run across a cat before, no telling what their reaction was going to be if one of the felines decided running was the best response to seeing two large, scary dogs.

Merlin was the first to blink open blue eyes, his gaze landing on the invaders in his home. Cody forced himself not to tense so that his dogs didn't pick up on his apprehension at what might happen next. Merlin yawned, and then stuck his nose back under his tail, apparently going back to sleep.

Sally and Pretty Girl had lifted their ears, their sights on the black cat. When Merlin ignored them, they both deflated as if totally disappointed they'd been deemed not worthy of attention.

"Pelli," Cody said. When the kitten didn't stir, he called to it again. Pelli sat up, eyed him, and then his Siamese crossed eyes fell on the dogs. He rose to his toes, the hair on his back sticking straight up. Cody pressed his hands harder onto his dogs' heads. "Easy. Friend."

The kitten hissed, then hid himself under Riley's hair. At Pelli's warning, Arthur awoke. He stretched his orange striped body, reaching a paw into the air. His yellow-orange eyes looked first at the sleeping Merlin, then to where Pelli had disappeared to, and then his gaze settled on Cody and his dogs. If Cody wasn't mistaken, the cat appeared delighted at what he saw. He jumped off the couch and marched toward the dogs.

"Friend," he said again, hooking his fingers around their collars to hold them in place while he waited to see what Arthur would do. The cat stopped a foot out of their reach, plopped down on his back, and peered at them upside down.

"You're a clown," he told Arthur. Still keeping his hold on the dogs, he let them stretch out enough to touch noses with the cat. Pretty Girl licked a slobbery tongue over Arthur's face. The cat purred. Not to be outdone, Sally belly crawled closer and gave the other side of Arthur's face a bath.

Riley slept on. He took the dogs into the kitchen with him and inventoried Riley's food supply. For a woman who lived alone, she had a ton of food on hand, both in her pantry and in her freezer. He rifled through the contents of the freezer, finding a container that had "chicken noodle soup" written on the lid.

"A cure all," he said, used to talking to his dogs. He put the soup in the microwave, punching the Express button several times until it was defrosted and starting to bubble. There was a loaf of wheat bread in the pantry, and he toasted some slices, slathering them with butter after they popped up.

After waking her, he helped her sit up. She ate half the soup and a slice of toast before her eyes slid closed. He picked her up and carried her to bed, liking how she wrapped her arms around his neck.

"Are you staying with me?" she asked as he pulled the covers over her.

"Try to get rid of me, darlin'. Back in a minute." He made a pit stop, went to the kitchen, rinsed and stacked the dishes in the sink, then collected his dogs from the corner where he'd ordered them to stay. In the bedroom, he showed them where they could sleep. Stripping to his briefs, he climbed into the bed and spooned her, dislocating the cats that were using her as a bed.

She snuggled against him. "Not quite how we planned our first time in bed together, is it?"

Her hair smelled lemony from the shower she'd insisted on taking as soon as he'd brought her home. "No, it isn't, but now we have something to look forward to."

"That we do."

She wiggled some more, and he groaned, putting his hand on her hip to still her. "You're killing me here, darlin'. Stop moving around." Her little giggle was cute, and he smiled into her hair. When she grabbed the hand he had on her hip and pulled it around her, tangling their fingers together, warmth curled its way around him. He experienced something he'd not felt in a long time. Good. He felt damn good.

It wasn't long before her breathing settled into the rhythm of sleep. He stayed beside her, holding her, thinking about her. He couldn't see a future for them, believing she would be the one who would be the first to say she'd had enough of him. What he did know was that for as long as she wanted him he was hers. He just had to make sure he didn't fall in love with her.

She had laughed when he had warned her not to fall for him, and at the time, his message had been intended for her, but he was beginning to fear that the laugh was going to be on him. She was feisty, caring, and fit perfectly in his arms. If he were smart, he'd run for the hills before he got any more attached to her, because something told him that in the end the joke would be on him.

When his eyes burned from keeping them open, he eased out of bed, snapped a finger at his dogs, and slipped out of the room. One thing he wouldn't do was fall asleep next to her and risk having a nightmare. If he woke up with his hands around her neck, he'd never forgive himself. He fell asleep on her sofa with Sally and Pretty Girl on the floor next to him.

Yelling startled Riley out of sleep, and she sat up so fast that her head protested the sudden movement by sending a sharp pain down the back of her skull. The cats scrambled off the bed and dove under it.

"Nooo!"

Cody? Puzzled, she slid her hand over the sheets. There was no lingering warmth from his body, and she remembered that he'd said he wouldn't spend the night in her bed because of his nightmares. She switched on her bedside lamp, then went into the living room and turned on a lamp in there.

"Don't. Please don't hurt her."

Pretty Girl sat near his head, her body shaking. Sally pawed at his chest, apparently trying to wake him. Cody had the afghan she'd left on the couch tangled around his legs as if he'd been fighting its confinement. He twisted his body from his side to his back.

Taking him at his word that he might try to hurt her if he didn't realize who she was, she was at a loss as to what to do. If she went up to him, would he grab her or fight her? If he did anything to her, he would hate himself. That much she knew about him already. He fisted a hand and aimed it for Sally. The dog dropped his belly to the floor before he was knocked across the room, and Riley let out a relieved breath, wondering if Sally expected Cody would come at him and was prepared for it.

That was so sad that tears pooled in her eyes for both of them, and for Pretty Girl as she cowered in fear. When Cody yelled again, Sally sat up and licked his face. He kicked off the afghan, giving Riley a view of his magnificent body. The man was all muscle from head to feet, and if she weren't watching him in the middle of a nightmare, she'd take the time to admire the hottest male physique she'd ever seen.

He grumbled something and pushed Sally's face away, and then turned onto his side with his back to the room. Since he seemed to be over his nightmare, and since he'd presented such a perfect view, she let her gaze roam over him, up his long legs, pausing at his butt, which unfortunately was hidden by his briefs, then over a broad back that she couldn't wait to get her hands on.

"You going to stand there and stare at me all night?"

"Oh, you're awake." She started toward him.

"Go to bed, Riley. Turn off the lamp on your way." He kept his back to her.

If she had to guess, she'd say he was embarrassed that she'd seen him having a nightmare. She hesitated, wanting to comfort him. He pulled up the afghan, covering his beautiful body, and buried his head under the pillow. Fine, she could take a hint. She switched off the light, and stomped back to bed, making as much noise on her wood floors as possible. Pissy, she knew, but he'd been there for her when she needed him, so why couldn't she return the favor? She left the door open so she could hear if he called out again.

Although her head still hurt, the pain had eased significantly, and she didn't feel as out of it as she had the day before. Even so, no matter how hard she tried, she couldn't go back to sleep, and finally gave up, letting her mind do what it wanted, which was to think about Cody.

Was she making a mistake wanting to be with him? Maybe his problems were too deep for her. Her biggest worry was that she didn't know how to help him. She could clip an animal's toenails, set a broken leg, treat pretty much any ailment, but delving into the mindset of a man having nightmares from his past was out of her league.

And who was *her*? He'd called out, begging someone not to hurt "her." Was it a woman he'd had a relationship with, someone he'd loved? Still loved? All questions she had no answers for, and if he had them, she doubted he'd share. More than anything, she wanted to know about the "her" that was haunting his dreams.

It was impossible to fall back asleep, and as light from the rising sun crept through the sides of the blinds, she gave up trying. Two of her cats had returned to the bed, Merlin in his usual place at her feet, and Pelli curled up next to her neck. Arthur was missing. When she sat up, the kitten opened one eye, blinked at her, then stuck his head under his tail and went back to sleep. Merlin's attention was on the open doorway, where Cody was visible. Riley peered out and found her missing cat. Arthur was snuggled between the two dogs, all three fast asleep.

"Silly boy," she murmured.

She went into the bathroom, flipped on the light, eyed herself in the mirror, and gasped at the rat's nest that was her hair. She'd washed the bottom half when she'd showered after returning home, but hadn't wanted to get shampoo in her wound. Along with the mess that was her hair, there were purple bags under her eyes.

"You look like crap, my friend," she told her reflection. She turned on the water to let it warm up, then returned to her bedroom to get clean clothes.

Feeling much better after cleaning the rest of the blood out of her hair, she came out of the bathroom, and as she smelled coffee and bacon, her stomach rumbled. When she followed the aroma to the kitchen, the first thing she saw was her cats eating their breakfast while Sally and Pretty Girl sat to the side, avidly watching. The second thing to catch her eye was Cody, wearing only his jeans, standing at her stove with his back to her, and she paused, captivated by the way the muscles in his back and shoulders flexed as he worked.

"Your coffee's on the table and breakfast is almost ready. Sit."

She saluted him.

"I saw that."

He had eyes in the back of his head? Then she noticed he was looking at her kitchen window where a fuzzy image of her was reflected back. "Sneaky," she said, heading for the cup of coffee. "I didn't know I had bacon and eggs."

"You didn't, but I did."

"Well, thank you." He still hadn't looked at her directly, and his tone was brusque. She stirred cream and sugar into the coffee while trying to think of how to bring up his nightmare. It was driving her crazy wondering who his mysterious *her* was.

"Eat," he said, shoving a plate in front of her.

If he wanted her to forget his existence—which she thought was exactly what he was aiming for—then he needed to put on a shirt. "Aren't you going to eat?" He stood with his back to the counter, leaning against it, his hands stuck into the front pocket of his jeans, his gaze fixed on her as if waiting for her to obey his every command. And wasn't he just the sexiest thing ever in his shirtless, bad boy bossy mode?

"Ate already."

Okay. That conversation was effectively shut down. Fine. She'd just go right to exactly what she wanted to know. "Last night, you said, 'Please don't hurt her.' Who's her?"

Caramel-colored eyes flared, then his gaze flicked from her to her cats, then to his dogs. "Apparently someone I can't remember," he said so quietly that she had to run his words through her head a second time to decipher them.

"You're having nightmares about someone you can't remember? Were you hurt or something?"

He lifted from the counter, his body expanding in a way that had her blinking her eyes in awe—and not just a little lust—and said, "I don't know, all right! Eat your breakfast. I'll be across the street if you need me." With a hand signal to his dogs, he walked out with the two canines on his heels.

"What just happened?" she asked her cats, but none of them seemed to have an answer as all three were busy with their after-breakfast baths.

And the strange thing was, she wanted Cody more than ever. He was a wounded warrior, and whether he knew it or not, he needed her. So, how to make him see that? Unless there was a woman he loved so much that he still dreamed about her out there somewhere. Had he lost her somehow? If so, that would change everything.

CHAPTER FOURTEEN

At his front door, Cody stopped and hung his head. Just because he was embarrassed that Riley had seen him lose it because of a nightmare didn't make it okay for him to talk to her the way he had. The coffee and food he'd downed sat like a fat clump of dirt in his stomach.

He was an idiot. He let Sally and Pretty Girl into the house, told them to stay, then headed back to Riley's. Not only was an apology in order, but he'd left Riley alone. As he stepped up to her front door, he heard a sound coming from the side of the house. When he went around the corner of her carport and saw her heading for her car, keys in hand, he blocked her with his body.

"Going somewhere?" he said.

Her nose smashed into his chest. "You need to put on a shirt."

"Ah, but I don't think you mean that." He put his thumbs under her chin and lifted her face. "Look. I shouldn't have stormed out like that, and I'm sorry. It's just that—"

"That you're having nightmares you don't know what to do with, and it's getting to you."

It was exactly that and more. He tapped her nose. "Inside with you, sneaky girl."

"Can I ask you a question, a personal one?"

He took her keys and opened the side door, following her into the house. "Might not answer, but fire away, darlin'."

"Okay, here it is." She huffed a breath as she stopped in the middle of the kitchen and faced him. "Is there someone in your life you love? If so, you need to tell me now."

That was one he could truthfully answer. "There's not."

"Good. I was a little worried about that."

He tucked a loose strand of hair behind her ear. "Only a little?" The gold in her hazel eyes flared, and he gave in to the need to kiss her. When she sagged against him, he slipped an arm under her knees and picked her up.

"I guess I'm not going to work after all."

"Guess not."

"I was only going to spend an hour or two catching up on paperwork. Nothing physical."

The woman couldn't be trusted, and it was a good thing he'd been given a few days off so he could keep an eye on her. "You obviously need a keeper. Didn't you listen to a word the doctor said? You rest until you see him again on Wednesday."

He got her settled on the couch, swallowing a smile at her grumbling about not being an invalid. To keep her entertained, he played poker with her, which wasn't easy when three cats thought the cards were things to play with. She didn't ask again about his nightmare, but her question had him thinking. Had he seen something he shouldn't have? It was maddening that he couldn't remember, but he supposed that was why he was seeing a head doc, which reminded him that he hadn't told Riley.

"I have an appointment this afternoon, and Maria Buchanan's going to stay with you while I'm gone. I'll stop by the store on the way back and pick up something for dinner."

She scowled. "I can stay by myself for a while."

"No, you can't. You can't be trusted. Have you forgotten already I caught you trying to sneak out? Besides, I understand you and Maria are friends. How'd that come about?"

"Maria's cool. I met her when she brought in her cat, and we hit it off. If I have to be babysat, I'd choose her."

"What am I? Chopped liver?"

"Oh, no! I didn't mean . . ." She tilted her head and eyed him when he cracked a grin. "You were teasing me."

"I was." And wasn't that interesting? He wasn't the teasing sort, but Riley brought out a side of him he hadn't known existed. He stacked the cards and set them on the coffee table.

"I've waited for you to feel better to talk about this. Have you given any thought to who might want to hurt you?"

"Maybe someone planned to mug me but something scared them off before they could grab my purse."

"Would that be the same person who tried to run you over?" Why was she being so stubborn about accepting someone was targeting her?

"I lived most of my life in fear, Cody. I thought once I was on my own, I would be safe. If what you believe is true, then I need time to process it all because it means I'll never really be safe." Her eyes misted, and she turned her face away, hiding her tears. "It means there'll always be monsters under the bed, and I don't want that to be true."

The woman was breaking his heart. "C'mere." He wrapped his arms around her, where he wished he could always keep her, safe from the monsters.

"Just give it some thought, okay? See if any names pop into your head." He heard a car pull up. "Maria's here. Give me a kiss before I go."

"Thought you'd never ask."

Without hesitating, she slid onto his lap, facing him, and gave him a smile that made his heart feel like someone had clamped a pair of jumper cables on it. The charge that sped through him was like nothing he'd ever felt before.

She lowered her mouth to his, and he cradled her neck with his hand, careful not to touch the bump on her head. Her lips were warm and lush, and he swept his tongue into her mouth, loving the taste of her. All too soon, the doorbell rang, and he lingered for a few more seconds before pulling away and staring down at her. Her eyes were dark with desire, and the last thing he wanted to do was leave. He wished to God that he were in a better place in his life, because he was going to find a way to mess up whatever this was between them. That was a fact.

The head doc's waiting room wasn't typical of any doctor's office that Cody had ever been in. The chairs were soft leather and comfortable, the assortment of magazines varied and some were even interesting, and jazz music played softy through ceiling speakers. The receptionist had offered him a choice of coffee, tea, or soda. He'd almost asked if she had any scotch, and he would have only been half kidding.

"Mr. Roberts."

Cody jumped up, eyeing the front door, wondering how fast he could get out. Pretty damn fast if he wanted. *Man up, dude. You've been through worse than this.* He wasn't so sure about that, but his job depended on doing this. He followed the woman who'd introduced herself as Norma when he'd checked in. She reminded him of the kind of grandmother you could tell all your troubles to, and then she'd feed you cookies and milk. Probably intentional on the doc's part. Trick you into liking it here, then sneak up on you when you weren't paying attention.

She led him to an office, and then backed out without a word, closing the door behind her. There *was* a damn couch against the wall. He so fucking didn't want to be here.

"I'm Tom Bledsoe," said a tall man maybe ten years older than Cody. He had black hair peppered with gray, and piercing blue eyes.

"Cody Roberts." He shook the man's hand.

"Have a seat." The doctor returned to his desk. When Cody hesitated, he chuckled. "The chair is fine. We're not at the couch stage yet."

"Not sure I ever want to be."

"Almost everyone says that. Do you prefer Mr. Roberts or Cody?" he asked after Cody was seated in front of the chrome and glass desk.

"Cody's fine."

"Good, because I prefer Tom." He steepled his hands and fixed on Cody with those all-too-seeing eyes. "Tell me why you're here."

And there it was right off the bat. The million-dollar question. "I was given an ultimatum by my boss. Get help or lose my job."

"I've known Kincaid for a few years now. I imagine he's a good man to work for."

"He is." For a while they talked about the similarities and differences between serving in Iraq, where Tom had been a medic, and Afghanistan, where Cody had been deployed.

"Why do you need help, Cody?"

The man was a trickster all right. He'd lulled Cody into relaxing before springing the question. He took a deep breath. "I keep having this nightmare, the same one over and over. Last week, on an operation, I had a flashback. Now I'm grounded until I figure things out."

"I see. That unfortunately happens to too many of our military men and women who've served in a war zone. It's not a weakness, and it doesn't mean you're crazy. Just that you're human. In your case, with the recurring nightmare, I'd guess something happened that you're suppressing."

"So what do I do about it?"

The doc smiled. "Exactly what you're doing by agreeing to see me. The reason I'm good for you is that I've been where you are. I served, I saw things I'll never unsee, and I understand where you're coming from."

"Did you suffer from PTSD?" For some reason Cody wanted the doctor to say yes. Not that he'd wish what he was going through on anyone else, but how was the man supposed to understand if he'd never experienced the night sweats, the feeling that he was losing his mind, and at his lowest moments, never considered biting a bullet?

"I did, and I was stupid about it for too long. I came too damn close to swallowing a bottle of pills. I was a doctor, not yet a psychiatrist, but still thought I could heal myself. It was Kincaid who made me see the light. The man's persistent if nothing else, and he practically dragged my ass to treatment. When I was thinking straight again, I knew I wanted to help others like me, so I went back to school and got my degree."

If Tom Bledsoe could get better, why couldn't he? "Tell me what I need to do."

"This first appointment is two hours. That gives us a chance to talk and go over how the treatment works. After this, you'll come see me twice a week for one hour. There are a few choices, but I've found that CPT works best. That's Cognitive Processing Therapy. Trauma has a way of causing us to struggle with our memories of an event, sometimes the result being that we're unable to make sense of something that happened. I've not yet delved into your nightmares and what you remember, we'll do that at your next appointment."

Now that he was committed to doing this, Cody was disappointed that they weren't going to jump right in. "How long does this all take?"

"That depends on you. How open you are to the treatment, how hard you work at it. I'll be giving you some tools to help you handle depression and learn how to become aware of your thoughts and how to change them. We'll get to the bottom of your nightmare, figure out how much of it is real, and how much of it isn't. Individuals returning from a battle zone often blame themselves for things that were beyond their control, especially if someone died. You were a sniper, and that's right up there for messing with your mind."

Cody didn't think that was his problem. "I never lost sleep over killing an insurgent. My worry was more that one of our guys would get hurt or worse because of me. You know, that I didn't kill the bad guy first."

"And that was your job and an honorable one. Don't ever let anyone tell you different."

"Not even my parents?" Why had he brought that up? He'd long ago accepted he would never have their approval for what he did.

Tom eyed him with interest. "Not even them. That's always easier said than done, though, and we'll talk about your relationship with them."

"I'm good there." He was here to get to the bottom of his nightmare, not to discuss the relationship with the professors. "They're entitled to their opinion."

"They are, even when it's a wrong one. My concern, Cody, is how much their lack of approval affects you."

"I don't need their—"

"But we won't get into that today. The first thing I want you to do is to write down your nightmare and bring it with you to your next appointment. Do it right after it occurs so you remember every detail. Also, write out the flashback you had as much as you remember. What led up to it, what you heard, smelled, saw, thought. That's your homework for this week."

Cody had no desire to discuss his parents, but he'd deal with evading that discussion when it came up. He stood when Tom did. "This is gonna be different. I've been trying to forget it, to put it in a box and lock the lid."

"A problem never gets solved by ignoring it, it just takes root and grows. Make your next appointment with Norma on your way out."

"We didn't talk about what this was going to cost me. Don't get me wrong, I'm gonna do it no matter how much, but—"

"The bill's paid. And before you argue, you're a valuable member of K2's team, and Kincaid believes in taking care of his own. If it makes you feel better, he gets a discount. He paid for my help when I couldn't.

When I tried to pay him back, he refused on the condition that I treat any of his men who needed it, and you're not the first. Someday, you can do good for someone who needs it by paying it forward."

Cody swallowed the lump in his throat, not knowing what to say.

"Yeah, the man tends to have that effect on you. Make your next appointment for Friday."

Appointment made, Cody sat in his truck in the parking lot and thought about the past two hours. He hadn't known what to expect, but he hadn't thought it would be easy, and delving into his nightmare was going to be a bitch. If nothing else, after meeting with Tom, he had hope for the first time since the nightmares started. And he liked the man, which was surprising since he'd steeled himself not to appreciate anyone messing around in his head.

Another car pulled into the lot, likely Tom's next appointment. Cody turned the key in the ignition and drove away. He'd planned to stop at the grocery store, but remembered he still had the food he'd bought for Riley and him to eat last Saturday night. Anxious to be with her, he headed home.

Riley enjoyed Maria's company, but she hadn't been left alone since she'd woken up in the hospital, and she craved some downtime. Cody had been gone for over two hours, and she wondered when he'd return.

"You like him, don't you?" Maria asked.

Riley glanced at her friend. "Who?" Like she didn't know Maria meant Cody, but she was feeling ornery.

"The man who has you staring out the window watching for him to come home."

"Oh, him." She shrugged. "What's not to like?" Not a thing she could think of, and where was he? "I watched that SEAL movie, you know the one about the sniper? Do you think Cody's having trouble dealing with life after the military?"

"Mmm, you need to ask him that question. I'll just say that I haven't seen any of the guys I know who served make an easy adjustment back to civilian life."

Riley didn't doubt that Maria knew more about Cody than she did and that rubbed. She wanted to know everything about him, every tiny detail. Never mind that there were things in her life she never wanted him to know. That was her past, over and done with.

She had run away from foster homes where men had lurked, watching her with a dangerous gleam in their eyes, lived on the streets, been picked up by the cops more than once and returned to Child Protective Services, and run away some more. The only time she regretted running was that one time with Reed. If she could pick one thing to do over again, it would be that. But she'd loved him as much as a sixteen-year-old knew how to, and she'd believed him when he'd said they would make a new life where nothing bad could touch them.

"There he is," Maria said, bringing Riley back to the present.

Riley's gaze hungrily followed Cody as he entered his house. A few minutes later, the door opened and the dogs ran into the yard. She smiled when he stepped out behind them and stretched his body like a cat that had been too long confined.

"You got it bad, girlfriend."

God, she so did. "I do not."

Maria snorted. "Whatever." She stood and tossed her thick, dark hair over her shoulder. "Call me tomorrow. Oh, almost forgot. Tell Cody to check his e-mail."

"Will do. Thanks for hanging out with me."

"It was fun. We should do it more often."

Riley waved a good-bye to her friend, but her attention was on the man across the street. He would come over as soon as he saw Maria leave, and knowing that spurred her to hurry to her bedroom for a quick change of clothes and a peek in the mirror to see if the purple bags under her eyes were still there. They were, but they were not nearly as bad, and a touch of makeup helped.

After slipping on a sleeveless, pale-blue maxi dress made of soft cotton, and doing a quick check on her hair, which was in a ponytail to hide her bald spot, she returned to the living room. The material of the dress felt strange in all the places usually covered by a bra and panties. That she wore nothing underneath was daring and exciting.

Her head hadn't ached for a few hours, and come hell or high water, she was going to have sex tonight. All she needed to make that happen was the man walking across the street with his dogs at his heels and a plate of something in one hand. He stopped at her mailbox and collected some envelopes.

"Have you ever in any of your nine lives seen anything hotter?" she asked her cats, the three of them perched on the windowsill, watching along with her. When Cody and friends approached, Pelli took off for the bedroom. Merlin yawned. Arthur leapt down and parked himself at the door, his tail twitching with what Riley interpreted as excitement. She totally got it. If she had a tail, it would definitely be twitching.

"Hey," she said, opening the door. "Let me take something."

Her mail was thrust into her hand. When he stepped past her, she smelled soap and the spicy aroma of aftershave, making her mouth water. His face was lacking that scruffy bad boy look that melted her bones, but the smooth skin was just as tempting. Before the night was over, she was going to rub her face all over his. That she promised herself.

When he headed for her kitchen, his dogs staying with him, she followed and was almost tripped by Arthur, who hurried to catch up with Sally and Pretty Girl. "My cat's in love," she said.

A body made up of all bones and muscles turned. "And?"

His eyes raked over her, then lifted to hers, and the heat shimmering in them made her stomach flip. Just stick a fork in her right now and call her done. "And just this."

As if he'd fully expected her to come at him like a missile locked on target, he reached behind him, set the plate on the counter, and opened his arms, wrapping them around her when she snuggled into him.

He leaned back and peered down at her, a slow smile forming on his face. "Hello."

She grinned, feeling like a giddy teenager. "Hello back."

When he slid his hands down her spine to the curve of her butt, he stilled. "If I'm not mistaken, you're not wearing any panties."

"You're observant, Mr. Roberts."

"And you're a naughty girl, Dr. Austin, but I like that about you."

She rubbed against him, going all tingly inside when she felt the hard length of him against her stomach. He lowered his mouth to hers. Mother Mary, the man could kiss. The envelopes she held drifted to the floor as she let go of them to free her hands for the exploring she'd been dying to do. She slipped them under his T-shirt, and trailed her fingertips up his sides, feeling the indentation between each rib. His skin rippled against her palms. She flattened her hand over his heart and felt the fast beats, and a thrill shot through her that she could make his blood pound.

"Darlin'," he said, pulling his mouth away, chuckling when she tried to follow. "We're not doing this until the doctor says you're okay."

"Yes, we are." She took his hand and tried to drag him toward the bedroom and promptly bounced back against him. He hadn't moved an inch.

"Tell you what. Let's get the animals fed, eat a little dinner ourselves, and then we'll talk."

"About having sex? We don't need to talk, we just need to do it."

Laughter poured out of him, and he hugged her. "You're good for me, Riley."

That warmed her more than anything he could have said, and she hugged him back. "I'm glad. Let's get to it. The faster we get it done, the faster we can christen my bed."

He let go of her. "You just get a new one?"

"Nope. Been too busy this past year getting my practice set up to think about doing the dirty deed." Something flashed in his eyes, and she thought he was both surprised and pleased.

"Dayum, girl, we need to fix that."

"That's what I've been trying to tell you." She bent and picked up the envelopes, carrying them to the counter.

"You have a seat while I take care of feeding these creatures, and then we'll eat." He opened the pantry door.

"The cat food—"

"I know where everything is."

Riley slid onto a stool, liking how at home he was in her kitchen. She watched him for a few minutes, enjoying the view. He had a way with the animals. Pelli slinked into the room and tried to climb up his legs. Cody pried him off and held the kitten in front of his face.

"You need to learn some manners, my little friend," Cody said. He set Pelli on the floor and tapped his pink nose. "Stay."

While Cody was giving her cat a lesson on manners, Riley flipped through the envelopes, set two bills aside, and grinned when she saw one with her last foster mother's name in the corner. Pat's letters were usually long and chatty, and she'd read it later. Eyeing the last envelope, she flipped it over to see if there was a return address on the back. There wasn't. Opening it, she pulled out a single sheet of paper.

"Ack!" Slinging away the paper, she tried to back away, got the hem of her long dress caught under her foot, and fell off the stool.

CHAPTER FIFTEEN

At Riley's yell, Cody dropped the cat food, splattering it on the floor. Somehow, he made it around the counter, catching her before she hit the floor.

"Is it your head? Are you having a relapse?"

She shuddered. "Spiders."

"Huh?" Still holding her in his arms, he followed her gaze. "What the hell?" Taking her to the sofa, he set her down, then returned to the kitchen. Merlin jumped up on the counter and swatted at a dead spider. There were dozens of the things, different sizes, different kinds, all dead. *The fuck?*

He picked up Merlin and set him on the floor. "Those aren't toys for you." The other two cats were busy eating their dinner from the spilled can. "Go grab some grub before they eat it all." He gave the cat's butt a push. Sally and Pretty Girl were still in a corner of the kitchen where he'd put them, their ears perked up, and their eyes locked on the food spilled on the floor. "You'll get yours soon," he told them.

"Where's your plastic baggies?" he called to Riley.

"In the pantry, bottom shelf. Who would send me dead spiders? That's just creepy."

The same person who tried to run you over and hit you on the head with a rock? She was still in denial if she had to ask. And whoever it was, they were messing with the wrong woman, and were going to be very sorry when he found them. Baggie in hand, he grabbed a paper towel, using it to lift the sheet of paper. The letters had been cut out of a magazine and taped on like something out of a bad B movie.

Next time they won't be dead

Using the paper towel, he slid the spiders to the end of the counter, letting them fall into the baggie, then added the sheet of paper and the envelope. Once sealed, he put it on top of the refrigerator before going to the living room and sitting next to Riley.

"Are you calling Mike?" she asked when he put his phone to his ear.

"No, my boss, Logan Kincaid."

"I think we should call Mike or that detective."

He held up a finger. "I'll tell you why I'm calling the boss first in a minute." When he got Kincaid's voice mail, he left a message, asking for a return call. After setting his phone on the coffee table, he slipped an arm around her, and tugged her close. "The first thing you need to know is that whoever this is, they're not playing a practical joke on you. They mean business. The second is that K2 has more resources than any police department could ever hope for, which is why we're bringing them in on this. After I talk to Kincaid, we'll give your cop a call."

"Mike's not my cop." She burrowed into him, and he felt a shiver pass through her. "Ugh. Spiders. Hate the things."

"Yeah, me, too." He pulled her onto his lap and wrapped his arms around her. "Did you have a nice afternoon with Maria?" he asked, hoping to get her mind off the spiders.

"Oh." She lifted her face from where it was buried against his neck, pulled her long dress up to her thighs, and straddled him. "I almost forgot. Maria said to tell you to check your e-mail."

"Probably sent the list of possible cars." He reached for his phone, latching onto the excuse to keep from doing what he really wanted, and somehow managing to keep his eyes off her bare legs.

"Cars?"

"Yeah, here you go." Turning the screen so she could see it, he scrolled down. "Looks like there's around twenty possibilities in Escambia County." While she skimmed the list, his eyes gravitated to the long, satiny legs hugging his thighs. If he touched them, he wouldn't stop, so he forced his gaze back to her face.

"This really is all connected, isn't it? The poisons, the car, the spiders?" The last was accompanied by a shudder.

'Bout damn time it sunk into her pretty head. "Yeah, so we need to figure out who's targeting you and why."

"You know what?" She took the phone out of his hand and placed it back on the coffee table. "Let's talk about this tomorrow."

With that, she lowered her mouth to his, and when her tongue made a slow slide across the seam of his lips, he decided tomorrow was a perfect day to discuss cars and poisons and spiders. When he tried to take control of the kiss, she clamped her teeth down on his bottom lip, and lust took a straight path to his groin.

"Riley." He'd already noticed that she liked being in control, and he wondered if that had anything to do with bouncing from foster home to foster home, always at the mercy of others. Whatever the reason, he was more than happy to let her take over, curious to see what she had in mind.

"I love how you growl my name." A sultry smile curved her lips as she slipped her fingers under his T-shirt and tugged it up.

Cody leaned forward so she could get the shirt over his head. "I think you've cast some kind of magic spell on me, darlin'," he said, staring into her hazel eyes, watching the gold flecks in them darken. She fascinated him, this woman who hadn't been loved as a child but felt so deeply that she cried when she couldn't save someone's pet. He wanted to know everything about her. What had happened to her parents? What made her want to be a veterinarian? Had she ever been in love? He wanted to know it all, down to the smallest detail.

"I want you so much," she said.

"The feeling is mutual." He brushed a strand of hair from the side of her face and tucked it behind her ear. "But you know we can't. Not until you see the doctor, and I have to tell you that it's killing me to say that."

She pressed her forehead to his and sighed. "I know, and it's not fair. A sexy, mysterious man moves in next door, and I finally get my chance at him, and someone conks me on the head. Just not fair." A sly gleam appeared in her eyes. "But you're not under a sex ban."

That got his attention. "Whatcha got in mind?" And if she said what he hoped she was going to, he might explode on the spot.

"Just this." She undid the button on his jeans and lifted an eyebrow. He lifted one right back at her, and she laughed. "I take it you approve?"

"Oh yeah, baby. Gotta say I do." He put his hand over hers when she started to pull his zipper down. "But you can only use your hand. Can't have you bouncing your head around."

"I'll be careful."

She batted her eyelashes, and he laughed. "What are you doing to me?" he asked, his voice a mere whisper. Did she have a clue that she had him wrapped around her finger?

"That very question has been on the tip of my tongue to ask you," she answered.

He hissed when her hand circled him. "Ahhh, been . . . ahhh." It was true what they said about a man's blood rushing south when aroused because Cody was pretty damn sure not a drop was left from his waist up. Talking was next to impossible, but he tried again. "Been too long. N-not gonna last."

"I want you so badly," she said as she slid her hand down the length of him.

"The minute you're pronounced okay, darlin'. The very minute." Her gaze lowered to her hand and what she was doing to him, and watching her watch him was flat-out hot. He zoned in on her lips, so soft and kissable, and he cradled her neck, pulling her face down. He brushed his lips over hers before fusing their mouths. Everything about her enticed him. Her lemony scent, her warm, soft skin, her taste, the gold flecks in her eyes that changed to topaz when she was aroused or annoyed—both of those emotions a big turn-on. Her taste was one a man could sustain his life on.

"Riley," he gasped when she rubbed her thumb over the head and spread the evidence of his arousal around, making him slick so that her hand glided easily up and down his length. He was close, and he put his hand over hers, showing her how fast and hard he needed it.

Riley loved the feel of his big hand over hers, both of them touching him. A hungry moan sounded low in his throat, and it was as if fuel had been thrown on the low-burning fire inside her. She tightened her grip and felt him throb against her palm. He was big, and hard, and beautiful. When he thrust against the hand she had around him, making that moaning sound again, she stroked him faster.

"Jesus, Riley."

He grabbed his T-shirt and tried to cover himself, but she pushed the shirt away. Needing to taste him, she scooted off his lap and lowered her mouth at the moment he came. Air swished out of his lungs, and then he sucked air back in. She'd done that to him, stolen his breath. Surprised him, too, by the dazed look he was giving her. When his chest stopped heaving, he wrapped his fingers around her arm and pulled her up.

"You didn't have to do that, darlin'," he said, kissing her.

Oh, but she did. He slid his hand down the top of her dress and cupped a breast, flicking his thumb over her nipple as his mouth explored hers. The slide of their tongues over each other, the possessive press of his mouth on hers, and the way his hand palmed the curve of her bottom sent fiery heat to all *the* places.

He rested his forehead against hers. "No more or I'm gonna forget you're hurt."

Although he was right, she didn't like it. "So not fair," she grumbled.

"I'll make it up to you, I promise." He kissed her nose.

Before she could tell him he most certainly would, his phone buzzed. When he picked it up, she saw the name Kincaid on the screen. As he talked, she studied him, reaching up and sliding her fingers over his clean-shaven cheek. Although she thought he was crazy hot with a smooth face, she loved his stubbled look best. At her touch, he winked at her, which about melted her. If he put even a half-assed effort into making her fall for him she doubted she'd be able to resist. Sadly, he had heartbreak written all over him, yet she was beginning to believe he was worth the risk.

After a brief conversation with his boss, Cody set down his phone. "We're meeting with him in the morning. Once we do that, you can call your cop friend if you still want to."

Wow, she was going to get to meet the legendary Logan Kincaid. From the few things Cody had said of him, and the way Maria spoke of her brother as if he were some kind of hero who no one dared to mess with, she was as curious as a cat about the man.

Riley couldn't help ogling her surroundings as she followed Cody through the inner sanctum of K2 Special Services on Wednesday morning. She felt as if she'd stepped into a movie set of a military war room. There were digital maps on the walls, monitors all over the place, and workspaces where men and women wearing headsets sat in front of computers that were angled in such a way to prevent her from seeing the screens. Offices lined the large, open middle room, most with their doors and blinds closed.

And that receptionist? Cody had introduced the woman only by her first name of Barbie. She was tall, gorgeous, and looked like she should be walking the runway for Victoria's Secret with a pair of angel wings strapped to her back. After he'd punched in a code, then put his palm over a black box on the wall, and they'd entered the inside room, he'd leaned close to her ear and whispered that Barbie wore a gun strapped to her thigh.

"Remind me not to piss her off," she'd whispered back, causing him to laugh.

With his hand on her lower back, Cody led her to a conference room, the only furniture a long table with chairs around it. There was a large screen TV mounted to the wall and a small black refrigerator in the corner. He pulled out a chair next to the one at the head of the table.

"Have a seat. Want something to drink?"

"Water would be nice." She slid into the cushy black leather chair. Cody went to the fridge and returned with two bottles of water. She wondered if she'd asked for a slushy beer if they would've had one ready for her, lime and all. It just seemed like that kind of place, one where they already knew all your preferences and were prepared for you. Pretty cool but also spooky.

"This place is like being in some secret spy building. What did you say you people do?"

"Nice try, darlin'." He took the seat next to her, leaving the one at the head of the table empty.

That dimpled grin of his did its job again, making her stomach fluttery and curling her toes. "I bet if I tortured you, you still wouldn't tell me."

An unholy gleam lit his eyes. "Probably not, but might depend on just what you have in mind." He leaned over and sucked her earlobe into his mouth. "There's torture and then there's torture."

Which was exactly what he was doing to her by his words and his warm breath caressing her neck. Not to mention the tingling that shot through her as he nipped on her lobe. "Cody," she gasped.

"Giving her a physical there, Dog?" a man said as he entered the room.

Riley jerked away, and when Cody laughed, she swatted him. Cheeks burning, she turned to the stranger, who was eyeing her with interest.

"As the team's medic, I think I'm the one who should be examining her." The guy winked at her.

"Touch her and you die."

A wide grin split the man's face. "Thought you weren't going to drink the water," he said mysteriously.

"Shut up, Doc." Cody put a possessive hand on her arm.

What was that all about? The man was drop-dead gorgeous with his green eyes and beautiful smile. Another man walked in, and she recognized him as Maria's husband, and following him was a blond, blue-eyed man. All of the guys were big, muscled, and just as drool worthy as Cody. She could grow to like this place.

"Riley, the one with the funny green eyes is Ryan O'Connor, our medic, which is why we call him Doc."

"Nice to meet you," she said after Cody introduced him. His eyes were definitely unusual, with orange streaks in the green, but they were beautiful.

"The scary looking one is Jake Buchanan, aka Tiger, aka Maria's husband," Cody said. "And the pretty one is Jamie Turner, aka Saint."

The man he'd called Saint turned a beatific smile on her, and Cody was right. He was pretty in a very manly kind of way. Jake, she'd met once when he'd come into the clinic with Maria.

"If it isn't Mouse's favorite vet." Jake grinned. "Except when you give him shots. Hear you got a problem, Dr. Austin."

"Riley, please. Unfortunately, appears I do. Great seeing you again, but wish it were under better circumstances." She turned to the one called Saint—and wasn't that a perfect name for him? "And nice to meet you."

"Likewise, Riley."

The men took seats around the table, and she sent a questioning glance at Cody. Were they all here because of her? At his nod, she was overwhelmed that a team of men who appeared to be the take-no-prisoners types deemed her worth their attention. For a girl who'd had to fight her whole life to stay safe, who'd had to steal food in one of her foster homes to survive, who'd never had the kind of protection these men were offering, this scenario was beyond her comprehension. Tears stung her eyes and she swallowed hard.

As if he understood, Cody squeezed her hand. While she struggled to compose herself, and the men were razzing each other in a way that told her they were as close as brothers, another man walked into the room, taking the chair at the head of the table.

She would have known he was Logan Kincaid even if he hadn't taken that particular seat. Although he'd not said a word yet, there was an air of command about him. And jeez, he was as good-looking as the rest of them. She glanced at Cody, and he gave her a reassuring smile.

Even surrounded by some of the hottest men she'd ever laid eyes on, to her, Cody was the only one that called to something inside her. She smiled back before turning her attention to Logan Kincaid, only to find him watching her. Riley had the unsettling feeling that if anyone had eyes that could see into the soul, it was this man. With considerable effort, she didn't squirm.

"This is Logan Kincaid," Cody said. "Boss, Dr. Riley Austin."

"Dr. Austin, I hear you've got some trouble."

That was it. No exchange of pleasant talk for a few minutes, no getting to know each other. That was fine. Since she found the man intimidating, she wouldn't have a clue how to chat with him. "Riley, please."

"Riley it is. Because we all go by more than one name, we'll keep it to first names to prevent any confusion, so I'm Logan." He chuckled, making him seem more human. "See, you're already confused. Take my brother-in-law. Sometimes he's Jake, sometimes Buchanan, other times, Tiger, and always Dumbass."

Jake snorted. "Hey, be nice to me or I'll tell Maria."

"I'm shaking in my boots," Logan said. He shifted those inquisitive dark eyes back to her. "Cody's briefed us on the situation, so we don't need to go over that. Maria's working on narrowing down the list of possible cars. She'll be here in a few minutes."

"I'm here now." She pressed Riley's shoulder as she passed, sitting in the empty chair next to her husband.

With so much testosterone in the room, it was nice to have another woman at the table. Riley gave an inward snort. There wasn't a woman in the world who wouldn't think she'd died and gone to heaven to be surrounded by so much eye candy, and here she was feeling relieved to have female company. She'd likely be enjoying herself more if not for the reason she was here.

"I don't want to be an inconvenience." She had to get that said. If her guess was correct, K2 was some kind of secretive agency doing God knew what, and they probably had more important things to do. Like save the planet.

"There's one thing you need to understand," Logan said. "We take care of our own, and by your . . . friendship with Cody, that includes you."

Riley caught his hesitation at the word friendship, and her cheeks heated. The man was an oracle—or some such thing—and probably knew exactly where on Cody's body her mouth had been yesterday. *Gah, shut that vision down, or he really will know just from the bright red of your cheeks.* Cody's soft chuckle confirmed that at the moment, her face was an open book. She kicked him under the table, which made him grin. Daring to glance around, she saw that all the men and Maria were looking at her with amusement.

"Like being in a room with twelve-year-olds," Maria said. "Ignore them. I do."

Jake leaned over and kissed Maria. "Try and ignore that, Chiquita."

Logan gave a huge sigh. "I hate it when you kiss my sister in front of me, Dumbass."

"Don't care," Jake said.

Maria rolled her eyes. "See what I mean?"

Riley laughed. So far, she really liked these people. She also believed that Logan allowed the nonsense knowing it would help calm her. Except for Cody and Ryan, the men wore wedding rings, and she'd love to meet the women strong enough to take them on.

"Playtime's over," Logan said, drawing her attention back to him. "Cody, what's your plan to handle this situation?"

Riley was eager to hear that, too.

CHAPTER SIXTEEN

Because he'd put a lot of thought into how to protect Riley while hunting down their target, Cody didn't hesitate. Also, he knew the boss expected him to be prepared to answer that question. Since he was already on shaky ground, he wasn't about to screw up anymore, so yes he had a plan.

He shifted to face Riley. "The most important thing is your safety. The only way to achieve that is to have someone with you twenty-four seven."

"I have a practice to run. Are you going to follow me around while I clip toenails and neuter people's pets?"

"Not wanting to watch that," Jake said, and every member of the team shuddered.

Cody had the urge to cover his balls. "I think we'll all pass on that one."

"You guys are such babies," Maria said.

Jake laughed. "Where our junk's concerned, you bet your ass, sweetheart."

Riley and Maria shared a look as if to say these guys are idiots. Something inside him unfurled at seeing how well Riley was fitting in with his friends. He'd known she would, but watching it happen quite honestly scared him. She was working her way into his life without even trying, and how big of a hole was she going to leave when he went and screwed things up?

"No, we aren't going to get in the way of your work. Most times you'll forget we're even there," he assured her.

She smirked. "I doubt that."

Well, they were an imposing bunch, but she had no clue. "Darlin', we're very good at what we do, and when that means we need to blend into the woodwork, we disappear from sight. Most of the time, that'll be me, but if I'm needed elsewhere, it will be someone in this room taking my place." He glanced at Kincaid to make sure one of the team would be available if needed and got a slight nod.

"I just don't want my pet owners to think they're in danger. You won't be packing guns or whatever, will you?"

"Oh, we'll be packing whatever," Jamie said, "but you or your clients won't see anything alarming. Like Cody said, we'll blend in."

The next thing Cody had to say was going to be the hardest. Before he got into the details of his plan, he needed to lay everything on the table. Debating how much to say had kept him awake most of the night, but it had to be done. Other than Kincaid and Ryan, the others didn't know he was dealing with some serious issues, and it was only fair they were warned, especially Riley, since it was her life on the line.

He probably should have told her privately, but he didn't think he could deal with speaking twice about what was going on with him. "Here's the thing you need to know. I've been grounded." His gaze was on Riley, his words for her, but even without checking, he knew his teammates were listening as he had sensed their attention, had heard the creaks of their chairs as they sat forward. As for Riley, by the way she was looking at him and only him, and the softness in her eyes as she waited for him to continue, he wondered if she'd forgotten there were others in the room.

"Why? Because of your nightmares?"

Trust her to get right to the point. He almost regretted not telling her privately as he'd like nothing more than to lay his head on her lap, close his eyes, and tell her all his secrets while she used her fingers to stroke his hair. "In a way. I had a flashback that mirrored my dream when Ryan and I were in the middle of an operation." He couldn't meet the eyes of his teammates. Every man here knew you never allowed a weakness to endanger a warrior brother's life. If that boy would have had a gun instead of a knife, the situation could have easily turned tragic.

Don't go there, Dog. Not here and not now. "I'm getting help," he said, finally meeting the gazes of his friends.

"Whatever you need from us, man, you know you got it," Jamie said.

The others echoed him, and when Riley put her hand on his leg and squeezed, he came close to losing it. He'd been alone and isolated since coming home from his last deployment, and until the day Kincaid had knocked on his door, offering him a job that reunited him with his team, he'd tried to numb himself with scotch, a lot of the stuff.

"Thanks," he said, hating how gruff his voice sounded. "So other than my doctor appointments . . ." he turned to Riley, "I'm all yours."

"Lucky me."

"I don't know about that, but let's hope so." The smile she gave him went straight to his gut. He cleared his throat. "Along with protecting you, we need to up our search for the target. Maria's working on the car angle, and if you would, boss, it might be helpful if you pulled in some favors with the police department to make sure they increase their patrols in the area."

"Done," Kincaid said. "I've also sent what we know so far to a profiler friend of mine. She's going to get something back to us by the end of the week."

"Thanks, boss. Appreciate it."

Riley twirled her bottle of water. "What can I do?"

"You and I are going to do a lot of dog walking, watching for anything suspicious."

"What about us?" Jake asked.

"Until we get some kind of lead on this character, I'm not sure what you can do. If you're bored and have a little free time, wouldn't hurt for you to cruise around the area of Riley's clinic, keeping an eye out."

"Charlie and I can take walks around there," Ryan said.

Riley glanced up. "Who's Charlie?" Was there another member of the team she hadn't met?

"My fiancée. She's an amazing aerobatic pilot."

There was so much pride in his voice that Riley couldn't help smiling. She looked forward to Saturday when she'd get to meet all the wives and girlfriends. These men were fascinating, and she wanted to see what kind of women they fell for. Growing up in foster care, moving from home to home, frequently changing schools, she'd not had friends, much less a bestie.

If asked to describe herself, she'd say that her first memories were of a little girl who was shy and scared. She didn't remember much of her parents. They'd been killed in a car crash when she was three, and she'd gone to live with her only relative, her grandmother. Nana, grief-stricken over the death of her only child—Riley's father—hadn't had room in her heart for a granddaughter confused over the drastic change in her life. Riley learned to be as quiet as a mouse least she anger Nana and get another lecture on what a burden she was.

When she was six and about to start school, Nana had had a heart attack and died. There were a lot of things Riley had learned in the following years, and how to push past the shyness was the first. It was only because she had learned to stand up for herself that she'd remained mostly untouched by people who were supposed to protect and care for her. When she wasn't allowed enough to eat and was sent to bed hungry, she'd learned how to steal food in a way it wouldn't be missed.

That lesson, she'd discovered the hard way during her stay in the first foster home when she'd eaten some leftover fried chicken.

As she grew into her teen years, and the fathers or older boys in whatever home she was living in had tried to touch her in a way that made her uncomfortable, she'd threatened to go straight to the mother or to call 911. When one of the boys hadn't believed her, she'd screamed her head off. Blaming Riley for coming onto her son, the mother had called Child Protective Services. Faster than she could pack her meager belongings in a garbage bag, she was put in a new home, which had been fine with her.

Another lesson had been learned. If a home she was sent to was intolerable, raise enough hell and she'd be removed. By the time she'd been labeled a problem child, she'd shut down any hope that a nice family would adopt her. It wasn't until Reed that she'd dared to love again, and after losing him, John and Pat had literally saved her life, taking her into their home and dishing out their no-nonsense love.

With the determination of a bulldog intent on keeping a bone, she'd chased her dream of being a veterinarian, and she'd succeeded. The day she'd received her doctor of veterinary medicine degree, John and Pat had been the only two people in the world who'd been there to celebrate with her.

She glanced around the table. Now here she was, in a room full of people who seemed to care about her safety. It was enough to make a girl cry. The discussion wound down, and Logan stood.

"Got a minute, Cody?" he said.

"Are you going to ask if I'm worried about having another flashback?"

Logan returned to his seat. "That was my intention. I thought you'd prefer to discuss it in private."

Under the table, Cody's leg bounced, bumping hers, making her think of an agitated tiger. That was the only way she knew the subject distressed him. Other than that, nothing showed on his face, and his hands were flat on the arm of his chair.

"I'd prefer not to talk about it at all, but I'm done hiding it." He glanced at her, and at the uncertainty in his eyes she smiled, nodding for him to go on. "I can't ask any of you to back me up if I'm not honest with you. So, yeah, the flashbacks scare the shit out of me . . . that I might have one in the middle of a situation again. The thing is, if Riley's life is on the line, I think I can power through it. My next appointment is Friday afternoon, and if the head doc disagrees, I'll tell you."

Riley could tell it was killing him to admit he had a problem, but he had, and in front of those whose opinions he valued the most. He was a beautiful, brave man, and she fell a little in love with him sitting there, surrounded by his teammates. She wished they were alone so she could wrap her arms around him and hold him close, but settled for putting her hand on his bouncing knee. His leg stilled, and he covered her hand with his.

"Fair enough," Logan said. He glanced around the table, his gaze landing on her last, and staying there. "Anyone have a problem with that?"

She waited until everyone else had chimed in, all of them good with Cody's offer, before speaking. "I trust Cody with my life." There was nothing to add to that, no caveat, no buts.

Cody's gaze landed on her, and she was probably the only one who heard his quiet expel of breath, as if he'd been holding it, expecting to hear her say just the opposite. It got very quiet, and she glanced around to see everyone watching her with knowing smiles on their faces.

"Welcome to the club, Dog," Logan mysteriously said, his eyes dancing with amusement. "Call me after your appointment."

After he left, the others filed out, each one touching both Cody's shoulder and hers. It felt like she'd just been initiated into some kind of society she knew nothing about. Maria was the last to leave, and she gave both Cody and Riley a hug. Then she left while humming the "Wedding March."

Riley frowned at Maria's back as she left. "What's up with that?"

"Damned if I know," Cody said right before he put his hand behind her neck, pulled her to him, and kissed her so hard and possessively that she wouldn't have been able to tell anyone her name if asked.

And guess what, she didn't care. All she wanted to do was forget her problems and lose herself in this man and the mouth he had fused to hers. Okay, she definitely wanted more than that, but jeez, they were at his place of work and it probably would be frowned upon if she threw herself onto the table and hollered, "Yes! Yes! Oh God, yes! Take me right here, right now."

Cody broke away and put his forehead against hers, his heavy breaths warming her face. "There are security cameras in every part of this place. Unless we want to be the X-rated show of the day, let's get out of here."

"I'm ready. We have just enough time to grab some lunch before my doctor's appointment, where I will be pronounced well enough to have sex."

He wrapped his arm around her shoulder, tucking her next to him. "Please, God, let it be so."

It wasn't so. "I'm sorry," she said for the third time as she and Cody walked up to her door. Although tempted to deny it, she'd admitted to still having headaches when asked. They weren't as bad as the first three days, but they hadn't gone entirely away, so she was still under a no-sex order. As a doctor, she understood the seriousness of a concussion and couldn't argue, but she was disappointed.

"Darlin', you're worth waiting for."

That was about the best thing he could have said. He put his hand on the back of her neck, and she leaned her cheek against his shoulder. She'd never been a touchy-feely woman, but she could change her mind about that where Cody was concerned. Everything about him called to her. She inhaled his spicy man scent as she leaned into his strong body, liking how well she fit against him.

"I sure hope so. The doctor said if my headaches are gone by Saturday, then I'm good to go. Wanna make another Saturday night sex date?"

"You really have to ask a man that question?" He grinned as he took her keys from her and unlocked the door, ushering her in with his hand on the small of her back.

"What was I thinking?" His expression changed from teasing to what she could only describe as warrior mode as he pushed her behind him, but not before she saw Arthur's lifeless body on the middle of the floor and the mess that was her living room.

"Arthur!" She was only dimly aware of Cody reaching into his boot and coming back up with a gun in his hand. When she tried to push past him to get to her cat, he put out an arm, stopping her.

"Easy, darlin'. I'll get you to him. I don't sense anyone still in your house, but better safe than sorry."

Although it seemed like it took forever, he led her to Arthur in only a few seconds, and she knelt, putting her fingers to his chest, letting out a relieved breath. "He's alive. Where're Merlin and Pelli?" They should have come to her at hearing her voice.

"Stay here. I'll go look for them." He eased away, his tense body alert to his surroundings.

"I have to get Arthur to the clinic." She grabbed the afghan from the sofa and gently nestled her sweet boy into it. Tears freely rolled down her cheeks. Who would have hurt such an innocent creature and where were Merlin and Pelli? If they were . . . no, she couldn't even think it.

"The house is clear," Cody said, returning. "Merlin's under the bed, but he won't come out. Can't find Pelli."

Riley handed an unconscious Arthur to Cody. "I need to get him to the clinic so I can take care of him, but I have to get Merlin and Pelli.

I'm not leaving them here." She ran into the guest bedroom, got the cat carrier out of the closet, and then raced to her room. "Hey, Merlin, it's all right. Come on out, baby." He let out a yowl as he crawled to her. She got him in the carrier and looked under the bed, hoping to see Pelli. He wasn't there.

"Pelli," she called as she headed back to the living room. The little thing could be hiding anywhere, but she couldn't take the time to search for him if she was going to save Arthur. Not seeing Cody, she glanced around, noticing that her kitchen door was open.

"Riley, come here."

She found him standing in the carport, staring at the doorframe with Arthur held in the crook of his arm and his gun still in his hand. If there was one thing Riley hated, it was guns, but at the moment, she appreciated that he had one. When they found the person responsible for so much heartache, Riley would be tempted to shoot that person herself.

"What?" she asked, frowning at the crunch of glass at her feet.

"They broke the window, and then it was a simple matter of reaching in and unlocking the door. You need a good alarm system. I'll take care of it."

The door had four small framed-in windows, and they'd broken one of the bottom ones. "Bastard."

"Find Pelli?"

"No." She tried calling him again, but didn't get even a small meow back from him. "He must be hiding somewhere, but I can't take the time to find him."

Cody pulled the door wide. "Let's get you to the clinic, then I'll come back and do a search while I'm waiting for the alarm company."

Two hours later, Riley settled a sleeping Arthur into the carrier next to Merlin. "He's going to be okay." She watched for a moment as Merlin gave his friend's face a bath before curling around Arthur as if to protect him. She'd almost lost him, and anger that someone had given him poison burned low in her stomach.

"I'm so glad," Maria said. She got up from the chair in the corner where she'd been sitting and came over, giving Riley a hug. "Ready to go home?"

"As soon as I get things cleaned up."

"I'll stay and take care of it," Brooke said from the sink where she was washing her hands.

The K2 team had jumped into action the moment Cody had called his boss. An alarm company was at her house, installing the best available system, and Maria's husband, Jake, was patrolling the clinic parking lot while Maria had stayed with Riley, giving her support whenever possible. The clinic had been closed until Riley could return, but Cody had called Brooke, and soon after both she and Michelle had shown up.

She gave Brooke a hug. "I'm planning to be here tomorrow, but don't schedule anything. We'll go over the appointment book and start rescheduling everyone we cancelled this week." She was tired and her head pounded like the devil, but that was nothing compared to what Arthur had just gone through.

"I'm going to go check on Jake while you're finishing up," Maria said.

She smiled at her friend. "I don't know how to thank everyone. You guys are like movie superheroes the way you spring into action. I really appreciate it."

"Like my brother said, we take care of our own." Maria waved as if it were nothing, and then left to go find her husband.

As a feminist, Riley thought she should probably resent that they believed she couldn't take care of herself, but she was also a realist. Whoever the person was, they had tried to run her over and had managed to sneak up on her, so she wasn't invincible. The K2 guys had circled the wagons with her in the middle, and she wondered how she'd ever thank them enough.

There was no sign of Pelli. Cody dreaded telling Riley her kitten was missing, and as he stood outside her front door waiting for her to get out of Jake and Maria's car, he knew it was going to happen in a minute. He watched as she reached over the backseat and gave Maria a hug, and then said something to Jake that made him laugh. Cody gave Jake a wave as the car backed out of the driveway.

Even with the puffy eyes from crying and her long hair pulled back in a messy ponytail, she was gorgeous. He met her halfway down the sidewalk and took the cat carrier from her, wrapped his free arm around her shoulder, and pulled her close.

"Jake called, said Arthur's gonna be okay. That's great news."

She leaned her face against his arm. "It was touch and go for a while, but he's a fighter. I was so scared I was going to lose him."

There was probably not another man who would understand her fear as much as he did. He was getting close to accepting that he'd never find Layla, and it was a hurt deep in his heart knowing he'd lost her.

"Even though he's a cat, I'm awful glad he's okay," Cody teased.

"You know you love him." He opened the door, following her inside, and her eyes darted around the room. "You found Pelli, right?"

The owner of the alarm company walked into the living room. "We should be done here in about an hour."

Cody welcomed the interruption. The last thing he wanted to do was tell her Pelli was gone. "Take however long you need to make sure it's right." Doug gave a two-finger salute before disappearing back into the bedroom.

"Who was that?" Riley asked.

He set the carrier on the coffee table. "Doug Villiers. He's here with two of his employees. They're installing a state-of-the-art alarm system. Tomorrow he'll do your clinic." While that had been going on, Cody had managed to straighten up her house. Fortunately, no lasting damage had been done, only upended things and Riley's stuff tossed to the floor.

"Oh, okay. Where's Pelli?"

He took her hand and led her to the sofa, sitting beside her. "I'm sorry, darlin', but he's not here."

"Maybe he's hiding." Tears pooled in her eyes.

"I don't think so. I've looked in every cabinet and hiding place I could find." When the tears overflowed and streamed down her cheeks, he wrapped his arms around her and held her close. "I think he's alive. We just have to find him." He wished he could be sure about that, but his gut said the bad guy would have left Pelli's body for her to find if they'd killed the cat.

There was so much hope and trust in her eyes that he silently vowed he'd find her kitten even if he had to tear the town apart.

CHAPTER SEVENTEEN

Friday afternoon, Riley slipped on a pair of black-and-gray silk pajama pants and a soft, light-gray pullover top after taking a shower. Hair dried and left down her back, face moisturized, and lips glossed, she decided she was done. Cody had taken care of feeding her since she'd come home from the hospital, but tonight she would make dinner.

One thing she never scrimped on was food. At any given time, her pantry and refrigerator were full. She was self-aware enough to understand that her reason for needing to have an abundance of food on hand was a direct correlation to her childhood.

She liked to cook, and on Sundays would often make a batch of freezable meals. After Cody left for his doctor's appointment, she eyed the possibilities in her freezer, settling on lasagna. That, along with French bread and a salad, should satisfy a man's stomach.

She wasn't sure what she would have done without him these past few days. He had stayed at her side, held her until she fell asleep each night, and true to his word, blended into the woodwork during her days at her clinic. She'd cut her day short so Cody could bring her home before he left to see his doctor, but parked in front of her house, guarding her, was a man from K2, one she'd not met.

One thing she didn't like was that Cody moved to the couch each night after she fell asleep. She wasn't afraid of him, didn't believe he would hurt her during one of his nightmares, but he refused to take the chance.

They still hadn't had sex and that was going to change tonight. Her headaches were gone, and she was more than ready. Her plan for the evening was a romantic dinner and then bed. Her only concern was Cody. He'd been quiet all day, and had spent most of the morning working on the homework he'd been assigned, which he'd declined to talk about.

As she set the table, she glanced at her two cats. Both were curled up with Pretty Girl and Sally, and it amazed her how well Arthur and Merlin had taken to Cody's dogs. The cats had searched for Pelli, especially Arthur, and they'd been subdued since he'd gone missing. Thinking of Pelli brought tears to her eyes. She was so worried about him. Cody believed that he was alive, and she prayed he was right.

She swallowed the lump in her throat, and went looking for where she'd put the candles, finding them on a shelf in the back of the pantry. They were a nice addition to her table setting. Salad made and the lasagna ready to go in the oven, she turned on some soft music, picked up a magazine, and sat to wait for Cody.

Only a few minutes had passed before she heard his truck, and she watched out the window as he got out and went to talk to her bodyguard. After a few minutes of conversation, Cody jogged to his house and disappeared inside, emerging a short time later wearing a different shirt, and she figured he'd probably showered. The man who had been guarding her had left.

At her mailbox, Cody stopped and removed her mail. As he began walking toward her door, he flipped through the envelopes, pausing to stare at one of them.

Please, not another one. She went to the alarm and turned it off before opening the door. "Is it . . . ?"

"Think so. Your address is in block letters and there's no return address." He pulled her into his arms. "Let's go inside."

His dogs trotted to him to welcome him back, and her cats, for the first time, nosed their way in. Cody gave them all equal attention. The man was an animal pied piper.

"Down," he said, and Sally and Pretty Girl plopped at his feet. Merlin, normally aloof, stepped onto Sally's back and sat. Arthur decided to follow the dogs' example, and flattened himself out next to Pretty Girl. It was so cute, the way the four of them had bonded, and it only made her miss Pelli all the more. He should be a part of the little family the animals had created.

Riley eyed the envelope. Was it proof Pelli was alive or something bad? "Open it."

"You have any rubber gloves?"

Oh, right, he'd want it checked for fingerprints. "Be right back." She hurried to the kitchen, sending up a little prayer that whatever was in that envelope wouldn't be something horrible. As an afterthought, she grabbed a paring knife for Cody to use as a letter opener.

Back by his side, she held her breath as he struggled to put on kitchen gloves that were sized for her hands. After sliding the knife under the envelope's flap, he pulled out a sheet of paper and unfolded it.

"Pelli," she whispered at seeing the photo. Her baby was peering out of a wire cage, and he looked so sad. But he was alive, at least when the picture was taken. At the top of the page were words typed in a funny script.

How Much Do You Love Him?

"What does that mean?" Unable to bear seeing him caged like that, she jumped up and went into the kitchen. She needed to start dinner, or cut a lime for beers, or would he rather have something different? Dammit, she didn't know. She burst into tears.

A pair of strong, masculine arms wrapped around her, and she turned, burying her face against Cody's chest. "I can't stand to think of him suffering."

"I know, darlin'. Why don't you make us both one of those slushy beers? I have some things to tell you."

She peered up at him. "Do you have a lead?"

"We have an idea of what kind of person we're looking for." He brushed her tears away with his thumbs. "Make those beers while I take the dogs out, then we'll talk. Grab your laptop, too."

Twenty minutes later, she sat, clutching her ice-cold bottle while trying not to get her hopes up. "What do you know? Do you have a name?"

"No, not a name, but a profile. I stopped by K2 after my appointment, and Kincaid gave me the profile he got back today from his friend at the FBI." He opened her laptop and inserted a thumb drive.

A page came up, and she frowned at seeing it was only a few paragraphs.

Cody angled the screen so she could see it better. "According to the boss, this profiler is one of the best, even when she doesn't have much to go on."

Riley had to agree that they didn't have a lot of information to pass on, but as she began to read, she was impressed with the profiler's insights.

This is personal to the perp, most likely a woman, age forty to sixty, possibly with a history of mild mental illness that has escalated after she suffered a loss. Perhaps more than one loss of someone or something close to her, such as a second family member, or her home, or possibly a beloved pet, which combined, triggered a mental breakdown.

The perp feels she has been tragically wronged in some way by Dr. Austin, and is attempting to make her look incompetent because she cannot save the animals being poisoned. It is my understanding that Dr. Austin has been able to save some of the pets, and this will enrage the perp. Therefore, I advise Dr. Austin to be on guard, as I expect the attacks will intensify and will be directed more at her personally.

Intensify? As if they weren't already intense. Riley leaned back against the sofa. "How can she possibly get all that from what little we know?" She glanced at Cody to see that he stared at the page—his lips compressed into a thin line—and there was a dangerous glint in his eyes. He didn't like that last line either.

"I was curious about that, too, and asked the boss." He closed the lid to the laptop. "He called her while I was there and put her on the speaker. She said a few things. One, that a woman is more likely to play games whereas a man is more likely to cut right to the chase. The poisoning of the animals was an attempt to make you look bad, which is what she means by playing games."

"Okay, that makes sense, I guess." This whole thing made her stomach sick.

"She stressed that even though her profile is based on years of experience and training that she could be wrong. That we shouldn't rule out any possibility until we have more to go on."

How had her life come to this? She loved animals. All animals, be they cats, dogs, bunnies, or even the brown mouse little Lindsey loved with her nine-year-old heart, and brought in every time it sneezed.

Riley squeezed her eyes shut. Her life's work was to keep her patients healthy, giving their humans as much time with their furry friends as possible. What she really wanted was to crawl into bed and pull a pillow over her head. Was it her fault she'd pushed someone already unbalanced over the edge?

She tried to think of a middle-age woman who had brought in a dog or cat—or hell, maybe even a rabbit or hedgehog . . . how was she supposed to know? "It makes me sick to think I did something to start all this."

"Come here, darlin'." He put his arm around her and tugged her to his side.

Snuggled up next to Cody, she rested her head on his shoulder, wishing they'd met under different circumstances. No crazy person after her, and no nightmares for him because of something that happened in Afghanistan.

"Tomorrow, you need to start going back through your files, see if there's anything in them that strikes you as odd or fitting to what the profiler said." He rested his chin on top of her head.

"I know, but I don't want to talk about this tonight. How did your appointment go this afternoon?" It was intimate, the way they were nestled together, and for one night, she didn't want to think about poisoned pets.

"Tell you what. Let's go out, have a nice dinner, and I'll tell you about my appointment later, after we get back." He nuzzled his nose against her hair. "You smell so good."

"I was just thinking the same thing about you." And he did smell great, the hint of soap from his shower, and the spicy aftershave scent that she could breathe in forever.

He chuckled. "Guess we could just sit here all night then, smelling each other."

"We could, but I have other plans for you." When he stroked his fingers over the skin on her neck, she shivered from the pleasure.

"Do you now?"

"Oh yes." She lifted her hand to her shoulder, lacing her fingers through his. "I'm going to feed you, then you're going to play for me and tell me about your appointment. After that, I'm going to reward you for talking about things I know you have no wish to."

"Mmm, sounds a little like bribery to me."

Cody had no desire to talk about Afghanistan, or flashbacks, or nightmares, or his messed up head. But Tom had told him this afternoon that one of the first things he needed to start doing was to share what was going on inside his mind with those close to him. *Share.* He hated that word. According to Tom, however, the longer he held everything in, trying to go it alone, the longer it would take to clean up the mess in his head.

Cody had laughed at that. "Clean up the mess in my head? Is that the kind of medical terminology they taught you in med school?" It was true, though. His head was definitely messy. And he wanted more than anything to clean it up, so he'd take Tom's advice and talk. He already had talked to Kincaid when he'd stopped by K2 after his appointment. It hadn't been as hard as he'd expected.

"Call it bribery if you want, but whatever works. I don't want to go out tonight, though." She turned her face and brought his hand to her lips, kissing his fingers. "I've already got dinner planned."

"Works for me, darlin'." He hadn't particularly wanted to go out either, but had felt like he should make the offer since her condition for getting her into his bed was that they date, which they'd yet to do. "Since you have everything planned, you're the boss tonight."

"Awesome." She let go of his hand and jumped up. "You've been taking care of me all week, so tonight, I'm taking care of you. Take a nap, read a book, or whatever, while I finish making our dinner."

"In that case, the first thing you can do to take care of me is to give me a kiss." He spread his legs, held his hands out, and waggled his fingers.

"Said the big bad wolf." She stepped between his legs, put her palms on his shoulders, leaned her face down, stuck her pink tongue out, and licked his lips.

"The big bad wolf wants to eat you up." He put his hands on her hips and tried to pull her onto his lap.

"Oh, no you don't. Dinner first. I'm in charge, remember?"

When she tried to push away, he slid his hands down the silky material of her pants, noting on his way to her thighs that she didn't have panties on. "Nice. I like this new thing you have against wearing panties." He let her go before he ended up dragging her down to the couch with him. "Can I help?"

As she walked away, she glanced over her shoulder, giving him a sultry smile. "No, just sit there and fantasize about what's going to happen between us tonight."

He could do that. Her hips swayed with each step she took away from him, and his gaze zeroed in on her ass. Did she mean what he hoped she meant? "How's your head?"

"Haven't had a headache for two days."

That he was about to have dinner with a sexy woman who he personally liked seemed something of a miracle, considering the last several months. Even more noteworthy, he'd only had two nightmares since bunking on her couch. Was that because she was near? He'd started thinking of her as his calm in the middle of an angry sea, and being with her soothed his soul. If he had to talk to anyone about his problems besides the head doc, he would choose her. What did that say about his feelings for her? Missing her even though she was only in the other room, he headed for the kitchen.

Dinner had been delicious, and now Cody sat on his porch with Riley, who was bundled up in a blanket, only her nose and eyes visible. She'd wanted him to play for her, and she'd wanted to sit on his porch while he did, even though the Florida weather had finally turned cold. She reminded him of a moth, snug in its little cocoon, and he swallowed a smile, thinking how he'd like to peel her out of all her coverings until the beautiful butterfly that was her was exposed.

He drank a few swallows of coffee, laced with Kahlúa—what he considered a girly drink. Wasn't bad, though, and that was another thing. Since he'd been hanging with her, he hadn't touched a drop of scotch, his only alcohol the one or two beers they'd drink in the evenings. He was learning to like the stuff, limes and all.

Dinner had been great, and they'd kept their conversation light. Now it was time to talk about important things. For the first time in days, he wished he had a scotch. He strummed a few chords, trying to think how to start. At the beginning. Wasn't that the best place?

"I came home from my last deployment fairly unscathed, or so I thought." He kept playing, the soft notes somehow keeping him grounded. "About a week later, I'd close my eyes to go to sleep, and things I'd done and seen started playing through my head like I was watching a movie. Every kill, every time I didn't pull the trigger even though the man I'd sighted through the scope of my rifle was an insurgent . . ."

He glanced at her and shrugged. "Don't even get me started about the Rules of Engagement."

"I understand a little of that from watching *American Sniper*." She slid her hand out of the blanket and picked up her coffee cup. "You knew he was a bad guy, but your hands were tied without irrefutable proof."

"Yeah, that's how it was, and how many of our guys were hurt or killed because of those rules? I leave him alive knowing what I know, and he comes back the next day and kills one of us. If anything, that's what I thought would haunt me, and it does when I let myself think about it. But that's not my nightmare."

"I'm listening," she said when he paused.

He smiled. "I know." He drank the last of his coffee. "So there I was, the only one left from my SEAL team, the guys you met at K2 having opted out by then, and I get assigned to a marine platoon. I was six days from returning home when I went out on one last operation. I'd already scoped out where I'd position myself on a rooftop building. The last thing I remember was heading there with my spotter before waking up back at camp in a bed with a doctor peering down at me. Apparently, I'd been hit on the head, and my teammates found me out cold on the street."

She set down her empty cup. "You don't remember anything?"

"Not a thing. Not then or now. So there I am, back home, having trouble sleeping, but not sure why. Then I had the first nightmare. Honestly, I didn't think much of it. Just leftover shit from a shit war. But it came again the next night and the next. Always the same, always waking up at the exact moment someone comes up behind me." He stood the guitar next to the wall behind him.

"When you told us about the nightmare when we were at K2, I thought then that it was real, that it really happened."

He'd fought against it being real for so long now, but he could no longer. "Yeah, I think it is. Tom, he's my head doc, thinks that it isn't just the concussion that keeps me from remembering, but that I saw something I don't know how to deal with. Something bad."

"Cody," she whispered, getting up and crawling onto his lap, blanket and all. "You don't even know what happened, but I'm guessing you think you're somehow to blame."

"That would be a good reason for not remembering, wouldn't it?" Because deep in his bones, that was his greatest fear, that he'd done something to cause an innocent girl to be hurt or worse.

"Bad things happen to the best of us or to someone we care about, and sometimes we might unintentionally do something to bring that about. That doesn't mean we're bad people or don't deserve happiness."

He'd have to work on that one, but there was something in her voice that caught his attention. "What was your bad?"

CHAPTER EIGHTEEN

Surprised by Cody's question, Riley shook her head. She never talked about that. Ever. "It's getting late. We should go in."

"So I bare my soul to you, but you don't trust me with your secrets?"

When he picked her up and put her on her feet, she knew she'd hurt him. "It has nothing to do with trust."

He stared at her, his eyes no longer holding warmth. "No? What then?"

Pulling the blanket tight around her, she walked to the railing. It was a clear, cold night, and billions of stars glittered against the black velvet of the sky. She and Reed had made wishes on those stars, had dreamed of making a life together. Their dreams had been made of dust, though.

Now a man she thought she could love—something she hadn't been sure would happen again—wanted to know her secrets. She had tried to bury them somewhere deep enough that they couldn't be found again, even with a bulldozer. To dredge up Reed and her role in his death would be like scraping a razorblade over her heart. It would be agonizing.

If she didn't, though, Cody would be lost to her. That she knew for a fact. He was a man who had trusted her with his hurts, and one who, if he ever fell in love with her, would settle for nothing less than all of her. Since Reed was a part of her, that meant telling Cody about her shameful past. God, she didn't want to.

A pair of strong arms circled her waist, and she leaned her head back on his muscle hard chest. "So, you want to know my secrets?"

He let out a long sigh, his breath ruffling her hair. "I want to know everything about you, Riley. Why is that, do you think?"

She turned, wrapping her arms around him and resting her head on his chest. "Because you like me?"

His chuckle vibrated against her face. "Like is a mild word, darlin', and not at all what I think I'm feeling for you."

"Do you call all the women you've been with darlin'?"

"No. I've called them by their name. You're my first darlin'." He pressed a kiss to the top of her head. "That's the truth. It popped into my head when my sexy, nameless neighbor gave me the finger."

No wonder she was falling for this man. "In that case, go sit and I'll tell you about a time in my life that I swore I'd never talk about again."

When he dropped his hands, she felt a moment of panic. "No, don't go away. Just hold me." His arms came back around her, and she turned, putting her back against him. "I think I can tell you better this way." She couldn't look at him while telling her story, but having him behind her, strong and steady, made it possible to talk about things from a past that she'd done her best to forget.

"You know I was in foster care. My parents were killed in an accident when I was three, and I was sent to live with my grandmother. She never got over the death of her son, my father. Having me in her house was a reminder of him, and she hated me for that."

"Oh, baby."

"Yeah, sad, right? She died when I'd just turned six, and since there was no other family, I became a foster care kid. Not a life I'd wish on any child. Maybe someday I'll tell you about my experiences, but that's not what you're wanting to know tonight. What I've never talked about to anyone except Arthur and my last foster mother before now is the boy I fell in love with when I was sixteen."

"So Arthur is the keeper of your secrets?"

She nodded. "He is."

He rubbed his chin over the top of her head. "Give me Arthur status, Riley. Tell me your secrets."

"Damn you, Cody Roberts. How did you sneak into my heart?" His arms tightened around her. "Okay, here's my biggest secret. When I was fifteen, I was sent to a foster home where there were three other children. Two were foster kids like me, although younger, and there was a biological son a year older than me. His name was Reed, and he was the first person to be nice to me. It was a novel experience, let me tell you."

She pulled away from Cody. She couldn't talk about Reed while being held by another man after all. "Eventually we fell in love, which turned out to be his doom." Giving Cody a sideways glance to see his reaction to that, she saw nothing but a strong man patiently waiting to hear her story.

"Go on," he said.

She lifted her gaze to the sky. "We used to sneak out at night, put a blanket on the ground, and stare up at those very same stars up there and dream of a life together." Tears stung her eyes, thinking of Reed. If she could have one wish, it would be that he'd never met her, because then he'd still be alive.

"By that time, I was pretty wild. He'd always been a good boy— great grades, got along with his parents, loved by everyone . . . you know the type. One thing you need to understand. His parents were dirt poor and they took in foster kids for the extra money. I can't blame them for that, but the children they brought into their home were never valued for more than the income."

Telling her story was hard, and she paused to compose herself. The last thing she wanted was Cody's pity, but he needed to understand that she'd been the one to corrupt a beautiful boy. Cody put his hands on the porch rail and lifted up, sitting on it. He gave the appearance that he had all the time in the world to listen to her sad story. His calm patience steadied her.

"Their son was everything to them, their hope for a better life. He played baseball, was an all-star pitcher, and had offers of full scholarships to some of the best colleges. The world was his oyster until I . . ." She cleared her throat, and then pushed out the words naming her sin. "Until I turned him onto drugs." What would Cody say to that, this man who was a hero to his country? He'd probably never touched drugs in his life. She risked a peek at him, warmed by the compassion in his eyes.

"He could have said no. You get that, right?"

No, she hadn't gotten that. She was to blame. Reed had only smoked that first joint to please her. "He could have, I suppose," she said softly.

"Riley, there's no could have about it. I don't care how damn hot you are, which you are, by the way, but there's not a thing you could do or say to make me do something I didn't want to. He could have said no."

It was strangely appealing to hear him say that she couldn't make him do something if he didn't want to. If only Reed had been that strong in character. But where she had been able to take or leave the pot, thank God, Reed had taken to the stuff like a man on a mission. And Cody was right: Reed could have said no to that first joint she'd offered. That didn't make her blameless, but it eased her guilt a little.

"Thank you for saying that. I never really thought of it that way." She moved closer to Cody and rested an elbow on the railing. "At first it was fun, having someone to get high with. But where I thought of pot as a weekend recreational thing, Reed was smoking it before school, in between classes, and as soon as school got out for the day. It wasn't long before he added coke to the mix. I tried it once at his insistence, but didn't like how it made me feel. Reed started messing up at school and fighting with his parents. They blamed me, and rightly so."

"You're not responsible for his choices, Riley."

"I get what you're saying, but if not for me, he would have never started. Anyway, his parents called Child Protective Services to come get me out of the house. We panicked at the thought of being separated, and we ran away to Atlanta, figuring it was a big enough city to get lost in. With no money and no jobs, we lived on the streets."

"How long did that last?"

"Three months. Thankfully it was summer, so we weren't freezing. I was finally able to get work at a fast-food place, but Reed was too strung out to even think of holding down a job. I begged him to stop using, but I might as well have been talking to a fence post."

Cody reached out and brushed a wayward strand of hair from her face, and she leaned her face into his palm, soaking up his warmth. He was strong and honorable, and she wondered if she deserved such a man. She was almost to the end of her story, but she'd come to the hardest part to speak of.

"What happened to him?"

"He overdosed. We were living in an abandoned building with some other kids, most of them druggies, and Reed started going with them during the day, stealing purses, picking pockets, that kind of thing."

She'd sworn she wouldn't cry, but hot tears rolled down her cheeks. "I didn't even recognize him anymore. The beautiful boy I'd fallen in love with was gone. He didn't try to stay clean, he hardly ate enough to stay alive, and he had dead eyes. All that mattered to him was scoring." His lifeless eyes had haunted her for a long time, still did sometimes in the darkest hours of the night.

"I came back to the building one evening after I got off work and found him. He was barely alive, and all the kids had split, afraid of sticking around for the cops to come. Not one of them, the ones he considered his friends, cared enough to get help. Since I didn't have a phone, I ran down the street until I found a cop, but it was too late. When we got back to the building, Reed was taking his last breaths and I held him while he died." She swiped at the tears. Hadn't she already cried an ocean of tears for the boy she'd loved and lost? How did she even have any left to shed for him?

"What happened to you?"

"I got sent back to Florida, back into the hands of Protective Services. Honestly, I didn't care anymore what they did with me. But a funny thing happened. They finally got something right when they put me in Pat and John Haywood's home. I wasn't a fun kid to be around, but they turned out to be more stubborn than me. They were my salvation."

Cody caught Riley's hand and pulled her between his legs. She lifted the edges of the blanket and wrapped it around them, resting her face against his chest. Her story had just about ripped out his heart, and he was in awe of what she had made of herself considering what and where she'd come from. If she could recover from a life gone wrong, how could he do any less? From her, he took the determination to deal with what he faced.

"I'm sorry he died, darlin'." He kissed the top of her head. "But I'll say it again, he made the choice to take the road he did."

"I can't argue with that, but I'll always live with knowing that if he'd never met me, he would be alive today and happy."

"You can't know that either. Maybe he would be, or maybe he would have found his way to drugs some other way." When she shivered, he slid off the railing. "Don't move." He grabbed his guitar, putting it inside before locking his front door. "I think we've bared our souls enough for one night, don't you?"

She nodded, and the tears glistening on her cheeks tore at his heart. No sixteen-year-old should have experienced what she had. Hell, no child should have to live a life like hers—in and out of foster homes, an abandoned, unwanted little girl. He didn't think she had any idea just how strong and determined her character was. How beautiful she was.

Although he'd never understood his parents, or they him, he'd appreciated that they'd loved him, even if it was in their own way. They would never be different from who they were, would never understand the man he was, but that no longer mattered. He was blessed to have them.

Riley pulled the bottom of the blanket up around her waist, and they walked to her house, hand in hand. Not a man who had ever wanted a long-term relationship before, he now wanted one with her. Considering they'd yet to make love, his coming at this relationship with Riley from a friends-first angle was novel.

When they stepped inside her house, she dropped the blanket. Taking his hand, she led him to her bedroom. He kicked the door closed behind them to keep out nosy critters.

By unspoken agreement, they didn't speak. Maybe they'd talked themselves out. He didn't know, only knew that words weren't needed between them to understand what this night meant.

He was all for a little rough sex when his partner was of a like mind, but this brave, beautiful woman standing in front of him with warmth in her eyes meant just for him had not had an easy life. On this night of confessions, he wanted to worship her, wanted her to know that the world was sometimes soft and tender, even though she'd never known such a thing. Maybe she had with her Reed in the beginning, but he'd ended up abusing the love she had for him.

Cody cradled her face with his hands, leaned down, and brushed his lips over hers. Her eyes slid closed, and he smiled against her mouth. Although they'd kissed before, tonight felt like a new beginning, a chance to touch something magical. He moved behind her and flattened his palms on her shoulders, then with the barest of touches, slid his hands down her arms, lacing their fingers together when he'd reached her hands. As he did that, he nibbled on her earlobe. Goosebumps rose on her skin, and he felt a shudder travel through her.

Letting go of her hands, he gathered her long hair and moved it over her shoulder to trail down the front of her. Her neck exposed, he swept his tongue over her skin, eliciting more shudders from her. She was responsive to his every touch, and he wanted to bury himself in her heat right then, but tonight was for her. To show her that she was special, because he didn't think she knew that.

He reached for the hem of her top, and pulled it up. She lifted her arms, and he tossed the shirt onto a chair. There were still no words spoken between them, and he didn't want any. The skin under his palms as he slid them down her back—tracing the curve of her spine—was silky smooth. Waves of shivers rippled through her when he danced his fingers up her ribs. She leaned against him, and he rested his chin on her head, closing his eyes.

Using his sense of touch, of smell as he inhaled the essence that was Riley, and of sound—listening to her little gasps of breaths—he knew nothing, saw nothing, felt nothing but her. When his thumbs scraped under the soft flesh of her breasts, she made a little humming sound that had him throbbing with desire. He pressed his erection against her bottom, letting her know how much he wanted her.

But not yet. There was more to learn about her. He shed his shirt, needing to feel her, skin to skin. With her back against his chest again, he cupped her breasts, and flicked his thumbs over her nipples.

"Oooh," she murmured.

He would allow her that one word tonight. While he played with her breasts, he pressed his mouth to her neck and sucked, marking her as his. She lowered her hands, digging her fingers into his thighs when he gave her nipples a light pinch. Cody licked the red, irritated skin on her neck, soothing it. He couldn't remember the last time he'd felt the need to mark a woman, if he even ever had.

Still standing behind her, he slid one hand under the waistband of her silk pajama bottoms. He cupped her mound, and just held his hand there, feeling her heat. She tilted her head, looking up at him with eyes darkened by desire, and he covered her mouth with his. Keeping his hand cupped over her, he pressed his tongue to the seam of her lips, urging her to open for him. When she let him in, their tongues sought out each other, tangling in a demanding dance.

He could no longer keep his hand still, and he slipped a finger into her slick heat. She was so damn wet for him. There was something hot about both of them bare from the waist up, but clothed from the waist down. Half their bodies touched skin to skin, while the friction of the material separating their lower halves created a kind of pleasurable pain.

Finding her sweet spot, he toyed with her until her breaths were coming fast. When she came, it was as if her legs gave out, and he held her close until he was sure she would remain upright. He moved to stand in front of her, and when she opened her mouth, he put a finger over her lips, shaking his head. All that existed in her bedroom this night was the two of them. They didn't need words.

Understanding entered her eyes, and she lifted on her toes and kissed him. He didn't know why he wanted it this way, had never cared before how much a woman talked, but the quiet between Riley and him seemed . . . spiritual. Yes, that was the right word. She brought her hands up, cradling his face as she kissed him, and he covered her hands with his. The kiss started as gentle, but quickly became intense. He wanted to devour her, wanted her to climb into his skin and live there.

Was that love? He didn't know. All he did know was that she calmed him, that he desired her like no other, and that he couldn't imagine ever tiring of her. With her, he felt complete. Because of her, he was determined to conquer his demons. She didn't know it yet, but he was hers for as long as she would have him.

She lowered her hands to the button on his jeans, and he inched away, giving her room for her task. He'd gone commando after his shower, and decided he'd best take over the job of unzipping the jeans, considering he was already about to pop out of them. The thought of getting caught in the zipper made him want to squeeze his legs closed. He took out the condoms he'd put in his pocket, then pushed his pants over his hips, chuckling when Riley's eyes widened at the sight of him.

She had mentioned that she hadn't been with anyone since starting her clinic. He knew she'd been with the boy she'd loved, and he assumed there had been college boyfriends. But those were boys, and he would be her first man. He liked that.

After kicking his jeans to the side, he lifted Riley in his arms and carried her to the bed, dropping the condom packs on the bedside table. The lamp was on its brightest setting, and he dimmed it. Her gaze roamed over him when he knelt beside her, and he hoped she liked what she saw. She reached up and traced the Trident tat—an eagle clutching a U.S. Navy anchor, a trident, and a flintlock pistol—on his upper arm. He'd been proud when he'd made it through BUD/S, the SEAL training school. Only two hundred or so sailors out of a thousand made it through the rigorous course each year, and the first thing he'd done when he had was to get the tattoo.

Her eyes lifted to his when he pulled her pajama bottoms down. Every time she looked at him with those soft, desire-darkened eyes, he felt caught up in something he'd never known before, something magical, and he couldn't tear his gaze away.

The yellow glow of the lamp fell on her hair, spread out over the pillow, making the red and gold highlights shimmer. He wondered what she'd think if he told her that her hair reminded him of a German shepherd's coat. Coming from him, that was a high compliment, but he thought it wise to save that piece of info for some other time. It amused him, though, and a smile slipped out. To keep her from wondering what he was thinking, he kissed her. He'd been wanting to do that, anyway.

It was almost scary how attuned they were to each other without words between them. He hadn't been searching for *the one*, and maybe there was something in the water at K2. He no longer cared why Riley had walked into his life at a time when he'd thought he least needed that to happen, only that she had.

Without breaking the kiss, he stretched out alongside her, and because his fingers were itching to touch her, he allowed them free rein to roam. She sighed into his mouth when his hands slid over her skin, and she arched into his palm when he cupped a breast. It had been much too long since he'd been with a woman, and this one, Christ, this one brought him to the edge of losing control.

There were so many things he wanted to do with her, and he would, but if he wasn't inside her in the next minute, he was going to embarrass himself. He reached for a condom, tore it open, and rose to his knees. It was a turn-on watching her watch him put it on, and although it seemed an impossible feat, he grew even harder.

Moving between her legs, he put his hands on the insides of her thighs, caressing his thumbs over her flesh, a little surprised at how firm her legs were. But she was a runner, so she would be fit, another thing he liked about her. He pushed her knees farther apart, and took himself in hand, rubbing the tip over her, teasing her. She moaned, and he could take no more. In teasing her, he was torturing himself. He slid into her, pausing to let her get used to him, moaning at how hot and wet she was.

The discipline he'd learned as a SEAL was the only thing keeping him from going caveman and pounding into her with the insatiable lust of a beast. He had the feeling she could take that side of him, and they'd get around to crazy monkey sex soon enough. Tonight, though, he wanted gentle and tender, not only for her, but for himself. That was a first. He didn't do tender. Not until Riley, anyway.

When her eyes slid closed and she pressed her head back into the pillow, he covered her mouth with his, swallowing the little noises she made. She hooked her ankles behind him and dug her heels into his ass. Her hands were all over him, as if she wanted to touch and know each part of him. His SEAL discipline failed him. He grunted, giving into his need for her.

Sounds of sex filled the air, and he didn't want it to end, wanted to listen all night to their bodies slapping against each other and the mix of their harsh breaths. She squeezed her core muscles around him as her climax hit, and he hissed when the pressure that had built up in his lower back and groin gave way. As he sucked in air, he wondered if his entire insides were pouring out.

"Riley," he rasped. He fell over her, catching himself on his elbows, and stared down at her. What was it about this woman that had him thinking of forevers?

CHAPTER NINETEEN

Riley pressed a hand over her stomach in an attempt to calm the butterflies taking flight. She looked out the window of Cody's truck, watching as the houses became grander the nearer to the beach they got. Although she'd met his K2 friends, other than Maria, she didn't know any of their wives or girlfriends. In her entire adult life, she'd never attended a party with a group of grown-up couples.

As if making a good impression on his friends wasn't enough to worry about, she wished she hadn't let Cody talk her into wearing jeans. Wouldn't a blouse paired with a skirt or slacks be more appropriate for a dinner party at a rich man's house? She hoped Cody was right when he swore everyone would dress casual. She'd decided on a pair of black skinny jeans with a deep green turtleneck sweater, and black, flat-heeled boots. She'd left her hair down at Cody's request, and her only jewelry was large hoop earrings.

At least he'd been impressed, if his wolf whistle when he'd come to her door to collect her was any indication. Did it matter what anyone else thought? He looked pretty darn hot himself wearing a pair of blue jeans that hugged his hips and a black turtleneck sweater.

"Did you find anything unusual this morning when you went through the files?"

Jerked away from her thoughts on how sexy her boyfriend looked—had they reached boyfriend-girlfriend status?—she glanced at Cody. Unable to help herself, she reached over and ran her palm over his stubble, her stomach fluttering when he leaned his face into her hand. "I love that day-old beard look on you. Makes you appear dangerous."

He smiled, showing his sexy dimple. "But never to you, darlin'."

No, he never would be to her. They'd made love last night, dozed off, made love again, slept some, and made love again. He'd stayed in her bed, waking up next to her this morning. But she'd had to beg him to not move to the couch, and she knew he hadn't allowed himself to fall into a deep sleep. Her hope was that when he stayed over, she could eventually prove to him that even if he had a nightmare, he would never hurt her, even subconsciously.

"To answer your question, no, nothing struck me. I went through all the files from the first day I opened the clinic. Yes, I've had pets that I couldn't save for one reason or another, but I just can't see any of those owners gunning for me."

"Damn, I was hoping we'd get some kind of lead. There was nothing unusual at all?"

She shrugged. "There was one thing, but the owner doesn't fit the profile we got." He raised a brow, and she laughed. "You do that so well."

"What's that?"

"That brow-raising thing men do."

"Ah, that. We're born with the talent." He took her hand and put it on his thigh. "So what's the unusual thing?"

"We accidently sent the wrong dog to be cremated." Both of Cody's brows rose, making her giggle. He grinned and waggled them. As each day passed that she spent with him, he seemed to grow happier, lighter in heart. She liked to think she had something to do with that.

"I felt so awful about it. It was Brooke's first day, and we had two dogs die, one from old age, and the other from liver cancer. I had to euthanize both. The owner of the dog that was old wanted him cremated. The other owner wanted to take his dog home to bury him. He also accused me of not doing enough to cure the animal. Anyway, Brooke got the dogs mixed up. The man who wanted to take his dog home was furious about the mistake."

"Let me guess. You took the blame, didn't tell him it was Brooke who screwed up?"

"Of course. I wasn't going to throw her to the wolves. It was an honest mistake, and believe me, she learned from it."

"Was he married, the man who was mad?"

"I have no idea. He never had a woman with him, and we only get contact information from the owners. All our records are about the animals. I did check, but he didn't list anyone else as a contact."

"I agree he doesn't fit the profile, but tomorrow, let's go to the clinic and get the phone number. Call it, see who answers."

She should have thought of doing that today. "We don't have to. I can access the clinic files from my home computer. The profile could also be wrong, couldn't it?"

"There's always that possibility, but Kincaid said the profiler had never been wrong, that he knew of."

"I just want to find Pelli. It's killing me wondering if he's okay." She blinked against the burning in her eyes. She wanted her baby.

He covered her hand where it rested on his leg with his. "I know, and we'll find him."

And he sounded so sure that she believed him. Otherwise she'd fall apart. He turned onto a long cobblestone driveway where other cars were already parked along the sides, and her mouth fell open at seeing the huge two-story house.

"Wow," she muttered.

"Yeah, kind of amazing, isn't it? I've only been here once, but I can tell you that you ain't seen nothing yet."

The house was about twelve feet off the ground, built like that because of hurricanes, with a four-car garage under it. A wide set of stairs with what looked like polished, dark mahogany rails led up to a double front door. It had a beautiful, weathered copper roof, and ocean-blue shutters framed the oversized windows. The yard was covered in pale rose gravel, and the plants were palm trees, beach grasses, and succulents.

"Wow," she said again, not being able to think of another word good enough for what she was seeing. Cody laughed and bumped against her arm. She grinned up at him. "If my mouth falls open when I get inside, kick me."

"I'd much rather kiss you," he said as they reached the top of the stairs. "Like this."

When their lips met, she sighed. She had only kissed a handful of men, so she didn't have much to compare him to, but she'd bet her beers that there wasn't a man in the world who kissed as well.

"Ring the doorbell when you're done."

Riley jumped away—heat immediately flaming her cheeks—and turned to see Logan Kincaid standing in the doorway, amusement dancing in his eyes. "Ah . . . hi. We were just . . . we were . . ."

"We were kissing," Cody said, giving her a wink.

"I noticed." Logan stepped back. "Come in."

Could she be more mortified? She pinched Cody's arm in retaliation as she passed by him to step inside. His chuckle didn't endear him to her, and she glared at him. That got her a big grin. *Men!*

Logan closed the door behind them. "Good to see you again, Riley. Everyone's outside."

As she followed Logan through the house, she did manage to keep her mouth closed, but it wasn't easy. The place was freaking amazing. Floor-to-ceiling windows on the side facing the gulf provided a magnificent view of Pensacola's famous sugary sand beach, and the water sparkled an emerald green. The interior colors were beachy—blues, turquoises, and greens—and the floors were bleached wood. The great room opened up to a state-of-the-art kitchen and dining area, and stairs led to a second story.

"Wow," she whispered.

Cody put his mouth close to her ear. "Told you," he whispered back.

She elbowed him in his stomach.

"Ooof." He rubbed her bottom.

She sidestepped. "Stop it."

"Make me."

This playful side of him was new, and she liked it, but she wasn't about to tell him. Nope. Not giving him that satisfaction.

"You have a beautiful home," she said, increasing her pace to catch up with Logan, then was snatched back when Cody caught the waist of her jeans.

He tucked her against him. "You can't get away from me, darlin'."

Like she wanted to. "You're being a bad boy. Behave or I'll punish you."

His eyes lit with interest. "Yeah?"

"Well, that threat didn't have the desired effect."

"When you two children finish playing, join us. Everyone else is here," Logan said before opening one of the French doors and walking out.

"Does he have eyes in the back of his head?" She'd thought he was too far away to hear their whispering.

"Yep, and the best set of ears you'll ever find."

"That's something you should have mentioned."

"More fun letting you learn that on your own."

She rolled her eyes. It was funny, though, that his messing around with her had relaxed her. Maybe that had been his plan all along. When she stepped out onto the back deck and everyone looked over at her and Cody, she froze. Well, relaxed was good while it lasted.

Cody put his hand on her lower back, flattening his palm and rubbing his thumb over her. "There's not another woman in the world I'd be prouder to introduce my friends to than you, darlin'."

She shot him a grateful smile, and he dropped his hand from her back, lacing their fingers together. Glancing at the couples, she was relieved to see that everyone was wearing jeans. The temperature was in the high sixties with only a slight breeze, the sun was bright in the sky, and the waves made a gentle splash against the shore. A beautiful day to spend on the beach. The deck stretched across the entire back of the house, and flames danced in the fire pit that everyone sat around. She squeezed Cody's hand and got a return squeeze.

Cody didn't know why Riley was nervous about meeting his friends, but he could see that she was. She was beautiful and had a great personality—sassy and funny. He guessed because of her upbringing and then dedicating herself to getting her clinic up and running, she hadn't had much opportunity to socialize. But the death grip she had on his hand had him sending a warning glance at his friends. They better accept her. Because the team was so attuned to each other, they got his message, and the men gave an imperceptible nod. The women totally missed the communication happening between the team, but they all had warm smiles for Riley, so he relaxed.

He let go of Riley's hand and put his arm around her shoulder. "Everyone, this is Dr. Riley Austin. She's already met the team and is friends with Maria, so I'll just introduce the rest of you gorgeous ladies."

"My cat loves her," Maria said.

"Then that's good enough for me," Dani Kincaid chimed in.

"Riley, meet Dani Kincaid. Sitting next to her is Sugar Turner, Jamie's wife."

Sugar waved. "I'm pregnant." She patted her rounded stomach.

Riley laughed. "I can see that."

"Well, I meant that if I go into labor, it's good to have a doctor around." She glanced at her husband. "I don't think I'm fixin' to, honey, so get that worried look off your face."

Sugar was as southern as they came, and her accent with those drawn-out words was cute. "Ah, Riley's a veterinarian." Cody was positive Sugar already knew that because he was certain that everyone had been told about Riley by now. In her own way, though, she had put Riley at ease, and he liked Sugar for that.

"True," Riley said, "but I've delivered scads of kittens and puppies, so I'm sure I could figure out how to deliver a baby if it comes to that."

Jamie snorted. "She's got two months to go. Let's not even talk about delivering a baby today. Makes me want a drink."

"And he doesn't drink." Sugar patted her husband's knee. "You'll live through it. Probably."

Everyone laughed, and Cody thought the last of Riley's tension had vanished. "On the other side of Jamie is Charlie Morgan, Ryan's fiancée. Charlie's a stunt plane pilot."

Riley smiled at the petite woman. "That's really cool. I heard you actually fly in air shows?"

"Sure do. Have one tomorrow afternoon, in fact. If you're not doing anything, come out and watch."

"I'd love to."

As he and Riley took the two empty chairs, the whole group made plans to go to Charlie's air show. Kincaid had asked Cody Friday afternoon what he and Riley liked to drink, and a few minutes later, a young man dressed in black pants and a white shirt brought them beers with limes stuck in the neck.

When Riley showed surprise, Dani said, "I didn't want to be up and down taking care of drinks and food today, so we hired a caterer. Hope you like seafood. If not, you can opt for a steak."

Riley pushed her lime into the bottle. "I love seafood. Your home is beautiful."

Cody sat back, watching Riley get to know his friends. She was shy with them at first, but as the afternoon wore on, she seemed to be enjoying herself, and he was surprised at how much fun he was having.

Welcome back to the land of the living, Dog.

After a delicious dinner of fresh-off-the-boat cold boiled shrimp, grilled grouper that melted in his mouth, and raw oysters for anyone who wanted them—not him, but he learned that Riley liked them—everyone decided to take a stroll on the beach as the sun set. After the first ten minutes or so of walking as a group, Cody noticed that each couple began to wander off on their own. Holding hands with Riley, he slowed his steps.

Throughout the evening, he'd tried not to envy his teammates' happiness. It was blatantly obvious that every damn one of them was in love, and even more incredible, not embarrassed to admit it. A few years ago, when they were still a SEAL team, except for Ryan, who was already married to his first wife, not a one of them saw this day coming. He certainly hadn't. Yet, here he was, about to say something he thought would never come out of his mouth.

He tugged Riley to a stop. "Beautiful night. Beautiful woman. How did I get so lucky?"

She smiled up at him. "I could argue that I'm the lucky one."

Cradling her face with his hands, he angled his head and kissed her. She leaned into him, putting her hands on his waist. The breeze blew her hair around their faces, and he reached under her neck and gathered it up, wrapping it around his hand. He deepened the kiss, exploring her mouth, drowning in her sweet taste. When she rubbed her groin against his erection, he groaned.

"Careful, darlin'," he said, pulling away. "Another minute of that, and I'll be making love to you right here in the surf."

"Might be fun." She nestled her head against his neck. "When it's warmer."

"We'll put it on our bucket list."

"We have a bucket list?"

He wanted to make a list that would last them a lifetime. Wrapping his arms around her, he leaned his cheek on her forehead. "What would you say if I told you I think I'm falling for you?"

"I would say that I'm pretty sure I'm falling for you, too." She nuzzled her face against his chest.

"Think they'd miss us if we disappeared?" Needing to kiss her, he lowered his mouth to hers.

Kincaid walked past with his wife tucked next to his side. "Hey, you two. Time to toast the happy couple."

"Dammit, we weren't fast enough." He took Riley's hand, and they followed the others back to sit around the fire pit. A slew of off-color toasts were made to Ryan and Charlie amid much laughter, some causing the bride-to-be to blush.

"Something came up today," Kincaid said when the conversation trailed off. He turned those all-seeing eyes on Cody. "Something I need you for. Problem is, I need you back to the Dog that took no enemies. What can we do to get you there?"

Cody set his cup of coffee on the deck. He glanced around to see everyone's attention was on him. His first reaction was anger that the boss would shine a light on him like that, but the men sitting around the fire pit were his brothers. They loved him. He knew that. Where it had once just been the team, now significant others were involved. These women loved their men, and they needed to know that if he were involved in an operation, he wouldn't have a flashback, endangering whichever teammate was out with him.

Riley reached for his hand, tangling her fingers around his. She glared at the boss. "Do you have to do this in front of everyone?"

Damn, the woman was amazing. "Yeah, he does, darlin'." He pulled her chair closer, needing her near for what he was about to say. "I don't know what any of you can do to help, but before I met Riley, I'm not sure I would have talked to you about what's going on with me. She's incredible, my inspiration."

"He swore he wasn't going to drink the water," Ryan said.

Riley furrowed her brows. "You've said that before. What does that mean?"

Since Ryan was next to him, Cody kicked him.

"Saw that," Jake said.

At the smirks on his teammates' faces, including Kincaid's, Cody sent them all a glare. He wouldn't trade a one of those jerks, though. They were his family, one that had grown to include the women sitting with them tonight. They had his six. Always had. Always would. For these people he would bare his soul.

After discussing his nightmare, everyone agreed that he was suppressing his memories, but other than continuing his appointments with Tom, no one had anything new to offer. They hadn't been there that day, and he knew that bugged them, each believing he could have done something to protect their sniper.

Cody met Kincaid's gaze. "I want to be a member of the team. One thing Tom told me was to have a safe word that would bring me back if I ever had another flashback."

"Riley," the boss said.

If there was one word that would get through to him, it was that one. Cody glanced at Riley to see her reaction, and smiled at the shock he saw on her face. "He's right, darlin'. No matter how far gone I was, your name would get through to me." He sat back in his chair. "Riley it is." He turned back to the boss. "When is this operation?"

"Next month. If you don't think you'll be ready, you can refuse."

He wasn't about to. "I'll be ready." Come hell or high water, he was going to be the man they needed. Enough attention had been paid on him, though, so he said, "Where are your kids tonight?" Who knew the day would come when his SEAL team commander's eyes would light up with pleasure at the mention of children?

"They're upstairs with our housekeeper. Would you like to meet them, Riley?"

"I'd love to," Riley said, standing and pulling Cody up with her. Everyone followed Kincaid and Dani into the house.

Cody privately chuckled. He *had* gone and drunk the damn Kool-Aid, and was already imagining a miniature Riley running around his feet. He wasn't taking for granted that it would happen, though. He hadn't asked her to marry him, but the question was now on his agenda for the near future. As soon as he cleaned up the mess in his head.

Cody jerked awake to the feel of soft fingers caressing his cheek. It was so familiar that a fuzzy picture hovered at the edge of his mind, one from his past. As he stared, somewhat disoriented, at Riley's face as she leaned over him, he tried to recapture the memory. It seemed important that he did so, but it slipped away. They had come home, made love, and quickly fallen asleep, tired from a long day.

"You were calling out," she said.

He smiled at her before drifting off again.

"Soldier."

The muted voice stopped Cody. He motioned for his spotter to head on up to the roof of the building they'd scouted out a few days earlier. Cody was familiar with the occupants of the house across the alley. Covered in a burqa, Asra, the teenage girl who lived there with her parents and two brothers, beckoned him before disappearing inside.

He ran low to the other side of the street and ducked into the open door of her home, his Glock palmed in his hand. Taking off on his own was against regulations and foolhardy, but she'd given him good intel on the

Taliban twice now. Her only condition had been that no one know about her. He understood. The Taliban would kill her and her family if they ever learned of her treachery.

Adjusting his eyes to the dusty shadows of the house, he zeroed in on Asra, doubled over and holding her stomach. She yanked away the material covering her face. Blood dripped from a cut on her neck. Every hair on his body stood on end. The situation was bad, but he wasn't sure why. Had the Taliban somehow learned that she'd been passing their locations to him? He stepped toward her. It was quiet, too damn quiet.

The air behind him shifted, and he spun . . .

Soft fingers caressed his cheek, and he blinked his eyes open. Asra leaned over him, the blood on her neck now dried in crusty patches. "Wake up, soldier."

"Where am I?"

"We have to go before they come back."

"My head," he said, reaching a hand up and finding a large lump on the back of his skull.

"They hit you there. They think you dead, soldier. We must go." She pulled on his arm.

"Have to go." He struggled to his knees, and then the blackness descended.

He groaned at the pounding ache in the back of his head. Forcing open eyelids that felt as if they had been stapled shut, he frowned at seeing dusty, sandal-clad feet in his line of vision. Why was he facedown on the floor? Lifting his gaze, he saw Asra being held against a bearded man wearing a balaclava head wrap, saw the knife in the man's hands, saw the blood dripping down Asra's neck. He tried to sit up. Had to save her.

He made it to his knees when something hit the back of his head again, the searing pain sending him into oblivion. When he came to, he was face-down on the dirt floor staring into the dead eyes of Asra. She was on her back, her head turned his way, her accusing eyes open. He pushed up onto his arms, then fell into a sitting position. The room swam, and he thought he was going to throw up.

"Asra?" He shook her. If he could get her to their medic . . . His gaze fell on her stomach, cut open, revealing a bloody mess of organs.

Cody leaned over and vomited. His fault. His fault.

Voices sounded in the next room, men arguing in Pashto, the primary language of the Taliban. Cody tried to focus on the open door, but there were two of them wavering in his vision. He fumbled around for his pack and sniper rifle, but they were gone.

"I'm sorry, Asra," he whispered. "So fucking sorry."

He crawled toward one of the doors, hoping it was the real one.

CHAPTER TWENTY

N oooo!"
Riley shot straight up in bed, heart pounding. Cody?

"I'm sorry. So fucking sorry."

The agony she heard in his voice pierced her heart. She scooted onto her knees and turned the lamp on dim. Cody rolled from his stomach to his back, and his face was wet with tears. He was having his nightmare, and she wasn't sure what to do. If she tried to wake him, would he lash out? She felt strongly that he wouldn't hurt her, that somehow even asleep he'd know it was her. Then she remembered that her name was supposed to be a safe word.

It was something to try, at least. On the other side of the closed bedroom door, Sally, or maybe it was Pretty Girl, whined. Riley covered Cody's clenched fist with her hand, hoping her touch would calm him. Also, if he tried to punch her, she'd maybe be able to push his hand away.

"My fault. My fault."

He sounded so devastated, and whatever he was dreaming had to be something really bad, something he blamed himself for. She leaned her mouth close to his ear. "Riley." She waited a few seconds, then said it again. "Riley." He tried to shake off her hand, but she closed her fingers around his. "Riley." Each time she spoke her name, she said it a little more loudly and forcefully. "Riley."

His eyes blinked open, and he stared at her, but she knew he didn't really see her. "I'm Riley. It's Riley here with you."

"Riley? You can't stay here. It's not safe. They'll get you, too."

At least he was talking to her. "Riley's not there. You aren't either. She's here, in America, with you. Do you understand? You're with me, baby."

His eyes finally focused on her. "I had the nightmare, but it didn't stop like always before." His Adam's apple bobbed as he swallowed hard. "I-I remember everything."

"Will you tell me?"

When he brushed his fingers across his cheeks, he seemed surprised when they came away wet. He frowned as he stared at his fingertips. She hoped his tears didn't embarrass him. As far as she was concerned, when you cared for someone you should be able to cry in front of them without fearing they would think less of you.

Thinking he might feel more comfortable talking to her if she wasn't looking at him, she stretched out alongside him with her back to his stomach. He put an arm around her, and she laced her fingers through his.

"I screwed up something awful, and it cost a girl her life," he finally said after a few minutes of silence.

She brought his hand to her mouth and kissed it. "Tell me about it." If he blamed himself for the death of an innocent girl, no wonder he hadn't wanted to remember. But she knew him, and he would never have purposely put someone in danger. As she listened to his story, tears stained her own cheeks. No, he hadn't intentionally set out to put the girl in danger, but he'd not followed the rules, and the results had been tragic. Would he ever be able to forgive himself? If not, the guilt would eat him alive.

"She was gutted like an animal," he rasped.

He pulled away, getting out of bed, and she turned over, watching him get dressed. "Are you leaving?" Riley glanced at the clock to see it was five in the morning.

"Yeah, I need some time alone," he said, not looking at her.

The last thing she thought he needed was to be alone, but she sensed that if she argued the point, he would shut down. Although he already had. "You're still going to the air show, aren't you?"

He sat in the chair, his gaze on the shoes he was putting on. "No. I'm going to call Tom, see if he can meet with me this afternoon."

"That's probably a good idea." She bit down on her bottom lip, willing her tears to go away. He was closing down on her. It wasn't fair. She'd only just found him, and now it felt as if she was losing him.

"But you still should go. I'll call Jake. Ask him and Maria to pick you up." He walked to the bedroom door and paused, but didn't turn. "Set the alarm after I'm gone."

"Okay." She didn't really want to go anymore, but if she tried to speak, she would start crying. Her heart hurt, as if it had shattered into tiny pieces, for him and for her. *Please stay and let me hold you,* she wanted to say.

"I probably won't be back later, but I'll ask Kincaid to send someone over." He left without looking back, Sally and Pretty Girl trotting out behind him, and maybe it was her imagination, but all three of them, man and dogs, appeared dejected, their shoulders slumped.

She got out of bed, slipped on a robe, and went to the alarm box. Alarm reset, she curled up on the sofa, unable to hold her tears in any longer. She tried to convince herself that he really did just need a little time alone to think things through, but her heart wasn't buying it. There was finality in his voice, that of a wounded animal, off to lick his wounds, possibly never to be seen again. To heal, he needed his pack, and that was her and his teammates. Yet, a voice whispered in her ear that he'd already shut her out of his life.

Arthur jumped up and nudged his face against hers. "I know he's hurting, but so am I," she whispered to Arthur. Merlin sat on the back of the sofa, staring down at her. "You're worried, too," she said, and he blinked as if in answer. Pelli should be with them, and thinking of him caused fresh tears.

When she'd finally cried herself out, she rose, and started a pot of coffee. While it was brewing, she showered and washed her hair. Not really caring what she wore to the air show, she slipped on a pair of comfy jeans, a long-sleeved T-shirt, and brown cowboy boots. After two cups of coffee and a bowl of oatmeal, she felt a little better.

She walked to the window and lifted a blind. The sun was coming up, and it was light enough to see Cody sitting on his steps, his arms dangling between his knees as he stared at the ground. His defeated posture tugged at her. Pretty Girl and Sally sat at his feet, gazing up at him. The whole scene was one of the saddest things she'd ever seen, and even as much as he was hurting, she knew he was keeping an eye on her until Jake and Maria came by to pick her up.

She dropped the blind back in place. Yes, he was hurting, but he'd hurt her by leaving the way he had. Did she mean nothing to him after all? Afraid of the answer, she turned her attention to how to find Pelli. She was tired of waiting for her crackpot stalker to make the next move. Opening up her laptop, she accessed the file for Mr. Ziegler, the owner of the dog her clinic had mistakenly sent to be cremated. Phone in hand, she started to call the number, but paused. What would she say if someone answered? Or should she just hang up if they did? Deciding she'd apologize for calling the wrong number, she finished the call. It rang six times, then a recording picked up.

"You've reached the Ziegler residence. We can't come to the phone right now, so unless you're selling something, please leave a message," a man's voice said.

Riley disconnected. "We," he'd said, so she assumed that meant he was married. Now what? She pulled up the address, noting the location was two or three miles from her clinic. That still didn't tell her anything. She glanced at the clock, seeing that she had plenty of time to drive by the Zieglers' house before Jake and Maria came to pick her up.

Keys in hand, she got in her car, turned the ignition, and backed up. At the end of her driveway, she stopped. Chewing on her bottom lip, she thought about what she was doing. *Don't go off half-cocked, Riley.* Whoever was targeting her probably knew what kind of car she drove and might recognize her. It wouldn't be out of the way for Jake to drive by the Zieglers' on their way to the air show.

Where the hell was she going? She knew it was dangerous to take off by herself. Cody reached for his keys, planning to follow her, but then she stopped. After a minute, she drove the car back into her carport, got out, and went back into her house. What was that all about?

After leaving her, he'd sat on his porch, watching her house, while scenes from his nightmare flashed through his mind. The first time Asra had approached him with intel, she had slipped a note into his hand. He'd been standing on the street in front of her house, talking to her brother, one of their interpreters. Asra had stood behind Jalandhar, eyes downcast. When Jalandhar had turned away to go into his house, she had slipped a piece of paper into Cody's hand before hurrying to follow her brother.

His male brain thought she was giving him a love note of some kind, maybe asking him to meet her somewhere. He almost didn't open the folded page, but when he did, he'd stared at the words in shock. The Taliban had compromised her brother and was threatening to kill him and his family if he didn't give them information on the Americans he interpreted for. She'd begged Cody to find a way to help her family, and in return she would pass on anything she heard. At the end of the note, she said that if Cody told anyone that she was giving him information she would jump off the roof of her house, because the Taliban had ears everywhere, and it would mean death for her, anyway.

He'd debated long and hard about keeping her a secret. Reporting her to his commander should have been the first thing he'd done on returning to base camp. If Kincaid had still been his commander, he would have. But Kincaid was back in the states and no longer in the military.

Cody had been temporarily assigned to a marine regiment in Kandahar as their sniper. If he went to the base commander with this, or any officer for that matter, he knew how things would roll. They would use Asra without any concern for her safety, while bringing her brother in for questioning. He couldn't do that to her, so she stayed his secret. He passed on her intel each of the next two times she'd given it, saying he'd been in the right place at the right time to overhear the information. He'd never been sure the higher-ups had bought his story, but they hadn't pressed him on it.

Nor did he report her brother. The country was fucked. That was a given. The Taliban was merciless, and he couldn't blame Jalandhar for trying to keep his family safe. In the young man's shoes, Cody wouldn't have done anything different. To counter whatever info Jalandhar was passing on—there wasn't all that much that he was privy to—Cody frequently gave the young man false information.

Everything he'd done had been to save a young girl brave enough to try to help her family and country, and he'd failed her. She'd not been given a quick death, and because of him, she'd been horribly tortured. How was he supposed to live with that?

His stomach took a sickening roll, and his mind begged for numbness. He'd told Riley that he was going to call Tom and ask for a meeting. Instead, he went looking for the scotch. If he finished off a bottle, maybe he would forget there was a woman across the street who deserved better than to be dragged into his hellhole. He hadn't even been able to look her in the eyes after he'd admitted his part in getting

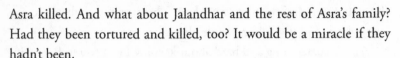

Asra killed. And what about Jalandhar and the rest of Asra's family? Had they been tortured and killed, too? It would be a miracle if they hadn't been.

Hands braced against the kitchen counter and head bowed, Cody tried to will away the image of Asra's mutilated body. It didn't work, and he eyed the scotch bottle. What the hell, Jake and Maria had just picked up Riley, so he was good to go. He filled a glass to the rim.

Sally whined.

"What? Now you're the booze police?" He glared at the dog peering up at him with worried brown eyes. Pretty Girl leaned her shivering body against Sally's. Damn dogs. They picked up on every stupid emotion, and right now, his emotions were paying a visit to hell.

Shit. Sally was right. If he started drinking now, he'd never stop. Ever. He poured the contents of the glass down the drain, following it with what was left in the bottle. "Happy?" Sally gave a bark that he took to mean yes. Pretty Girl wasn't so sure, apparently. She buried her face into the fur of Sally's neck.

"Dumb dogs." Didn't they know he needed a drink or five? He dug in his pocket for his phone, and finding it, he called Tom. His head doc was more than happy to see him after lunch. A few seconds after disconnecting, he got a text message ping.

> Might have a lead on Layla. Will let you know.

Cody stared at Wizard's text, afraid to believe she'd finally been found. It probably wasn't her, so he wouldn't get his hopes up. He answered, thanking Wizard for not giving up, grabbed his keys, and left to see his head doc.

As he pulled out of the driveway, he eyed Riley's house. His chest hurt at the thought of never walking across the street again. But he'd caused an innocent girl to be tortured, had seen with his own eyes what had been done to her, and he didn't think he could ever be at peace with that. He wouldn't wish himself on his worst enemy, so he wasn't about to drag Riley down with him. She was too special to wallow in his mud hole.

When he arrived, Tom was out front, waiting for him. Cody felt bad about bringing him out on a Sunday afternoon, but the man had said to call any time of the day or night.

"Coffee? Water? Soda?" Tom asked as they walked down the hall.

"I'm good, thanks." A lie. He was far from good.

"You remembered something?"

Yes, and I wish to God I hadn't. Cody wandered around the office, stopping to study two framed pictures that looked like a child had drawn them hanging side by side. Only a black crayon had been used in the one on the left, and best he could tell, Cody saw a kid with his mouth wide open, as if screaming. The top of his head was blown off, and black gooey stuff was oozing out. It was a raw cry for help, and too close for comfort to how he felt. He tore his gaze away to look at the one on the right.

With that one, he guessed the artist was a few years older as the picture was more refined. It was also a happy scene. A boy played with a small dog in the front yard of a pretty house surrounded by colorful flowers.

Tom came to stand next to him. "The same boy drew both of those, two years apart."

"Obviously, he wasn't well when he drew the first one. What was wrong with him?"

"He caused the deaths of his parents and baby sister."

"Jesus." Cody shifted his gaze to Tom. "And he's better now?" He had to be, or he wouldn't have been able to draw the happy picture.

"Yes. It wasn't intentional. It was his bedtime, but he wanted to finish a drawing he'd started, a birthday present for his mother. He snuck a candle and some matches into his room. Long story short, he fell asleep, and he must have knocked the candle over. The carpet caught on fire, and he was afraid he was going to get in trouble, so he hid in his closet. He was burned pretty badly, but he was the only survivor. He was five years old."

Cody tried to think of something to say, but he had no words. Finally, a question occurred to him. "I thought there was patient confidentiality or whatever. It's okay for you to tell me about him?"

"He gave me permission when he asked me to hang his pictures in my office. He said, and I'll quote him exactly, 'Nobody is as bad as me, and if I can get better so can they.' I think he has a strong message to share. He said I could show people his pictures and that if I thought it would help, I could tell his story. His aunt and uncle are raising him, and they love him like one of their own. His latest thing is visiting hospitals and taking sick kids crayons and coloring books."

Tom moved to the chair in front of his desk. "Come sit. Let's talk."

"How do you stand being around people like me and that boy every day? Isn't it depressing?" Cody sat in the second chair.

"Sometimes. But the reward is getting a picture filled with puppies and flowers. Makes it all worthwhile." Tom stuck out his right leg, rotating his prosthetic foot. "Damn phantom itches. Even after all this time, I still get them. Talk to me, Cody."

He took a deep breath, and then told Tom his nightmare.

"And you blame yourself?" Tom said when Cody finished.

"Of course I blame myself. Wouldn't you?"

"Absolutely."

That wasn't what Cody expected to hear. "I thought you'd try to convince me I didn't do anything wrong."

"Only you can do that. All I can do is help you talk through it and give you some tools to cope until you decide to forgive yourself. One thing you're going to have to accept is that you can't change the past. At some point, you're going to have to let it go because if you don't, you'll never be happy. Is that what you want? I ask because there are people who like being miserable. Are you one of those?"

"I want to be happy," Cody whispered.

"Good, that makes my job a lot easier. I'm assuming you won't be willing to take any meds to help control your depression?"

"No meds."

"Thought so, but if you ever reach a point where you think about taking your life, you call me. Day or night. If it comes to that, I'll insist on medication."

"No, I'm past that." And he was.

"The first thing I'm going to do is teach you some breathing exercises that will help relax you if you start feeling stressed or anxious. We're also going to talk your nightmare into the ground. Doing that will desensitize the event itself. That's called exposure therapy. It's possible now that you've remembered the event, the nightmare won't return."

"That would be my greatest wish."

"Ready to start?"

Cody nodded. "I've never been more ready."

CHAPTER TWENTY-ONE

R iley sucked in a breath when the engine of Charlie's red stunt
plane cut off after a straight-up climb, and then turned as if in
slow motion from nose up to nose down before spiraling straight for
the ground. "Wow!"

"It's called a hammerhead stall," Ryan said.

She glanced at him to see if the stunt scared him as much as her.
His eyes were glued to the plane. There was no way she could stand
watching someone she loved risk their life like that.

"Start the engine, Charlie," he said, when it seemed like there was
no way she could pull up in time.

As if on cue, the engine sputtered to life, and the plane crossed in
front of the grandstand so low that Riley thought Charlie was going to
land, but no, off she went up again. "She's amazing."

Ryan grinned. "She so is."

The man was besotted with Charlie. That was obvious by the pride
she saw in his eyes as he watched his girlfriend defy death. "Do you
ever fly with her?"

He laughed. "Oh, yeah. She leaves my stomach behind every time.
Wanna go up sometime?"

Riley snorted. "Not ever."

"Hannah wouldn't, but Sugar sure as hell would," Sugar said.

Jamie made a growling sound. "Hannah nor Sugar are setting foot in that plane."

"Who's Hannah?" Was there another couple she hadn't met?

Sugar waved a dismissive hand. "Long story. I'll tell you sometime."

Well, that cleared things up. Riley shrugged and turned her attention back to Charlie and her plane, as she raced past them upside down. When Cody had backed out, she hadn't wanted to come. She was glad now that she had as she really liked his friends.

For the afternoon, she was able to forget about stalkers and Pelli and a man who couldn't conquer his demons. She was even laughing, surrounded by men who were hot and scary at the same time. The women were funny and really nice, and she hoped she could stay friends with them even if she wasn't with Cody. The only ones missing besides Cody were Logan and Dani. Their little boy had woken up with a cold, so they'd stayed home.

Riley couldn't help envying the couples surrounding her. Ryan, with that light in his eyes as he watched Charlie wow the crowd, Jamie fussing over his pregnant wife, and Jake whispering naughty things in Maria's ear, if Maria's giggle and blush were any indication.

Over the loudspeakers, the air show commentator announced the finale, which was a precision parachute team, and Riley was as impressed with them as she had been with the stunt planes. As they were leaving, Ryan asked what she thought.

"It was awesome. I'd love to come to one again."

Ryan glanced at the planes coming in for a landing. "Great. I'll let you know the next time Charlie has one. I'm going to go meet up with her now, so I'll catch you later."

"Want to get some dinner?" Maria asked.

"I'm going home, taking off my shoes, and putting my feet up while my husband makes me a big fat cheeseburger," Sugar said. She laughed, patting her stomach. "It's what baby wants."

Jamie snorted. "This morning, baby wanted peanut butter pancakes with banana slices and whipped cream, and a slab of bacon."

Sugar grinned. "I love being pregnant. I can blame everything on baby."

She and Jamie headed off to their car, their arms wrapped around each other, and Riley walked toward the parking lot with Jake and Maria.

"You coming to eat with us?" Maria asked.

"I'll pass, but thanks for the invite." While she'd been with the group, she hadn't felt like a fifth wheel, but now she did. And what if they started asking questions about Cody? She wouldn't feel comfortable discussing him with his friends.

"Oh, come on. We'll go someplace quick and casual."

Riley's phone buzzed with a sound she'd never heard before. Puzzled, she fished it out of her purse, frowning at the screen as she read the text message from her new alarm company.

"What the . . . My house is on fire?"

"What?" Jake grabbed her phone, his eyes darting over the screen. "Let's go."

He started running, and Maria grabbed Riley's hand as the two of them chased after him. They piled into his car, and he tossed Maria his phone. "See if you can get ahold of Cody and your brother."

"My cats," Riley whispered as Jake used the grass shoulder to pass cars leaving the airport, ignoring the blaring horns. She estimated they were at least an hour from her house, and she choked down a sob at what she feared she would find when she got home. One hope that she held on to was the small sign at her front door for this very reason, stating that there were three cats inside. She knew that firemen paid attention to those notices.

"Cody's not answering, so I left a message," Maria said, peering around her headrest at Riley. "Logan's on his way to your house. You have cats, right?"

"There are two in the house. If they're scared, they hide under my bed in the front bedroom." She listened as Maria passed the information on.

If Cody was still with his doctor, he probably had his phone turned off. God, she wished he were home. Even if things were over for them, he would do everything in his power to save Arthur and Merlin. There was someone, though, she could call for help. She found Mike's number in her contact list and called him.

"My house is on fire," she said as soon as he answered.

"I know. Recognized the address as yours when it came over the radio. I'm here now."

"There're two cats inside. Have they found them?" Riley squeezed her eyes shut, afraid of the answer.

"No. They saw the posted notice, and they're inside looking for them."

"There are only two cats, not three, and tell them to look under my bed."

"Will do."

"I should be there in about . . ."

"Thirty minutes," Jake said. "Tell him I'm going way over the speed limit and to call the cops off me." He spouted off a license plate number. "In fact, if there's a cop near the I-10 eastbound lane from Alabama into Florida, an escort wouldn't hurt."

Riley passed the information on to Mike, along with a description of Jake's Jeep.

"I'll see what I can do."

"Thank you," she said. "If they find my cats, will you call me back so I can breathe again."

"Promise. Gotta go." He hung up.

Riley stared at her phone as panic swelled like a giant tidal wave, threatening to drag her under. Why did he have to go right then? What was happening?

Please, God, I beg you. Let them find Arthur and Merlin.

Cody turned his phone back on as soon as he walked outside. The session had been grueling, and he felt as if he'd been flayed alive. Tom hadn't lied. They'd rehashed Cody's nightmare until he could speak about it without thinking he was going to come out of his skin. The process had left him raw, yet in a strange way, cleansed. *Desensitized.* They'd done that all right. Now that he'd had a breakthrough, Tom wanted to see him again tomorrow afternoon.

He hit the remote to unlock his truck, and as he climbed in, his phone beeped, telling him he had a message. The hell? Riley's house was on fire? Was she back from the air show? He had to get to her. With a heart that felt like it might explode, he raced out of the parking lot, tires squealing.

Smoke was visible as soon as he turned onto their street, but a cop, who had his patrol car parked across the road, blocking traffic, stopped him. Instead of arguing that he should be let through, Cody pulled over, parking on the shoulder of the road. He got out, and ignoring the order to stop, ran past the officer. No one was going to stop him from getting to her.

Coming to a halt in her yard, he stared in horror as part of the roof collapsed just as two firemen ran out, each with one of Riley's cats draped lifelessly over his arm. Jesus, this was going to kill her. She loved those cats. He scanned the yard, looking for her. When he saw Mike Kilpatrick, Cody ran over to him, yanking on the cop's arm. "Where is she?"

"She should be here any minute. Highway Patrol's escorting her and her friends."

At that news, he inhaled air back into his lungs. She was safe. The firemen carrying her cats were kneeling under the tree in her front yard, and Cody headed toward them. Before he reached them, a Highway Patrol car came around the corner, his siren piercing the air. Close behind was Jake's Jeep, and Cody changed direction.

The back door flew open, and Riley tumbled out. "Oh God, Cody." She ran straight into his arms.

"Darlin', I'm so sorry." He pulled her tight against him. *This is where she belongs, Dog. You get that, right?*

She burst into tears. "They didn't . . . they didn't find my c-cats?"

"I meant about your house." The cats hadn't appeared to be alive, but he couldn't bring himself to tell her.

"My cats are safe?"

She peered up at him with such hope in her eyes, and he held onto her when she tried to pull away. "I don't know. They found them, but . . . but, I just don't know."

"Where are they?" Her eyes frantically scanned around them, pausing on the two firemen kneeling under the tree. When Cody tried to block her view, she jerked away from him. "Dammit, I'm a vet. Let me go do my job."

She was right. If anyone could save her cats, she could. He followed her, stopping next to her when she knelt. "I'm their owner and a veterinarian," she said to the fireman.

Cody was awed at how she'd put aside her grief to become what was needed, a doctor to her animals. Oxygen masks covered the cats' faces, and she placed her middle and index fingers on the inside of Arthur's leg.

"Why there?" one of the firemen asked. "I'm Dave, by the way, and this is Brent."

"I'm Riley. Wish we were meeting under better circumstances. To answer your question, the best place to check a cat's pulse rate is on the femoral artery, located right here inside the thigh, near the groin." She closed her eyes for some seconds before saying, "Thank God. He's got a pulse. Keep the oxygen on him."

Cody was pretty sure he was the only one who noticed the tremor in her voice.

She moved her fingers to Merlin. "His pulse isn't as strong, but it's there. I need to get them to my clinic," she said, looking up at Cody.

He could take her in his truck, but he wanted to stick around and find out what had happened here, because vacant houses didn't just burn themselves down. But he wasn't about to let her take off on her own. He glanced around to see who was here that he trusted could keep her safe.

"Be right back." The ones he wanted were standing next to Kincaid. "Jake, Maria, can you take Riley and her cats to her clinic? I'd do it, but I want to stay and get some answers. Tell her I'll come get her later. Don't let her out of your sight."

"You got it," Jake said.

"Thanks, man. You'll stay with them until I get there?"

Jake nodded. "Count on it."

A fireman came around from the back of the house, carrying two gas cans. Cody fisted his hands. "Arson. When we find whoever's doing this, might be a good idea to keep me away from them."

"Duly noted," Kincaid said. "Not that I blame you. Let's go talk to the fire chief."

Cody sat on his couch in his living room, as Riley stood at the window, staring at what used to be her house. She had been quiet ever since he picked her up at the clinic and brought her home. He wanted to hold her, somehow give her comfort, but when he'd tried, she had pushed him away. Not that he blamed her, considering he'd done the same to her that very morning when he had shut her out. The way her shoulders were slumped in defeat made him feel helpless.

"It was arson?"

"Yeah. I'm sorry, darlin'. You don't deserve this."

"You didn't do it, so why should you be sorry?"

Because he hadn't protected her, nor had he been there for her when she'd needed him. Those were his regrets, but he'd had a much-needed breakthrough during his session with Tom, and the goo in his head didn't seem as thick as it had before. So where should he have been? With her or with his head doc? He didn't know.

Although he still thought she deserved better than what he had to offer, he'd left Tom's office believing that if he worked hard at it, he could dig himself out of the black hole he'd been existing in. And by working really hard, doing everything his doctor said, he could become a man who deserved the love of an amazing woman.

When he'd read the message that her house was on fire, and didn't know if she was home or not, the thought of losing her made him feel like his chest had been cut open with a dull knife. Maybe he didn't deserve her, but he sure as hell needed her. From the beginning, he'd known he'd find a way to screw things up with her, and now, he just had to figure out how to fix everything.

He glanced over at their animals. The cats were resting on a large towel, awake and in the process of getting a bath—Arthur from Pretty Girl, and Merlin from Sally. The dogs didn't like the smell of smoke on their friends, and the cats didn't seem to mind getting washed. Both appeared to still be dazed, though.

"Are they going to be okay?" He lifted his chin toward the cats.

"I think so. I ran complete blood profiles and urinalyses, and the results aren't great, but they're not life-threatening numbers either." She bowed her head, as if in prayer. "I gave them both antibiotics to fight off any infection," she said, glancing at him. "I never thought I'd say this, but I'm glad Pelli was taken. He never would have survived the fire as little as he is."

Desperation and sadness dulled her eyes, and although he couldn't promise her cats would be okay, he could hold her, something he thought she needed. He opened his arms. "Come here, darlin'." For a few seconds, he thought she was going to refuse, then she came toward him.

Tears streamed down her cheeks as she crawled onto his lap. "I don't have a house, or clothes, or a car. The few photos I had of my parents are gone. Everything's gone, gone, gone. Up in smoke. What if she . . . he, whatever, burns my clinic down? Then I really won't have anything."

She had him, but that was something he'd have to prove to her. "As we speak, Kincaid is arranging around-the-clock security for your clinic. That's one thing you don't have to worry about."

"I don't know how I would have gotten through this without you and your friends. I'll pay all of you back somehow."

"Hush. That's a worry for another day. Jake said you came up with a name, Ziegler?"

She toyed with the hem of his T-shirt sleeve. "Yes. He owned the dog that was accidently cremated. I was going to drive by the Zieglers' house this morning, but realized that was a stupid move. Jake drove us by there on the way to the air show, but there was nothing to see."

"Don't ever go off someplace on your own like that without me . . . or at least, someone. But preferably me."

She leaned back and stared at him. "From the day my parents died, I've only been able to depend on myself. Then you came along and I thought . . ." She shook her head as she pushed off him. "It doesn't matter what I thought. When you left this morning, the way you left, it hurt. When you needed me the most, you wouldn't let me in. You walked away, Cody. How do I know you won't do it again?"

CHAPTER TWENTY-TWO

Two days had passed, and she and Cody still hadn't talked. Not that he hadn't tried, but she'd put him off. So much crap was stuffed into her head that Riley thought it might explode. Worry about Pelli, no home, no car, meetings with her insurance company, an arson investigation . . . the list was endless, and there was just no room left for dealing with what was going on between her and Cody.

At least she had new clothes, having gone shopping with Cody trailing alongside her, his eyes constantly scanning the mall for a monster that burned down houses and stole kittens. It had been nerve racking, and she hadn't bothered to try anything on, only wanting to get what she needed and return to the safety of Cody's house.

The problem that she couldn't get past—trusting him to not shut her out the next time he fell into his black hole. Each time she put him off when he tried to talk about their relationship, she was hurting him, could see it in his eyes. But she would be the first to admit she had trust issues.

Almost everyone in her life had let her down. Her parents by dying before she even had any memories of them, her grandmother for resenting her, an endless line of foster parents who didn't give a shit about the kids they brought into their homes. And then there was Reed, the one person she'd thought would stand by her side forever. Instead, he'd chosen drugs over her.

Cody had walked out on her Sunday morning, and who was to say he wouldn't do it again? Like everyone else in her life, he had left her, and it hurt. A nagging voice said she was punishing him for the crimes of others, and maybe she was. Had she overreacted to his leaving the way he had? Everything was just so confusing right now.

He had spent the morning at K2 presumably to begin planning the operation his boss had mentioned last Saturday night. What if something bad happened and he had a relapse of some kind? Would he walk out again? This afternoon, he was meeting with his doctor, getting Tom's opinion on how ready he was to go back to active status. In her opinion, Cody wasn't ready, but she kept that to herself.

They'd slept in the same bed the last two nights, but other than hold her, nothing else had happened between them. That was at her request, and it was killing her. She wanted him so badly that there had been a constant ache in her heart. But until they worked things out—if that was possible—she didn't want to fall in love with him. She huffed a breath. As if she had control over her heart.

"Stupid heart," she muttered.

"Your first afternoon patient's in room one," Brooke said, stepping into Riley's office.

"Thanks. Be there in a sec." She scooped the last bite of yogurt out of the cup as she glanced at the day's schedule, which showed that it was a new patient. Before she went to the exam room, she made a detour to check on Pretty Girl and her cats. Unwilling to leave them alone and vulnerable to a madman, or madwoman, as the case might be, she'd brought the entire crew to work with her. The K2 man sitting in her lobby, pretending to wait for his appointment, was using Sally as a prop. Because they got along so well, Riley had let her cats and Pretty Girl stay together in one of the large dog kennels.

Her phone vibrated, and she pulled it out of her lab coat pocket to see Cody's name on the screen. She debated answering, but she had a new patient waiting, so she let it go to voice mail. After a minute, it beeped a message. She peeked around the corner to see that Pretty Girl and the cats were curled up together, napping. Not wanting to disturb them, she headed down the hallway, listening to Cody's message.

So Mr. Ziegler had been married. Cody also said that he had died a year ago, and that Mrs. Ziegler fit some of the points on the profile. He ended the message by telling her he'd come straight to the clinic after his session with Tom.

Was it possible they had found the person making her life miserable? Being afraid all the time was exhausting. Hope blossomed that she would have Pelli back soon, but would an honest mistake in cremating the wrong dog send someone over the edge? Somehow, it didn't seem likely, but if the woman was already unbalanced, maybe the death of her husband had contributed to her mental state.

There was no way of knowing until someone talked to Mrs. Ziegler, and since she had a full afternoon ahead, Riley shelved her questions. Just as she put her hand on the doorknob to enter the exam room, a ping sounded that she had a text, and she paused to read it.

`I'm missing us darlin'.`

So was she. How long was she going to hold on to her hurt feelings? It was time to trust her heart, and tonight when they got home, she was ready to have that talk. She texted him back.

`I'm missing us too.`

A heart and a smiley face appeared, and she grinned as she dropped her phone back into her pocket.

With a smile on her face, and a new bounce in her step, she entered exam room one. She glanced at the new patient form for the owner's name. "Mrs. Napier, I'm Dr. Austin." A tall, thin-as-a-rail, somewhat disheveled woman turned from the cat carrier she was leaning over.

Riley gasped. "Mrs. Decker?"

"So you remember me?"

"Of course, I do. How-how are you?" Riley was taken aback by the malice in the woman's eyes. She shouldn't be surprised, though, since Mrs. Decker blamed her for Reed's death. Why was she here?

A plaintive wail sounded from the carrier, and Riley froze. She knew that meow. "Pelli?" she whispered. The odor of urine and feces coming from the carrier reached her nose, and she rushed over, opening the door. Pelli sprang out, right into her arms. As a thinner Pelli snuggled against her neck, Riley turned, intending to give Reed's mother a piece of her mind. The words died at the sight of a gun pointed at her chest.

"Stupid cat cries all the time," Mrs. Decker said. "Here's how this is going to go." She tossed a canvas tote onto the exam table. "You're going to put on a wig and glasses, and then we're leaving by the back door."

"I'm so sorry about Reed, but I'm not going anywhere with you." It had not once occurred to her to suspect Reed's mother, and it now seemed stupid not to have considered her. But she'd tried so hard to bury her past, leaving any thoughts of him and his family behind.

"Now, Riley."

She shook her head. If they left through the back, the K2 guy would never know she was missing until it was too late. With a gun pointed at her, though, did she have a choice?

"I have no problem with shooting you right here." She swept her arm across the counter next to her, knocking things to the floor, causing Riley to jump. "You took everything away from me. Reed was going to make it to the pros and give us a better life. After our son died, Larry got depressed, lost his damn job. He worked odd jobs here and there, but we fell behind on the mortgage, and the bank foreclosed on our house. Six months ago he sat in our car in the garage with the motor running. You took everything away from me." Spittle flew from her mouth as she yelled the last part.

Riley had never seen so much hate in another person's eyes, and she backed up a step. Because she'd made a point of not keeping tabs on the Deckers, she hadn't known that Reed's father was dead, which was another reason she hadn't considered Mrs. Decker when she'd read that damn profile report. As far as Riley had known, Mr. and Mrs. Decker were alive and well at their home in Gainesville.

Mrs. Decker waved the gun. "Put the damn wig on."

Although she'd always heard you should do anything possible to keep from going anywhere with your abductor, she wasn't willing to take the risk. If she tried to stall and Brooke came in to see why things were taking so long, what would happen? She could be taken hostage, too, or worse, be shot.

As much as she didn't want to put Pelli back into the nasty carrier, she did so. He would be safe left behind. Brooke or someone would find him soon. His pitiful cries tore at her heart, but it was for his own good. She just wished he understood that. The wig was a shorthaired, red one, and once she had it on, she put on the oversized glasses.

"Take off the lab coat."

"I can't. I don't have anything on under it." Not true, she had a T-shirt on, but her phone was in the lab coat, and she might have a chance to call for help at some point.

"No matter. If anyone sees us leaving, I'll just shoot them."

The woman had always been high-strung, but now she was acting deranged, which made her frightening. "You have a chance to walk away before you do something you can't take back. What you're considering won't bring them back." Even though Mrs. Decker had never shown her any affection, Riley felt sorry for her. She'd lost so much, and

Riley had played a part in that happening. "I'm so sorry. I loved Reed, too, and I'd give anything to bring him back." As soon as she said it, she knew she'd made a mistake.

"Shut up! You're not worthy of saying his name. I never should have allowed you in my house. What my son saw in you, I'll never understand." She sneered. "It was probably because you put out when the nice girls didn't. He didn't love you. It was lust, nothing more."

If Riley knew nothing else, it was that Reed had loved her until the day he loved his drugs more. But the words still hurt. She'd often wondered why Reed, one of the most popular boys at school, had chosen her. But all that was history, and she loved another man now. She almost chuckled. It took having a gun pointed at her and facing death for her to admit the truth. She loved Cody, deeply, truly, and irrevocably, and she'd spent the last two days shutting him out. If she didn't make it through this, that would be her big regret.

Mrs. Decker gestured toward the door, using the gun. "Time to go. You so much as step wrong, I'll turn this place into a shooting gallery, starting with you."

Riley believed her, and she had no choice but to obey.

Cody was happy. Tom had agreed that he could handle going back to active duty. Cody knew his issues hadn't evaporated into thin air. He still had a lot of work to do, and he would keep his appointments with his head doc. But remembering the rest of his dream had been the breakthrough he'd needed to move forward. The nightmare hadn't returned either. It seemed he had only needed to remember the rest for it to go away.

The guilt was still there for his part in what had happened, but as Tom said, "It was war, man. Instant decisions are made based on what is known at the time, and your intention was to protect the family. You didn't go to the Taliban and tell them Asra was feeding you intel. It was her decision to do that. She had to know the risks. How they found out, you'll probably never know, but you're going to have to forgive yourself and let it go."

He was going to damn well work on that. And if a successful therapy session wasn't enough, Riley had answered his text. On top of that, Wizard had e-mailed, saying that the lead on Layla was a strong one. Life was looking pretty damn good.

As he made the turn into the clinic parking lot, a police car—siren blaring—raced up, coming in behind him. A sick feeling churned in his gut, the instincts he'd honed in a war zone screaming that Riley was in trouble.

Mike Kilpatrick exited the police car, arriving at the clinic door at the same time as Cody. "What's going on?" Cody asked, pushing in ahead of Mike.

"Not sure. Brooke called in a panic. Said she couldn't find Riley."

"How long?" And where the hell was Baker, the K2 guy assigned to guard her today?

"About three minutes ago. I was cruising the area. Why I got here so fast."

Brooke skirted around the corner and ran right into Mike's arms. "We can't find Dr. Austin anywhere." She burst into tears.

Mike wrapped his arms around Brooke. "We'll find her, I promise."

They damn well would. Cody turned in a circle, looking for Baker. Why hadn't the man called him? As soon as the question entered his head, his phone vibrated, Baker's name showing up on the screen. "Talk to me."

"You need to get to the clinic. Dr. Austin's missing."

"I know. I'm here. Where the hell are you?" At Baker's hesitation, Cody knew the man had taken offense, because yeah, his question had been an accusation. Baker's job had been to protect Riley.

"In her office, getting ready to watch the security feed."

Cody disconnected. "Come with me," he said to Mike and Brooke. The other employee—Michelle, he thought—was standing behind the counter, tears streaming down her face. "Cancel the rest of her appointments for today and send these people home," he told her. Fortunately, there were only two women waiting, one with a dog, and the other with what looked like an iguana sitting on her lap. Both were staring wide-eyed at him and Mike.

"What should I tell them?"

"Just say there's been an emergency and that you'll call them tomorrow to reschedule."

Anxious to see the security recording, he headed to Riley's office, Mike and Brooke following him. "Tell me what happened." To keep from putting his fist through the wall or going off half-cocked, he fell back on his SEAL training. Get intel. Analyze. Act.

"We were running behind, and I poked my head into the room to see if Dr. Austin needed any help," Brooke said, two-stepping to keep up.

Cody stopped at the open door to Riley's office. "And?" It wasn't easy to curb his impatience, but he managed it.

"And she wasn't there. Mrs. Napier wasn't either."

"Mrs. Napier?"

"Yes. She brought her kitten in. It's still in the room in the carrier."

"Have you touched the carrier?"

Brooke shook her head. "No, why?"

He stuck his head around the doorjamb. "See if you can find where Dr. Austin goes missing on the feed. I'll be back in a minute." He'd have a talk with Baker about how he'd lost track of Riley later, but he had a funny feeling about exactly what he'd find in the carrier.

At Baker's nod, Cody turned back to Brooke. "Show me this carrier that was left behind."

"Unless the woman wore gloves, we can get fingerprints off it," Mike said.

"Yep, but I'll have someone from K2 do it." At Mike's frown, Cody said, "We can process them immediately. How long will it take the police department?"

"Point taken," Mike said, "but the detective on the case since Riley was hit on the head is on his way. He might have some problems with you guys ramrodding right over him and the department."

"Tough shit." No one cared as much about finding Riley as he did, and he had resources the police department didn't even know existed, not to mention a team consisting of the best of the best if he needed them.

Mike gave him a hard look. "Should get interesting then, but I'm of the opinion you people know what you're about, and finding Riley is all that counts. I'll back you up as much as I can."

"Appreciate it, man."

Brooke opened the door to an exam room. "Here it is."

"Christ, that smells," Cody said, peering into the carrier. A long meow responded to the sound of his voice. "Grab me a paper towel." When Brooke placed one in his hand, he used it to open the carrier door so as not to add his fingerprints. A cross-eyed Siamese kitten bounded out and latched onto his arm. "Well hello, Pelli."

Brooke's eyes widened. "Oh my God, that's Dr. Austin's missing cat."

"Yes. Where are my dogs and her other cats?"

"In the kennel. They're together."

He peeled the kitten's claws out of his shirt and handed him to Brooke. "Get him cleaned up, and then put him with the others. They know him." The poor thing was a mess and stunk to high heaven. "See if he's hungry." Who knew the last time he'd eaten. To Cody's eye, Pelli was thinner than when he'd last seen the cat.

"Let's go see what we can learn," he said to Mike.

Mike eyed him. "You're being damn calm about this. If Riley were my girl, I'd be freaking out." He swiped a hand through his hair. "Hell, I'm freaking out, anyway. I've never had a friend kidnapped before."

"You think I'm fucking calm?" Cody stilled, holding out his arm. "Cut open a vein and you'll see how furiously my blood is boiling. But rage won't find Riley. Intel is what we need, and I'm counting on the cameras providing that." Before he did lose it he entered Riley's office.

"Start the feed." At his abrupt command, Baker opened his mouth, then apparently thought better of whatever he was going to say, which was wise of him, since the man currently headed Cody's shit list.

Baker pushed Play, and a woman carrying a cat carrier entered. She paused and looked around before going to the farthest corner of the waiting room. A dog whined, and Cody shifted his gaze to the opposite side of the screen where it showed Sally straining against his leash, his ears straight up and his tail wagging.

Damn. Sally knew it was Pelli in that carrier. Cody pressed his lips together. If he'd been with Sally right then, he would have understood what his dog was saying.

"Sally was with you? Whose idea was that?"

Baker paused the video. "Dr. Austin's. She said I'd look like I was waiting for an appointment that way." He glanced up at Cody. "Look, man. You can't make me feel any worse than I already do for losing Dr. Austin. It's not an excuse, but unless I shadowed her every move, which she wasn't having, there was no way I would have guessed that woman was our target. When she came in, the smell coming from that carrier was god-awful, and I thought that was what your dog was reacting to."

There was no way Baker could have known that Sally was reacting to Pelli being close. Not only that, but Riley had refused to allow any of her guards into the exam rooms with her. None of them had considered that would be how the woman would get to her. Some of Cody's anger at the man eased.

"That's what I would have thought, too," Mike said. "Your dog knew, though, didn't he? That the missing kitten was in there?"

"Yeah, he knew." Cody could beat himself up all day for not being the one sitting in that waiting room when the woman came in, but that wouldn't help them find Riley. "Where is he now?"

"Brooke put him back with your other dog after we realized Dr. Austin wasn't anywhere in the clinic," Baker said.

"Okay, good. Start the video over." This time, he zeroed in on the woman's features. She was tall and skinny, with dirty brown and gray hair and a long, thin face. Along with Baker, there were two other women with pets in the waiting room, and both of them wrinkled their noses as they turned their faces away. Did Mrs. Napier—and who the hell was Mrs. Napier?—let the carrier get so disgusting that people would stay away from her?

On the screen, Brooke called Mrs. Napier's name. "Speed up the video," he said after Riley entered, closing the exam room door behind her. He watched until the door opened. "Stop it." According to the timer, Riley was in the room with Mrs. Napier for ten minutes.

A woman stepped out, wearing large glasses and what was obviously a wig. "Stop." He leaned closer to the screen. "That's Riley. Start it again." Right behind her, Mrs. Napier appeared. "Stop it again."

"She's got a gun," Mike said.

Cody took several deep breaths, his hands fisting at seeing Riley with a gun stuck into her back. "Start it." He had to figure out who Mrs. Napier was and fast. They watched the two women walk down the hall to the back before they disappeared. "Go to the parking lot camera."

That video showed the women walk toward an older model Chrysler. "Is that a Sebring?"

"Yeah. My dad had one," Baker said. "Let's see if we can get a license number."

Mike huffed out a breath. "Dammit, there's mud smeared over the tag."

There was, but Mrs. Napier hadn't done a good job of it. The partial outlines of some of the numbers were visible. Cody thought they could decipher the tag at K2 with the resources at their disposal. He was counting on it.

The women got in the car, Mrs. Napier driving and Riley in the passenger seat. They drove past the security company's car that Kincaid had hired, the man sitting in it giving them a wave. Cody wanted to scream at the man to open his eyes, but he'd been hired to guard the building, not the people in it. That had been his job, and he'd screwed up. Again.

A rabbit hole opened up, welcoming him with open arms, and he almost let it take him. He'd let both Asra and Riley down, and how was he supposed to live with that?

A strong hand clamped onto his shoulder. "We're going to find her," Mike said.

He took deep breaths, the way Tom had taught him. "Whatever it takes."

Since an IP camera—an Internet protocol camera—had been installed at his request, he said to Baker, "Send everything to Maria and tell her I'll call her. You stay here and keep an eye on things. Send Brooke and Michelle home. There's a kid who comes in around six, I think. He spends the night. Stay with him and guard this place with your life. I won't have Riley losing this, too."

"I won't let you or her down," Baker said.

Cody nodded. "Good man." He headed for the door, Mike on his heels. If the cop thought he was coming, the man needed to think again. When they reached the waiting room, Cody said, "We'll need that cat carrier so we can dust it for fingerprints. Why don't you go grab it while I call Maria at K2 and tell her we're on the way in?" Mike wasn't going to be happy about being ditched, but tough. The last thing he needed was a cop telling him what he could and couldn't do.

"Be right back," Mike said.

The front door opened, and the detective that Cody recognized from before walked in.

"I need a status report," the man whose name he couldn't remember said.

Cody walked past him. "Your officer's down the hall. He'll bring you up to speed."

"Hey. Where you going? I need a statement from you."

"Just getting something out of my truck. Be right back." Cody got in his truck and turned left out of the parking lot, the same direction Mrs. Napier had taken. He instructed his Bluetooth to call Maria.

"It's Cody," he said when she answered. "Riley's been taken—"

"What?"

"Someone has kidnapped Riley. All I know is that it's a woman named Mrs. Napier. We just sent over the video with the woman's car in it. There's mud smeared on the tag, but can you see if Kent can do his magic and laser trace the numbers or whatever it is he does?"

"Where are you?"

He hated lying to her, but if Kincaid knew one of his men was going rogue, he wouldn't be pleased. "At the clinic. Call me as soon as you have a number for that tag or any other information you come up with."

"Okay, but you need to come in. Logan will want to start planning a rescue."

And that was the problem. The boss operated on the theory that there couldn't be enough planning for an operation. What if Riley didn't have that much time? "We got some things to finish up here, then I'll be there."

"I'll see you soon. I'm sorry, Cody."

"Yeah, me, too. Call me when you come up with something." He clicked off before she could say more. When he came to a traffic light, he pulled over. Which way?

CHAPTER TWENTY-THREE

Riley shook her head. "I'm not taking that."
Mrs. Decker had pulled into the parking lot of an abandoned warehouse after leaving the clinic, and now held the gun in one hand and a pill in the other. She pointed the gun at Riley's feet and pulled the trigger.

Riley screamed, and expecting to feel pain, she squeezed her eyes shut.

"Next time, it will be your knee. Take the damn pill, Riley."

Nothing hurt, and Riley opened her eyes and peered down, shuddering when she saw the hole in the floor not two inches from the toe of her shoe. Given a choice between a bullet and a pill, she'd opt for the latter. "Pills make me gag. I have to have water to take them." That was true; she'd never be able to swallow it without something to wash it down.

"You always were a pain in the ass." Mrs. Decker pointed the gun at Riley's knee. "You have until the count of three to swallow the damn thing."

Riley held out her hand, and Mrs. Decker dropped a white capsule into it. "What is it?"

"A sleeping pill so you don't try to jump out of the car."

Which was exactly what Riley had planned to do—should have already done—when the gun wasn't pointed at her.

"One . . ." Mrs. Decker said, when Riley hesitated.

"I'm taking it!" She popped the pill into her mouth, squeezed her eyes shut, and forced it down her throat, gagging as she did so. *Stupid. Stupid. Stupid.* Why hadn't she thought to stick it under her tongue and spit it out when Mrs. Decker wasn't looking?

"Who's Mrs. Napier? Is that a name you made up?" How was Cody supposed to find her if he only had a fake name?

"My maiden name, not that it matters."

And that, Riley hoped, was her first mistake. Surely Cody and his friends, with all the resources at their hands, would be able to find that out. Although Mrs. Decker might be right. Would it really matter if they did? Unless Mrs. Decker had rented a house in Pensacola under Napier, nothing would show up.

"Now another one."

Riley eyed the second capsule in horror. Two would knock her out cold, and she wasn't sure she could swallow another one. At least with only one, she might manage to stay somewhat alert.

"One . . . two . . ."

This time, she put the pill under her tongue, making a gagging sound as she pretended to swallow. When Mrs. Decker pulled the car back onto the road, Riley turned her head toward the window and pushed the capsule out, letting it drop onto the seat to her right. She palmed it, dropping it into her lab coat pocket. When her fingers touched her phone, she wanted to slap her forehead for not thinking of trying to call for help.

At a quick glance at Mrs. Decker to see her gaze was on the road ahead, Riley took a chance and slipped out the phone, keeping it to the side of her thigh.

"What are you doing, Riley?"

Riley froze, hearing the suspicion in Mrs. Decker's voice. How to answer? Something that would divert attention. "I'm hating you, is what I'm doing. You're Reed's mother, and I don't want to hate you, but I do." Her eyes drifted closed as the pill began to take effect. She forced them open. "Please don't make me hate you."

"You don't know what hate is, but you're going to find out."

Riley couldn't decipher the woman's words. Her mind was too fuzzy. When her head fell forward, she realized she wasn't going to be able to fight the sleeping pill, and only had seconds to call someone before she conked out. Pretending the pill had done its job, she closed her eyes to slits, and with her chin resting on her chest, she went to the recent-calls screen and put her finger on Cody's name. Her fingers lost feeling and the phone slid out of her hand, back into her pocket. As her eyelids closed, she wondered if she'd actually connected with him.

Cody sat in his truck, hidden among other cars at a strip mall, waiting for Maria to call. He needed a location, some kind of hint for which way he should go. Thirty minutes had passed since he'd talked to Maria, and sitting on his ass doing nothing was killing him.

Be strong, Riley. I'm coming for you.

Just as he decided he'd start driving up and down streets, his phone buzzed. "Talk to me," he said at seeing Maria's name on the screen.

"Where are you?"

"Who wants to know?" Was Kincaid getting suspicious? The man wasn't stupid and would be wondering why Cody hadn't arrived at K2 yet.

"Logan does. You need to come in, Cody. The team is gathered and ready to help."

Cody did some fast thinking. If Kincaid hadn't made the call, demanding he come in, then the boss knew exactly what Cody was up to and was unofficially sanctioning it. "Tell the boss I'm doing what I have to do."

"He knows," she softly said. "Kent's still working on getting a tag number. Says he's close. But I do have something for you. I hacked into some security cameras in the area of the clinic, found the suspect's car, and then followed it through other security cameras until I lost it. She appears to be headed to either Pace or Milton."

Yes! He hit the steering wheel with his palm. He finally had a direction to go. "Thanks, Maria. You're awesome."

"I know. I'll call you as soon as I know more. Be careful, okay?"

"Always am."

Someone was talking to her, but the person sounded as if they were speaking from the bottom of a well.

"Riley!"

"Leave me 'lone. Sleepy." She tried to push away the fingers digging into her arm, but her hands felt like they weighed fifty pounds each and refused to work right.

"You haven't changed, Riley. Still a pain."

She didn't like that voice. Never had. Always yelling at her, finding fault with everything she did. If she didn't love Reed, she'd run away.

"I probably shouldn't have made you take two pills before I had to get you out of the car," the voice muttered.

Pills? Was Reed taking pills again? She tried to open her eyes, but someone had glued them shut. Her arm was jerked hard, and she was pulled from her bed. She hit the floor, her hands scraping on gravel. Why was there gravel on her floor?

"Damn bitch. Get up."

She hated when Reed's mother was angry with her, which was most of the time. Riley managed to get her arms under her and pushed up.

With great effort, she forced her eyes open, only to find herself on her knees, staring down at rocks. Where was she? Something hard and cold pressed against her head.

"You can either crawl or walk into the house. I don't care which, but if you don't start moving, I'll just shoot you here."

A gun pressed against her back as she walked out of her clinic, then a gun pointed at her as she swallowed a pill flashed into her mind. Oh, God. She wasn't back living in the Decker's house, and Reed was dead. She needed to be alert and smart, but the sleeping pill Mrs. Decker had made her take made her mind fuzzy. She needed to think if she were going to survive whatever Reed's mother had planned for her.

"Move, Riley."

By sheer force of will, she stood on wobbly legs. Hot tears burned her cheeks as they rolled down her skin. She wanted Cody. He wouldn't let Mrs. Decker hurt her if he were here.

"Cody, please come find me."

"What did you say?"

"Don't know." She didn't like it at all when Mrs. Decker put an arm around her and helped her walk, but without the support, she would probably have fallen on her face, so she let the woman guide her into a house.

A few minutes later, she was pushed onto a small bed, and she fell over, snuggling her face into the pillow. How long she had slept, she didn't know, but when she woke up, it was to see Mrs. Decker sitting in a chair, staring at her with those hate-filled eyes.

"I didn't make him take the drugs," Riley said.

"No, but you introduced him to them. I'll never forgive you for that."

She probably was to blame. Yet, how was she, a teenager, supposed to have known there were people who couldn't take or leave the marijuana as she could, and would go looking for bigger and better highs?

If she'd had any clue Reed was one of those, she would have buried her supply of pot in a twenty-foot hole.

"I'm so sorry," she whispered. The slap across her face came out of nowhere, and she jerked, putting her back against the wall. Instead of being cowed, though, she got mad. "He could have said no." Cody had reminded her of that, and it was true. "I never gave him any hard drugs, he found those all on his own. I tried to save him, but he didn't want saving."

The gun that had been resting on Mrs. Decker's leg was suddenly pointed at her. "Shut up." She swung the barrel of the gun toward a table next to the bed. "There's a pill there." One side of her lip curled in a sneer. "And a glass of water so you can swallow it without all the dramatics."

Riley shifted her gaze to the table. Another sleeping pill? She was still half out of it from the last one. This one had the letters OC stamped on it. "That's an OxyContin." She gave a vigorous shake of her head. "I'm not taking that."

Could she manage to slip it under her tongue, and then into her pocket? Thinking of the pocket of her lab coat, she remembered she'd turned on her phone. At least, she hoped she had. Was Cody even looking for her? Yes, he was trying to find her. She had to believe that.

"Remember what I said, Riley. Your knee will be the first to go. Take the pill."

Riley considered her chances of getting the gun away from Mrs. Decker. If she could take the woman by surprise, maybe she could, but as out of it and sluggish as she was, she'd probably end up getting shot.

"Do I have to start counting again?"

"You're really making me hate you, Mrs. Decker." Riley grabbed the pill and stuck it in her mouth, slipping it under her tongue.

"Do you think I'm stupid, girl? Swallow it."

With a glare at the woman, Riley pretended to swallow.

"Open your mouth and lift your tongue."

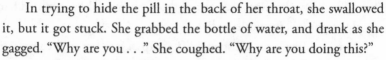

In trying to hide the pill in the back of her throat, she swallowed it, but it got stuck. She grabbed the bottle of water, and drank as she gagged. "Why are you . . ." She coughed. "Why are you doing this?"

Mrs. Decker sat back in her chair, and although she rested the gun on her lap, she kept her hand on it. "I want to see you suffer the way Reed did. At first, I was just going to kill you outright, thought I had with the rock, but then I decided that would have been too easy for you. When you're addicted to the drugs I'm going to make you take, when you're begging me for them, when you no longer care about food or being clean, then you'll know what my son's last days were like."

"I was there. Believe me, I know. He refused to eat or bathe no matter how much I begged." Her lips trembled. "I was there! It broke my heart to see him like that."

"Well, I can tell you right now, it's not going to break my heart to see you slowly die in your own filth."

Riley pulled the thin pillow to her chest. God, she was sleepy. "Go away. I don't want to talk to you anymore."

"Not until you fall asleep. Don't want you trying to throw up the pill."

There went that plan. If she didn't do something, and do it now, she would be too out of it to attempt anything. "I need to use the bathroom."

"Tough."

Rage proved stronger than the pills in her body, skyrocketing her blood pressure, and she lunged at Mrs. Decker, managing to take her by surprise. They both landed on the floor, and Riley struggled to get her hands on the gun, desperately fighting against the sluggishness making her limbs feel like they were sloughing through mud.

She had her fingers around the barrel, could see them there, but couldn't feel them, and Mrs. Decker was able to jerk the gun away. Using the handle, she hit Riley on her head where the stitches had recently been taken out. Pain exploded in her face and skull, and she gasped as she tried to catch her breath.

"Stupid girl. Get on the bed."

Somehow she managed to crawl onto the mattress, but it felt like her brains were going to leak out of her pounding head. As soon as Mrs. Decker left, Riley reached into her pocket and pulled out her phone, squinting at the screen. She wasn't connected to anyone, which meant she'd failed in her attempt to call for help. With trembling fingers, she found Cody's number and pressed Call.

"Riley?"

His voice washed over her as tears filled her eyes. "Cody, I-I love you."

"Talk to me, darlin'. Where are you?"

"Dunno. Drugged. She . . . she gave me Oxy . . . Oxy . . ."

"OxyContin?"

"Yeth." What was wrong with her tongue? She lost the battle to stay awake, giving in to the lure of nothingness that the drugs in her body were offering. The next time she woke up, she tried to move her arms and legs, but they refused to obey. Squinting her eyes against the bright light coming in from the window, she lifted her head and stared down at her feet, then at her hands. She was on her back, spread eagle, tied to the bed somehow. Funny, she thought that should concern her, but she couldn't quite seem to get her mind in order.

The door opened and Mrs. Decker walked in, pulled the chair next to the bed, and sat. "I found your phone, Riley. Bad girls get punished." She held up a needle.

"Wha-what's t-that?"

"Oh, you'll like this. It will make you feel wonderful, and then when you learn to crave it, I won't give you any more. Or maybe I'll give you enough to kill you. Haven't decided yet. To answer your question, it's heroin." She eyed the needle. "It's surprisingly easy to get, but I suppose you already know that."

"Please, don't do this." The tears leaking from the corners of her eyes burned. She wanted Cody. Wanted to curl up against him with his strong arms wrapped around her, where she'd be safe. Sad. That's what she was. So damn sad. She didn't have Reed or Cody, and if that wasn't worth crying over, nothing was.

"Oh, it's too soon to give you a shot of this. You'd probably OD if I did, what with the other drugs already in you. I just wanted you to know what you could look forward to. You're going to suffer just like my son did."

"But I love him," she whispered.

"You killed him," Mrs. Decker screamed. "You deserve everything I'm going to do to you."

She'd meant Cody, but even in her drugged state, she knew to keep that to herself.

CHAPTER TWENTY-FOUR

Cody pulled over to the side of the road, got out of his truck, and slammed his fist down onto the hood, not caring that he'd put a dent in it. He'd had her on the phone, but after telling him she loved him, and that she'd been drugged, all he'd heard was her breathing. For fifteen minutes he'd listened to Riley's labored breaths while begging her to talk to him.

But she hadn't responded, and the call had been disconnected. He grabbed his phone and pulled up a map of Pace. Milton was about nine miles farther, and both were small towns he'd driven through on occasion but wasn't familiar with. Since he could see the Pace city limit sign from where he stood, all he could do was wait for more intel.

Riley had said she'd been drugged with OxyContin, and something he'd seen on TV a while back occurred to him. He called Ryan O'Connor.

"Hey, man, where are you?" Ryan said in greeting.

That seemed to be everyone's favorite question today. "Trying to find Riley. Where the hell else would I be?"

"Easy, dude. I'm not the enemy. We're loading up, about to head out as soon as we know where to go."

"Sorry, Doc. I'm a little wound up right now. Listen, I seem to remember hearing about a drug that can reverse the effect of narcotics. Know anything about that?"

"You're talking about Naloxone. Why?"

"Riley managed to call me, but she was really out of it. Said she'd been drugged."

"With what?"

"OxyContin. Can you get a hold of some Naloxone and bring it with you?"

"I'm on it. See you soon."

Cody clicked off. Unable to stand around twiddling his thumbs, he decided to drive around some of the streets, keeping an eye out for the woman's car. Before he could start the engine, his phone buzzed and Maria's name came up on the screen.

"Got something?" he said.

"An address do it for you?"

"Christ, yes." He programed the address into his GPS as she gave it to him. "Kent's a genius."

"Actually, he's still working on getting the license plate numbers. He got the first four so far. I took those and went back to the list I'd made of suspect vehicles, using the search words Napier, Sebring, Chrysler, and the four numbers. Bingo. It came right up. The car is registered to a Connie Napier Decker. That name mean anything to you?"

He pulled onto the street. "Not a thing."

"This is personal, Cody. She's connected to Riley somehow. I'll keep on digging. As soon as I give the address to Logan, the team will be headed that way. You should wait for them to get there, you know."

"Can't promise that. Depends on what I find." It would take them about forty-five minutes to catch up with him, and he wasn't leaving Riley in that bitch's hands a minute longer than he had to.

"Well, I pretty much knew you'd say that. Stay safe, okay?"

"You bet."

According to the GPS, he was only eight minutes from the target address. As he left the populated area of the town, he followed a two-lane road into a rural area of older ranch-style houses sitting on what he guessed were one-acre plots of land. The homes were mostly run down, many of the yards overgrown. At one place, an old truck was up on blocks, and at another, chickens busily pecked at the dirt. Several abandoned houses had rental signs posted. It was the kind of neighborhood where people minded their own business.

He made a slow drive by the address Maria had given him. The Chrysler Sebring was parked under a carport that looked like it might collapse at any moment. It was all the confirmation he needed that he had the right place. At the end of the block, he pulled over, considering how to approach. It probably wouldn't be a good idea to pull his truck up to the house, announcing his arrival. As he debated where to leave it, a man mowing the yard across the street eyed him with suspicion.

Cody studied the house and the man. It was one of the few places on the street that was better maintained than the others, and the man had a military haircut and wore a long-sleeved T-shirt with "Navy" imprinted across the front. Could he be that lucky? Only one way to find out.

"If you're selling something, not interested," the man said over the noise of the mower as Cody approached.

"I'm not. Could you turn that off a minute? Need to talk to you."

"About?" Although his expression was one of annoyance, he cut the engine.

"Cody Roberts, former SEAL." He held out his hand.

Annoyance turned to puzzlement. "Tadd Singleton. Great to meet you, but I'm not sure I want to know why you're here."

"Smart man. Listen, I need to park my truck in your driveway for a while."

"Because?"

How much to tell him?

"Look, you SEAL dudes are cool and all that, but I don't want trouble and you got trouble written all over you. I have a wife and daughter in the house. Is parking your truck in my driveway gonna put them in danger?"

"No, that I can promise. Here's the thing." His phone buzzed, and he pulled it out of his pocket. "Stand by a sec," he told the man. "Hey, Maria. What's up?"

"I have some history on our Mrs. Napier . . . or Decker. Whatever. Anyway, several years ago, her son died of a drug overdose. Sometime after that, her husband lost his job, then they lost the house. I guess he couldn't deal with all of that because on the day the house was fore-closed on them, he sat in his car in the garage and carbon monoxided himself."

"What was the son's name?"

"Reed Decker. Why?"

Ding. Ding. "Reed was Riley's high school boyfriend. Now we know what this is all about. Great job, but gotta go."

"Cody—"

He hung up. "Here's the thing, Tadd. A woman's life depends on me getting to her ASAP. The woman I love to be exact." He removed his truck key from the ring and tossed it to Singleton. "Either move my truck or don't. If you don't, I'd appreciate it if you kept an eye on it." Without waiting for an answer, he went back to his truck and took his gun out of the glove compartment, along with his spare key.

"I'll park it in my driveway," Singleton said, coming up next to him. "I'm not sure what's going on, but my gut says you're righteous, so anything I can do to help a brother warrior?"

"Just take care of my truck. Appreciate it, man." He gave a wave as he walked away. There was an overgrown hedge between Decker's house and the one next door, and he used it for cover to get close to the carport where the Chrysler was parked. He wished it were dark when it would be easier to make a stealthy approach, but that was almost three hours away, and every bone in his body was telling him that Riley didn't have that much time.

When he was even with the carport, he slipped through the hedge, and ran to the side of the house, plastering his body against the wall. Easing up to the door he thought led into the kitchen, he wrapped his fingers around the handle and tried to turn it. Locked. He wasn't surprised, but a flimsy lock wasn't going to keep him out.

He removed his shirt and wrapped it around his fist. Using only enough force to break the small windowpane, he reached in and turned the lock. When the door wouldn't open, he ran his hand along the inside door edge, finding a deadbolt. Once he slid it back, he slipped into the house.

The kitchen was dark, and with his gun in hand, he crept to the entrance of the living room. A lamp burned on a table next to a well-worn sofa, and he cocked his head, listening. A voice that wasn't Riley's sounded from the direction of the bedrooms, but he couldn't make out the words. Sticking close to the wall, he made his way to the hallway, paused, and listened again.

"You'll have to tell me how it feels to have heroin in your body, Riley. I hear it's wonderful until you try to stop. Then it's hell." The woman laughed. "I guess you could say I'm sending you to hell with a little bit of heaven."

"Please don't. I-I tried to save him."

"But you didn't, did you?"

Heroin? With his blood pounding in his ears, Cody growled as he moved toward the sound of the voices. The sight before him chilled him to the bone. Riley was on her back, spread eagle, and tied to the bed. Decker leaned over her as she inserted a needle into Riley's arm.

"You push that plunger, you die," he said, his gun aimed at her head.

The woman froze, looked up at him, and then a sly smile appeared on her face. "Too late."

He pulled the trigger at the same time Decker pushed the plunger with her thumb, then she crumpled into a heap on the floor.

"Riley!" He rushed to her side and gently pulled the needle from her arm. "Darlin', talk to me," he said as he yanked a knife from his boot and cut her ties.

"My hero." She giggled.

She was so high that she could touch the moon. "Can you sit up?" He didn't know what was best, to keep her prone or to get her up and walking?

The scrape of fabric over wood caught his attention, and he looked down to see Decker reaching for the gun that had fallen out of her lap. As tempted as he'd been to kill her, he'd taken a shoulder shot instead. He stepped hard on her wrist, ignoring her cry of pain.

There was something he had to do first, before he secured Decker. With his foot still pinning the woman to the floor, he leaned down and kissed Riley. Kissed her hard because he had to.

She giggled again and grabbed his neck with her hands. "Make love to me, Cody."

"Oh, that's definitely on my list of things to do, but not yet." He smiled as he untangled himself from her hold. "Be right back."

He picked up Decker's gun and slipped it into the waistband of his jeans, then looked around for something to tie her up with.

"Need some of these?"

Cody glanced toward the doorway where Kincaid dangled plastic ties in his hand. "She's all yours." He removed his foot from Decker's wrist as the boss knelt next to the woman, Jake and Jamie following him in. "Where's Doc?"

"Right behind us. He's got that stuff you asked for."

"Wowdy! So many hot guys in one room," a giggly Riley said.

Cody rolled his eyes as the team shared amused glances. "She's stoned."

Jake chuckled. "No shit."

"Am not." Riley protested. Or was she? Didn't know, didn't care. Just wanted Cody to kiss her again. She loved his kisses. Adored them. "Are you going to kiss me again?"

"Cody would kill me if I did."

She tried to focus on the man leaning over her. Oh, right. Ryan O'Connor. "You have really beautiful eyes, but I want Cody."

"And you shall have him in a minute. I'm just going to give you a little something to combat the drugs in your system, okay?"

"No, no more. Weird stuff." She pressed her lips together, turning her head away.

"You won't have to swallow anything."

She felt a prick in her arm, but euphoria still streamed through her body, and she didn't really care.

"Riley. Look at me."

"What? Told you I want Cody."

"I'm here." Cody slipped his fingers around hers. "Listen to Doc, okay?"

"Kay."

The man with the beautiful green eyes smiled. "I just gave you a shot of Naloxone. It's some amazing stuff. In a few minutes you should start to feel normal."

"Kay." She shifted her gaze back to Cody. "Now will you kiss me again?"

"Soon, darlin'. Soon."

"He wasn't real happy, was he?" Riley said as Detective Margolis made his exit. It was absolutely wonderful to be home—well, at Cody's home as she no longer had one. Even that wasn't going to get her down, at least not today. She'd been examined at the emergency room, and pronounced in good-enough condition to come home.

The first thing she'd done on arriving at Cody's was to take a long, hot shower. When she'd walked into the living room—wearing a pullover sweater and a comfortable pair of lounge pants, her hair wet—three men had stood at her appearance, Cody, Logan Kincaid, and the detective. That had startled her as only Cody had been with her when they'd returned.

She hugged sweet Pelli against her neck. The kitten had been glued to her from the moment she'd walked in the door, had even sat outside the shower door crying for her to come out. Merlin perched on the sofa behind her head with his nose pressed into her hair, and Arthur was curled over her leg, staring up at her with worried eyes. Cody's dogs sat near his feet, their alert gazes seeming to follow the conversation.

Her biggest relief was learning that one injection of heroin wasn't likely to make her addicted to the stuff. She was tired, though, and she leaned her head onto Cody's shoulder, wondering when Logan would leave.

Logan stood. "He'll get over it, not to mention we handed him Decker on a silver platter, giving him the credit for tracking her down."

The details were fuzzy in her mind, but after the team had secured Mrs. Decker, Cody had called Mike. Thirty minutes later he'd shown up at the house with Detective Margolis in tow. A heated conversation had ensued between Logan and the detective, and from what Riley could tell, the detective had come out on the losing end. No surprise there. Logan Kincaid made a formidable opponent. Everyone but Cody and Detective Margolis had left, and shortly after, two ambulances had arrived, one for her and one for Mrs. Decker.

"Let me get this straight. On the arrest report, Detective Margolis gets the credit for finding me?"

Logan nodded. "Officially, yes, but the police commissioner is aware of the circumstances."

"Doesn't seem fair. The police would probably still be looking for me, and I shudder to think of the condition I would have been in by the time they did find me. You guys are heroes."

He smiled. "We're just men doing what we do best. I expect to see you at Ryan and Charlie's wedding, Dr. Austin."

"Wouldn't miss it."

"Come here, darlin'," Cody said, wrapping his arms around her after Logan left. "I need to hold you. Reassure myself you're here and safe."

She set Pelli next to Arthur and scooted onto Cody's lap. "I know my mind's still a little fuzzy, but I don't think I ever got that kiss you promised me."

"We'll just have to correct that, won't we?" His eyes locked on hers with an intensity she'd never seen in them before. "Do you remember what you said when you managed to call me?"

"I called you? When?" At the expression that flashed across his face, she knew her answer had disappointed him. "What did I say?"

"Doesn't matter."

Before she could protest that it must matter if he'd brought it up, his mouth covered hers, stealing any other thoughts in her head but how his lips felt pressed against hers. "Cody," she whispered.

He slid a hand under her sweater. "I'm here, darlin', for as long as you want me." His fingers danced up her spine, raising goose bumps on her skin.

She rested her forehead against his. "I think that's going to be a long, long time." Hopefully for the rest of her life, but she wasn't that sure of him yet. The most he'd ever said was that he was falling for her, but *falling* wasn't exactly a love declaration. She wasn't going to worry about that now, though. Only hours ago, she had been in fear of her life, and for tonight at least, all she wanted was to lose herself in Cody's arms.

"About that kiss I promised you . . ."

"Still waiting." Her body was sizzling from the lazy caress of his hand over her spine.

One side of his mouth curved as he put his hands on her hips and pulled her closer, so that they were touching, groin to groin, his erection pressing into her. When she rocked against him, he groaned and attacked her mouth, giving her the most erotic kiss she'd ever had. From there, his lips trailed a damp path to her neck. She leaned her head to the side, giving him better access, and his gentle bites and nips made her achy and wanting.

Her breath hitched when he slid his hand inside her panties, burying a finger inside her and stroking her. She watched for a moment, then lifted her gaze to his. "Take me to bed, Cody."

Faster than she could blink, he was standing with her legs straddled around his waist. "Are you sure you're up for this?" he asked, stopping at the edge of her bed.

"Oh, yeah." With a gentleness she found amusing, he lowered her onto the mattress. "I'm not going to break, you know."

"Indulge me, darlin'. I've had a very trying day, and I have this need to take care of you."

"Well, put that way . . ." She lifted up, resting on her elbow. "You could start by taking your clothes off."

He grinned, showing his sexy dimple. "And that's taking care of you how? Not that I'm objecting."

"Not sure, but I'll come up with an answer. In the meantime, clothes off."

The sweatshirt he wore came off, exposing a white T-shirt that did nothing to hide the stretch of muscles across his shoulders and chest. When that was removed, she licked her lips in appreciation.

"Nice," she purred.

"Just nice? I'm wounded."

Her gaze fell to the bulge straining at the zipper of his jeans. "Very, very nice."

"That's better, but not quite there." He toed off his shoes and socks, pushed his jeans down over his hips, and kicked them away. "Now?" He held out his hands and lifted a brow.

She burst out laughing.

He fell on top of her, catching his weight with his arms. "Not at all the reaction I was going for, Dr. Austin." He grabbed her hands and held them captive above her head. "Hurts a man's pride when his woman laughs at the sight of him naked, you know."

She hadn't meant to laugh, wasn't even sure why she had. Only knew that she was alive, no more pets would be poisoned, and the man she loved was staring down at her, trying hard not to laugh, too, but his twitching lips gave him away. She was just so damn happy.

"I love you, Cody Roberts." She hadn't planned to blurt that out, but her love for him was no longer possible to keep to herself. Her heart was bursting with it, her mind was overflowing with it, and her mouth wanted to shout it to the world.

His eyes turned the color of molten chocolate, and still keeping her hands prisoner with one of his, he cupped her face with the other. "I don't know if I deserve you, Riley, but damn if you didn't just make me a deliriously happy man."

His mouth covered hers then, and he kissed her with a possessive fierceness that stole her breath. He let go of her hands, and before she knew what was happening, he had her clothes off. "Sneaky," she said, when they came up for air.

"One of my many talents, darlin'. Wanna see another one?"

"Yes, please," she said, secretly thrilled with his playfulness. The man whose eyes were alight with happiness and an inner peace had come far from the tortured soul she'd first met.

He chuckled. "So polite, but that won't do. I want you wild and begging."

With the sneaky stealth she was coming to learn he excelled at, he had his face buried between her legs and his mouth on her, and true to his word, had her wild and begging. She fisted the sheet as a tidal wave roared through her.

"Oh God, Cody." She gripped the top of his head.

Her body trembled from the force of her orgasm and the wet trail of his tongue as he licked a path up her stomach to her breasts, sucking a nipple into his mouth. As his tongue toyed with her, he clasped their hands together, lacing his fingers with hers, and the intimacy of their palms pressed together brought tears to her eyes. She had once thought she would never love again the way she had loved Reed, but that had been puppy love compared to the soul-deep feelings she had for Cody.

"Ahh." She tightened her fingers on his when he moved to her other breast. He grunted what sounded like male satisfaction. He should be satisfied, considering he was playing her body with the finesse of a maestro. His strong body covered hers, and he nudged her thighs apart, settling himself between her legs.

She rocked her hips, straining for the touch of his arousal. "Make love to me, Cody. Please." The last word came out sounding like a whine, and she felt his lips curve against her skin.

"Told you I could make you beg, darlin'."

"That wasn't begging. It was a polite inquiry."

He lifted his head and grinned at her. "Sure, keep telling yourself that." He let go of her hand and reached into the nightstand drawer, pulling out a condom, tearing it open with his teeth before dangling it in front of her. "Want to put it on me?"

"I do." She'd never put one on a man before, and as he lifted onto his knees, she took the condom from him. "How do I do this? Roll it on?"

"Exactly." He covered her hands with his and guided her in sheathing him. When he was covered, he reached down and palmed her, then slipped a finger into her. "Christ, baby, you're so damn wet for me."

"Always for you," she said, falling back onto the mattress.

He stared hard at her for a moment, then took himself in hand and slid into her. When he was buried to the hilt, he stilled, caught her gaze, and held it. "The first time we met, I was in a bad place." He kissed her. "Even though I didn't know you, I wanted you. Crazy wanted you." He kissed her again. "But I didn't want to bring my crap into your life. Yet, here we are." Another kiss. "You and me, darlin'. I want you to know that what I'm about to say, I've never said to another woman." He kissed her hard and long. "I love you, Riley. Fucking love you."

That was the best declaration of love she'd ever received. She kissed him then because it was only fair that she got to initiate at least one kiss.

Much later, both of them sated, he spooned against her back as his hand made lazy explorations over her body. "When do you want to get married, darlin'?"

His question made her smile with pure joy, but her man needed to be taught a lesson. That wasn't a proper proposal. "When you figure out how to ask that question, I'll say yes."

CHAPTER TWENTY-FIVE

CHRISTMAS EVE

After eating a delicious dinner of prime rib, mashed potatoes, and green beans that he and Riley had cooked together, they had moved to the sofa, enjoying their spiked mocha lattes topped with whipped cream while transfixed by the Christmas tree lights.

"Okay, I admit I was wrong," Cody said, tucking her closer to his side.

She tilted her head and peered at him as if she'd never seen him before. "Yeah? About what?"

"Two things, actually. First, this latte. It's better than I expected, but it's still a girly drink."

"We'll just keep it our secret. Wouldn't want your friends making fun of you."

Damn, he loved her laugh. "*Our* friends, and I'm man enough to take whatever they throw my way."

"You sure are. What else were you wrong about?"

"The Christmas tree lights. I'm liking all the colors."

She gave a soft sigh. "Thank you."

He knew why she was thanking him. When they'd gone tree shopping she'd been as excited as a girl getting her first pony. He had even gotten teary eyed when she'd said it would be her first real Christmas since her parents had died. Although his parents had always put white lights on their trees, claiming they were classy and not gaudy like the colored ones, he'd given in to Riley's every wish—the tallest, fattest tree they could fit in his house, boxes and boxes of colored lights, and more ornaments than he'd ever seen on any Christmas tree, topped off by a pure white angel.

The monstrosity tucked into the corner of his living room was god-awful, and he loved it because she did. Another thing she'd asked for was to start a tradition, and she'd asked what his family's was. "Wait for my parents to get up on Christmas morning so they could watch me open presents," he'd said.

She had scowled at that. "That's it? Nothing special on Christmas Eve? No Christmas breakfast? Nothing else?"

"We would go out for a turkey dinner. Does that count?"

Turned out that it didn't. Later that day, she'd handed him a piece of paper that he'd now memorized.

Cody and Riley's Christmas Traditions

Put up a tree the week before Christmas.

Lots of presents for Riley under the tree. Cody gets lots, too. Presents for our dogs and cats.

Christmas Eve is just for the two of us, a romantic, candlelight dinner that we make together.

We get to open one present Christmas Eve.

Make love on a blanket next to the tree. All lights out except for tree lights.

He was particularly fond of number five.

Pancakes, strawberries, and mimosas for breakfast Christmas Day.

Open presents after breakfast. (Riley gets to open one first and last.)

Christmas night, drive around and look at lights.

Strangely touched by her list, he was determined to make their first Christmas together one she'd never forget. He wasn't taking for granted that she'd be with him next year because he'd caught her looking at apartments for rent in the classifieds. If tonight went as planned, she wouldn't be going anywhere.

"Time to open our Christmas Eve presents." He took her empty cup and set it along with his on the coffee table. "Which one should I open?"

She clapped her hands, scrambled off the sofa, and hurried to the tree. As he watched her search through the pile of presents, it occurred to him that his life was near about perfect. His head was almost back to where it should be, although he continued to see Tom once a week, and would for a while. He'd also convinced Riley to see Tom even though she had claimed she was perfectly fine. Cody hadn't agreed. She needed to come to terms with her childhood and Reed's death.

Then there was Mrs. Decker. Fortunately, she had accepted a plea bargain at the urging of the attorney Riley had insisted on retaining. That was good because it meant one of Kincaid's men wouldn't be involved in a trial, which the boss was definitely happy about. Cody was positively relieved that he wouldn't be testifying.

That Riley had sympathy for the woman had at first made him angry, but as his temper cooled and he could think rationally again, he understood why it was important to her to do that. Riley had heart, and he could only respect that.

"Found it!" She held up a beautifully wrapped box. She brought it with her, sitting back on the sofa with her legs curled under her and her eyes bright with excitement. "Where's mine?"

"You want to go first?"

"Yes! Where is it?"

She was going to bounce right off the sofa in a minute. He stifled a grin. "Don't move." Before dinner, he'd closed their animals up in his bedroom, using the excuse that he didn't want their noses in every-thing. That wasn't the real reason, though, and he hoped Pelli would go straight to Riley the way he usually did. He slipped the ribbon with the diamond ring on it around the kitten's neck.

"Go do your thing, Pelli." He opened the bedroom door and a scramble of four-footed creatures made a mad dash down the hallway. Following them, he grinned at seeing Pelli climb onto the sofa.

"Hello, sweet boy," Riley said, picking him up. "What's this?" She lifted Pelli into the air, her gaze on the ring dangling from his neck.

Cody dropped to one knee. "Will you marry me, Riley Austin?" Tears welled in her eyes, and he put his hand on her knee. "You said when I asked the question right that you'd say yes. Did I get it right this time, darlin'?" His damn heart was going to need a hit from defibrillators.

She slipped the ribbon over Pelli's head. "It's beautiful, Cody. Yes! Yes, you got it right, and yes, I'll marry you."

In her excitement, she jumped on him, and they both landed on the floor with a gaggle of animals wanting to join in this new game. He tried to kiss her, but they ended up laughing at all the tongues licking their faces.

"I love you, Cody."

He rolled them so that she was on top of him and pulled the band out of her ponytail, letting her hair fall down around them. "The first time I saw you, when you marched over to give me hell, I knew you were trouble, darlin'." When she opened her mouth, likely to protest, he put a finger on her lips. "Trouble to me. I wasn't looking to fall in love, thought it was the last thing I needed. I've never been so glad to be wrong. I love you with all that I am, and I pray that I'll always deserve you. Now kiss me."

"That was beautiful." She lowered her mouth to his, and he poured his heart into the kiss, wanting her to know that he belonged to her, heart, body, and soul. When she lifted her head and smiled down at him, her beautiful eyes shimmering with tears, he knew he'd love her to his dying day.

"Is it time for number five on your list?" At her blank look, he said, "Make love under the Christmas tree. I've been waiting for that one all night."

She laughed as she sat up, straddled his hips, and held out her hand. "I'm sure you have, but not yet. You still have to get your present, but first, I want you to put my engagement ring on my finger."

He took it from her and removed the ring from the ribbon. With her hand in his, he slipped it on. "With this ring I pledge my love, my loyalty, and my protection."

"I swear you're going to make me cry yet." She held out her hand and admired the white gold two-carat emerald-cut diamond ring. "Isn't it beautiful?"

"Yes," he said, looking at her. "Beautiful."

"My pledge to you is to always love you, to always be your friend, and to always stand by your side no matter what."

"Now you're going to make me cry," he teased.

"That might happen before the night ends," she mysteriously said, pushing off him. "Time for your present." She showed each of the animals her new ring. "What do you think, guys? We're going to be a family." She did a little dance, twirling around the room, waving her hand in the air.

He could have eaten her up right then, she was so damn cute. On one of her spins, she scooped up the present she'd taken from under the tree earlier and handed it to him. He took it and moved to the sofa. It hardly weighed anything, and he shook it as a delaying tactic simply because he knew it would drive her crazy.

"Is it an empty box?" Did she just growl?

"You'll never know if you don't open it, will you? And stop laughing."

"Can't help it. Your happy is contagious." Before she climbed out of her skin, he unwrapped the present and opened the lid. Sitting on silver tissue paper were three brown-leather dog collars with ID tags, and he picked one up. Tooled on the collar was the name "Pretty Girl."

Riley grabbed the box out of his hands, eyed the remaining two, and picked one up, handing it to him. That one said "Sally." His heart ached, knowing what the third one said. It was thoughtful of her to include a collar for Layla, but he wished she hadn't. This wasn't a night for a reminder of the dog he'd lost.

"I don't . . ." He cleared his throat. "I don't know what to say. Thank you."

Her eyes softened as if she understood his pain, and she picked up her phone, turned the screen away so that he couldn't see it, and texted someone. He waited for her to explain, but she only held out her hand, palm out as if telling him to stay. Confused, he watched her walk to the door.

"Be right back," she said.

"What's going on?" he asked his dogs, not bothering to include the cats as all three were batting ornaments under the tree.

Five minutes passed, but he stayed where he was as he held the collar for Layla in his hand, staring at it. It wasn't possible, was it? Yet, he couldn't imagine that Riley would be so cruel—even unintentionally—by giving him such a gift. Hope tried to blossom, but he crushed it. He would know if Layla had been found because Wizard would have e-mailed him.

Another thought occurred to him, and he hoped to God he was wrong. Had she gotten him a new dog, thinking to replace Layla? Would she believe that would make him happy? Sally tilted her head, her gaze focused on the door, and then Pretty Girl did the same, giving a whine.

Cody's fingers tightened on the collar. What he did know based on their reactions was that there was definitely a dog on the other side of that closed door. His heart thumped a stomach-lurching beat as he waited for it to open. It finally did, and Sally and Pretty Girl went wild at seeing Layla pressed against Riley's leg. They ran to their long-lost friend, barking wild greetings. Layla left Riley's side, meeting them halfway across the room, and the three dogs yelped and jumped around each other, tails wagging like crazy.

Blood rushed to Cody's head as he stood. There had never been a time in his life when he thought he might faint, but he supposed there was a first for everything. "H-how?" He swallowed the lump in his throat. At hearing his voice, Layla's ears perked up, and her eyes zeroed onto him.

"Layla," he managed to say past the lump in his throat. He knelt and about sixty pounds of dog landed on him. Laughing at the furious licks to his face, he wrapped his arms around her, and looked up to see Riley watching with tears running down her cheeks.

"Merry Christmas," she said.

"How?"

She sat on the sofa, pulling a handful of tissues out of her pocket. "I knew I'd need these."

"I don't even know what to say. You have . . . you have no idea what this means to me." He stood with Layla in his arms and sat next to Riley. "How did you do it?" His other two dogs, knowing they weren't allowed on the furniture, crowded against his legs. As for the cats, Pelli had gone to the top of the tree when the strange dog had entered, Merlin had perched himself on a bookshelf, and Arthur was cat-creeping toward the newcomer.

"It's Logan and your team you really need to thank. From what I understand, Jake was talking to someone named Wizard, or maybe Lizard . . . you people and your names."

"Wizard." He buried his nose in Layla's fur, breathing her in. She'd obviously been bathed and groomed since leaving Afghanistan, because she hadn't smelled this good even when he'd been there with her.

"Right, Wizard. So, Wizard happened to mention during the conversation with Jake that he was as certain as he could be that he'd found Layla. Coincidentally, Logan was in Jake's office at the time, and it was

Logan's idea to bring her here without telling you. According to Maria, who I got the story from, Logan wanted to be certain it really was Layla before getting your hopes up. Since the team knew Layla while you were in Afghanistan with them, they figured they'd be able to recognize her."

"Why didn't any of them tell me after she'd arrived?"

Riley shrugged one shoulder. "Because I asked them not to, thinking she would be the best possible Christmas present ever for you. Also, I wanted a few days with her at the clinic to check for the kind of problems a dog coming from a third-world country might have. She's been wormed, had her shots, and been defleaed. She's underweight, which isn't surprising, but she's in good health considering." Riley scratched Layla's chin. "Remarkably, she seemed to love getting bathed, like she knew she had to get all pretty for you."

And dammit, he fucking cried.

Riley peered out the window of the limo that Logan had hired to drive past the best Christmas lights in Pensacola. Obviously, the driver knew where all the coolest lit houses were. Although it was a little crowded with five of the biggest men she'd ever known, along with their significant others, she had never had a better Christmas. Cody had his arm around her and she lifted her hand, curling her fingers around his. On New Year's Day, she and Cody would attend Ryan and Charlie's wedding. Ryan and Charlie had picked that particular day because, as they said, "It was a day for new beginnings."

She and Cody had decided on a spring wedding, when life sprang anew. In the last few days, as she'd gotten to know the K2 team, she'd learned that each of them had a story, one that had a happily ever after, but didn't have an end. That was her fantasy, anyway, that there was no end to true love, even into eternity.

EPILOGUE

Riley huddled with the women who'd become as dear to her as blood sisters. Their men were coming home today after a successful mission to get a group of doctors out of Syria. It was Cody's third mission since coming to work at K2. The first one that Logan Kincaid had been concerned about Cody being involved in had gone off without a hitch. According to Maria—who knew everything there was to know about secret K2 stuff—Cody had performed to Logan's expectations. Riley had never thought otherwise.

In four days, she would be married to the man coming toward her, and her heart turned over at the sight of him walking down the concourse with his teammates. He was laughing, they all were, actually, and she guessed either Jake or Ryan had cracked a joke. There was nothing better than seeing Cody Roberts happy, and her breath hitched when he caught her gaze and held it, hunger shining in his eyes. Oh yeah, she knew what they'd be doing the minute they were alone, and she couldn't wait. It had been a long week of missing him.

Baby Griffin let out a wail. "Ah, sweetie," Sugar cooed, rocking her son in her arms. "I know you're hungry, but Daddy's here." She held him up. "See. There he is. Soon as we get in the car, you can chow down."

Jamie jogged to his wife and son and wrapped his arms around them. "Missed you both so much."

Sugar laughed. "We need to get gone before people start throwing tomatoes at us," she said, speaking over Griffin's wails. She looked over her shoulder as she and Jamie walked away. "See y'all at the wedding."

Jake and Ryan headed straight to their wives, and heedless of all the attention on their group, grabbed their significant others, soundly kissing them. Riley shivered as Cody prowled toward her, his gaze locked on hers, reminding her of a wild cat on the hunt.

The man was seriously bone melting, and when he reached her, he bent his mouth to her ear. "Want to know what you do to me at the mere sight of you?" Without waiting for an answer, he pressed his erection against her thigh. "You should get me out of here before I embarrass us both."

Fortunately, the team traveled light, so they didn't need to go to baggage. Riley and Cody waved good-bye to their friends, and laughing and holding hands, they ran to the SUV she'd bought with her insurance money.

Cody took the keys from her as he backed her up to the door. "I missed you like crazy, darlin'. Not one more minute's going by without a kiss."

His duffel bag thudded against the pavement when he dropped it before cupping her face with his hands. He angled his head, stared into her eyes for a moment, then covered her mouth with his, and, oh God, she'd missed this—his mouth, his strong body pressed against hers, his scent, his taste.

After a long, devouring kiss, he raised his head. "I really am going to embarrass myself if we keep this up here. Let's go home, darlin', and get naked."

Inhaling air back into her lungs, she laughed. "Sounds like a marvelous plan."

The church Riley had chosen for their wedding was one of the smallest and oldest in Pensacola. It was quaint and charming, and as Cody stood at the front, waiting to see his bride for the first time that day, he glanced around at those in attendance. There for Riley was Mike Kilpatrick, sitting with Brooke, along with Michelle and Riley's foster mother, Pat Haywood. His parents had arrived the day before, and he didn't know if it was Riley's influence or if he'd finally matured, but he was getting along with them better than he ever had.

The rest of the church was filled with his teammates, their wives, and the rest of the K2 staff. His professor mom, whom he'd never once seen cry, wiped her eyes with a pristine white handkerchief. He shared a smile with his father over that.

Ryan O'Connor, Cody's best man, caught his attention as he searched his pockets. At Ryan's frown, Cody narrowed his eyes. "If you lost the ring, I'm going to take you down right here in front of God and everyone in this church," he whispered.

"You could try, dude." He opened his coat and stuck his hand inside the pocket. "It's here somewhere. Well, I thought it was," he said as he tried another pocket.

"Doc, you better be kidding if you know what's good for you."

Ryan grinned and held up Riley's wedding ring. "Scared you, huh?"

"You're not funny, man." The pianist began to play, and as everyone stood and looked to the back, Cody elbowed Ryan.

"Oomph." Ryan rubbed his stomach.

They grinned at each other, then Cody turned. Maria, Riley's matron of honor, walked down the aisle and came to the front. Next was the flower girl, Regan, Dani Kincaid's daughter. She was adorable and seemed to take her job of dropping rose petals seriously. When she reached him, she stopped in front of him and smiled prettily as she handed him her basket, and then skipped to where her mother was sitting. Cody wondered what he was supposed to do with it.

"I'll take it," Maria said, and he handed it to her.

And then, there she was, his heart. As Riley walked down the aisle on the arm of John Haywood, her foster father, Cody thought he'd never seen anything more beautiful. Her hair flowed down her back in a beautiful cascade of curls, and the white scoop neck, off-the-shoulder dress she wore was elegant in its simplicity.

What he liked best, though, was that she only had eyes for him, and when she smiled, his heart bounced in a crazy dance. Her foster father put her hand into Cody's, and then took a seat next to his wife.

Later in the day, if someone had asked him about his wedding, Cody wouldn't have been able to tell them a thing. All he knew, all he cared about, all he saw was Riley. It wasn't until Ryan nudged him and put the ring in his hand that his awareness of his surroundings returned. After the rings were exchanged, and they were pronounced husband and wife, he was told he could kiss his bride. He gave her a chaste peck on the lips.

"You can do better than that," she said.

He gave an adamant shake of his head. "I don't think I can stop kissing you if I start." He seriously meant that, and hadn't intended to make a joke, but from the laughter of their families and friends, everyone else seemed to think it was funny.

Hand in hand, they came out of the church to birdseed being tossed at them. More than anything, he wanted to take her straight home and make love to her as her husband, but the boss was hosting a reception for them at his house. Cody figured it wouldn't be cool to be no-shows.

"To Cody and Riley," Kincaid said, raising a crystal flute of golden champagne.

"To Cody and Riley," their friends echoed, the sound of clinking glasses filling the air.

"An Irish toast," Ryan said. "Here's to fire: not the kind that brings down shacks and shanties, but the kind that brings down slacks and panties."

After the laughter quieted, Jamie lifted his flute filled with soda water. "May your ups and downs be done between the sheets."

"I'm all over that one," Cody said, grinning at his blushing bride.

Jake tapped on his glass. "I was told a toast should only last as long as the groom's love-making . . . so thank you and good night."

"Hey, dude, you only wish you were as manly as me," Cody fired back.

"Don't be making fun of my husband," Maria said. "He tries hard. Real *hard*." She giggled.

After several more naughty toasts, and the hilarity had calmed down, Cody's father and mother stood. His dad raised his glass of champagne. "To our son and new daughter." He smiled at Riley. "Welcome to the family, Riley. Your husband is an amazing man, one that his mother and I are very proud of, although I'm not sure he's aware of that." He shifted his gaze to Cody. "We may not understand why you chose the life you did, but we respect the man our baby became. We love you, son."

Damn. Cody blinked, trying to clear away the burning in his eyes. Riley squeezed his hand, and he got her message, loud and clear. He stood and went to his parents. "Thank you for that. I love you both." After what was his first hug with his parents that he could remember, he reached for Riley's hand, bringing her to stand with him and her new family.

The mushy love stuff going around, though, made him uncomfortable. "How soon can I steal my bride away and prove none of you know dick about my stamina?" As he'd intended, the mood reverted to fun.

Two hours later, Cody, his teammates, and their wives were the only ones still sitting around the fire pit. They'd circled it with five lounge chairs, each wife held snug against the chest of her husband. The evening was chilly, but between the fire, the hot coffee they'd switched to, and the warmth of bodies pressed together, they were comfortable.

Kincaid raised his coffee cup. "To the ladies who dared to take us on."

Five men lifted their cups in the air. "To the ladies," they all said.

"When men like us who live on the edge fall in love, we fall hard," Jake said, his gaze on his wife.

The team nodded, and Cody said, "And we fall forever."

Riley squeezed his hand. "Hoorah."

"Hoorah," the other wives echoed.

Acknowledgments

The more times I write one of these acknowledgements as my writing career progresses, the more I'm amazed by how my world has expanded since the day I published my first book. I've made so many new friends, both readers and authors, and I'm humbled by your love and support.

To the fans of my K2 Team series, I'm crying right along with you that the time has come to say good-bye to these five heroes. I'm going to miss them! To each one of you who has taken the time to e-mail me and/or friend me on social media sites, please know that I treasure our connection, and that I love each and every one of you. Don't be too sad, though. Another series of heroes is headed your way.

To my author friends, you all are rock stars, and I'm so proud to know you. Many of you have been there for me when I needed to solve a problem plaguing me during the creation of a story. Special thanks and love goes to my critique partners, Jenny Holiday and Miranda Liasson. I can't imagine what I'd do without you.

This is my fifth book published by Montlake Romance, and it has been an amazing experience. Thank you Maria, Jessica, Marlene, Melody, Lauren, Scott, and . . . well, just every single one of you at Montlake Romance for being so awesome!

My family knows they're superspecial to me, but I'll say it here . . . Owens peeps, you are my heart and soul. I couldn't do this without your love and support.

To my special friends, Lindsey and Felice, my Golden Heart® Lucky 13 sisters, and my Montlake Romance sisters, my life is better for knowing you.

It has become a tradition to save my agent for last because she's the best. Courtney Miller-Callihan, we've come a long way since we met at RWA 2013, and I'm thankful you were at my side every step of the way. May the journey continue! xoxoxo

About the Author

A bestselling, award-winning author, Sandra Owens lives in the beautiful Blue Ridge Mountains of North Carolina. Her family and friends often question her sanity but have ceased being surprised by what she might be up to next. She has jumped out of a plane, ridden in an aerobatic plane while the pilot performed thrilling stunts, and flown Air Combat (two fighter planes dogfighting, pretending to shoot at each other with laser guns). She's also ridden a Harley motorcycle for years. She regrets nothing. Sandra is a 2013 Golden Heart finalist for her contemporary romance *Crazy for Her*. In addition to her contemporary romantic suspense novels, she writes Regency stories. Connect with Sandra on Facebook at www.facebook.com/SandraOwensAuthor, on Twitter @SandyOwens1, and through her website, www.sandra-owens.com.